LIMINAL

Born in Liverpool to a rambling Irish family, Bee Lewis now lives on the south coast between Brighton and Eastbourne. She has a number of publishing credits including *British Short Stories* 2015 (Salt), *Flash Fiction Magazine*, and *Rattle Tales*. In 2016, Bee was shortlisted for the Brighton Prize, winning the Sussex Prize category, and graduated with an MA in Creative Writing from MMU. *Liminal* is her debut novel and she is busy working on the next one which is set in Sussex.

LIMINAL

BEE LEWIS

CROMER

PUBLISHED BY SALT PUBLISHING 2018

2 4 6 8 10 9 7 5 3 1

First published in Great Britain in 2018 by
Salt Publishing Ltd
12 Norwich Road, Cromer, Norfolk NR27 0AX United Kingdom

www.saltpublishing.com

Salt Publishing Limited Reg. No. 5293401

A CIP catalogue record for this book is available from the British Library

ISBN 978 1 78463 138 3 (Paperback edition)
ISBN 978 1 78463 139 0 (Electronic edition)

Typeset in Neacademia by Salt Publishing

Printed and bound in Great Britain by Clays Ltd, Elcograf S.p.A

Salt Publishing Limited is committed to responsible forest management.
This book is made from Forest Stewardship Council™ certified paper.

For Sophie 1970–2012

And for Estelle, Fin, Davis, and Adele
who picked me up and put me back together again.

Each thing changes, but nothing ever dies. The spirit wanders, roaming here and there, and takes possession of a creature's limbs, whatever body it desires, passing from savage animals to human beings, from human beings to beasts, but spirits never are destroyed. Just as pliant wax shaped in a new form does not stay the same as what it was before or keep its shape, and yet in essence does remain the same.

OVID – *Metamorphoses*

I

SATURDAY

WINTER HAD COME late leaving harsh scars across the countryside and, even now at the closing of March, there was no sign of it abating. The days were short and the cold soaked into the soil, along with the icy rains, leaving the frost-shocked earth battered and exposed. The bone-numbing wind tried to breathe new life into the ancient landscape, but Spring was not yet ready to be roused and instead pulled a cloak of frost around her.

Beneath the wintry quicksilver water of the loch, the mottled pike lurked, its torpedo body unchanged by the centuries, impervious to the cold. Patient as the ages, a pitiless water-wolf who had seen many winters and hunted for prey with a singular compulsion, even choosing its own offspring as targets.

The mountain hare looked with hope towards the sky. Her white winter coat marked her out against the bleak mountainside and she waited for stars to fall, eddying to the ground, covering the earth with their crystalline flakes. Driven by instinct to the higher ground, she shrank back into the brutal boulders as the golden eagle wheeled overhead. Food was scarce for all creatures and her white coat marked her out.

Winter endured. The mistle thrushes bickered with the silver birches who had long played host to clumps of shining, green mistletoe. Berries dropped to the forest floor in the tussle and the birds scattered, leaving the spoils for the army of grouse below.

High up on the mountainside, an auditorium of oaks rustled in muted shusherings to each other. From their vantage point across the glen, they watched as a lone vehicle snaked around the hillsides, hugging the curves in the road, heading towards Rosgill. The water in the burn babbled to the blades of grass on the bank in childish excitement. The grass in turn, stiffened against the cold, lifted lazy tendrils in half-hearted applause and the old station building sat low on its haunches, as it had for decades, waiting.

The Scots Pines, thrust up from the frozen ground, tilted closer to listen to the whisperings of the old building. The pleated landscape eavesdropped and, in the purple light between day and darkness, a young stag paused, sniffing the air as he sensed the change.

She was coming.

❧

The lights, buildings, shops and houses of Invergill gave way to the empty road ahead. The further they drove from the town, the more they were aware of being alone. Esther and Dan had been travelling since early morning and for most of the day before. Fatigue oozed from their skin and clothes. As usual, Dan insisted on doing all of the driving and so, having nothing else to concentrate on, Esther's focus shifted to finding things that irritated her. It was quite a list. The air conditioning in their silver Toyota was too cold. The door pocket jabbed into her left leg, causing her to wriggle and twist throughout the journey. Her corduroy skirt rode up, leaving the skin on the backs of her thighs to rub against the grain of the plush fabric as she fidgeted.

She should have listened to Dan when he'd suggested she wear jeans, but it had felt like such a small and inconsequential act of rebellion in the face of other, larger decisions she could do nothing about. She wondered again whether they were just running away from the problems they'd left behind in Bristol. The city was her touchstone, its roads were rooted in her veins, its houses in her cells. Yet she'd agreed to leave her sanctuary, trading the strident city streets for the cool mountain air and yawning expanse. She'd heard her rational self trotting out the reasons why: new life, fresh start, fantastic opportunity, support for Dan. But she couldn't ignore the small voice deep inside her that invaded her dreams and called her out for the coward she was.

The vanity mirror on the sun visor taunted her. She flipped it back up, not wanting to see how the weak light accentuated the shadows under her eyes, or how her normally sleek bob kinked out at the ends. She should have had her hair cut before leaving Bristol; it would be all blue rinses and perms in the salons up here.

The pressure from the stump collar added to her discomfort and, for a moment, she considered removing Peggy, the childish name she'd given to her prosthetic leg. Deciding there couldn't be much further to go, she tried to divert her thoughts, but the combination of tiredness and discomfort channelled into irritation at petty things she'd usually ignore. The radio kept de-tuning. Dan was driving too fast, braking too late, the road was too bumpy. Finally, she jabbed at the off button.

'Hey! I was listening to that.' Dan kept his focus on the road but didn't reach to switch the radio back on again.

'We've been listening to it all day. I just want a bit of silence.'

'You don't want to know the football scores? Or whether they've found that girl that went missing?'

She didn't respond.

'What about whether they've captured that escaped prisoner, then?' He grinned.

'You mean the escaped prisoner that absconded about six hundred miles from here and is probably half-way to Spain by now?'

'But he could come and murder us in our beds!' He emphasised the word murder, in the style of low-budget Scottish crime dramas.

In spite of her discomfort, she smiled at his attempt at an accent. 'You'll need to be careful round here. People won't like you taking the piss like that. How long till we get there?'

'Twenty minutes.'

She settled back into her seat and tried to take in the expanding countryside around her, conscious that every turn of the wheels took her further away from their old life. These mountains, these glens, her home now, were so very different to their waterside apartment in Bristol. In the beginning, she hadn't liked the apartment much either, but after she'd softened some of the hard, architectural lines with plants, art, and cushions, and injected some colour into the vacant space, she felt as though it had taken on some of her personality, not just Dan's. She glanced at Dan; softening him wasn't so easy.

A lump of unhappiness nestled in her windpipe, and she tried to swallow it down as it threatened to either choke her or to spew out her true feelings. They'd been away from the city for less than 48 hours, but she could still feel its pavements solid beneath her, reminding her where and who she was. She'd have no such comfort here, the hidden obstacles lying in wait to snare her: pitted ground, animal dens, roots, branches. The physical environment brought fresh dangers, but it was the emotional landscape that troubled her more.

Leafing through the magazine she'd bought at the last fuel stop, she skim-read an article called 'Surviving Stress – Techniques to Put You Back in Charge.' It listed the top five causes of stress: death, illness, job loss, moving house, and divorce. Mentally ticking them off as she went, she skirted around the fifth – divorce. In one way or another, their lives had been irreversibly changed in the last twelve months. There was nothing new that a magazine article could tell her.

She she glanced at Dan, trying to assess how he might be feeling. She'd always believed herself to be more mutable than him, but she allowed herself to admit that even she was feeling overwhelmed. Perhaps she should take her cues from him. For someone who didn't adapt well to change, it had been his idea to uproot them, and he showed no outward signs that he was struggling. Now here they were, just minutes from their new home, and he seemed more relaxed than she did. More relaxed than he'd been for months. Even so, she was on her guard for the micro-expressions that would help her gauge how to respond, how to diffuse any tension.

The snow-topped mountains seemed to form a protective

cloak around them as the car beetled along the black ribbon of road bisecting the mountainside – an attempt to tame the landscape with a feat of engineering. Esther knew that if she asked, Dan would tell her how the road was constructed. Not just what it was made from, but the techniques used to cut into the slopes, how the machinery was choreographed into place, and how much the endeavour would have cost in relative terms. She decided not to mention it, feeling a spark of satisfaction from denying him such a small pleasure.

His hands were at their customary ten-to-two position on the steering wheel, exactly as his driving instructor had taught him. She watched him as he drove, noticing a scratch on his left wrist. It looked fresh, probably a result of putting the boxes into the car. She'd bought him a watch once, in the early days of their relationship, but he'd only worn it a few times. As she'd slowly discovered more about him, she realised how inappropriate her gift had been – he was a walking atomic clock, regimented to the second. Everything about him was logical, precise, measured. He was a welcome antidote to the chaos of her childhood and she loved that she could count on him. Solid, consistent, dependable Daniel. Right up until the day she couldn't.

A mustard-sting of tears peppered the back of her nose. Her eyes dropped to his left hand as it rested on the wheel, his wedding ring glinting at her, accusing. She looked down at her own undecorated left hand, then resumed staring out of the window.

He slowed the car and peered into the hedgerow. 'Somewhere along here is the turnoff for Rosgill. Ah, there it is.' He pointed to a small white sign, with faded black lettering, partially obscured by the hedge. He indicated, though they hadn't passed another vehicle for several miles, then turned the car down a narrow, unmade road. The car lurched and juddered as they drove down the pitted lane. She doubted whether she'd ever be able to walk up to the road on her own given how rough the terrain was, but at the same time, tendrils of excitement crept along her veins. She was about to see their new home for the first time.

'You weren't kidding when you said it was remote. Will anyone even be able to find us here?'

'That's kind of what I had in mind. Just you, me, and the great Scottish wilderness.' He reached across to put his hand on her knee, but at the last minute, seemed to change his mind and patted her arm instead.

'And Bump.' Esther stroked her stomach. 'And the paying guests who are making all of this possible.'

He smiled across at her and smoothed his hand over her flat stomach. 'And Bump,' he said, softly. 'Though Bump's a misnomer just now. He's no bigger than a grape.'

As they pulled up at Rosgill Halt, the wind blew across the glen to greet them. Whether it was in welcome or in warning, she couldn't tell, but Esther shivered as she got out of the car and pulled her cardigan close around her, hands crossed in unconscious protection over her stomach. The pink sandstone building, rooted into the landscape, stared back.

Years of neglect scarred the station façade. Paint blistered like psoriasis from every wooden surface; sage green for the doors and white for the canopy and window-frames. One of the windows to the old ticket office had cracked. She remembered Dan telling her that many of the original signs and features had been stolen some years back, the souvenir hunters coming like grave-robbers in the night to make a profit at the auctions, selling items to collectors and interior designers. All colour had bled out of the signage that remained and she wondered if the souvenir hunters had stolen that too, pocketing the pigments and tints like stardust to be sprinkled in new places – places with promise, encouraging people to congregate and commune. Buddleia and bindweed invaded the disused track-bed, while more vines spilled in through one of the windows to the side. There were more buildings on the opposite platform, a mirror image of where she stood. The symmetry was pleasing even though it could have been a scene straight out of a gothic horror movie.

'Do you want your stick out of the boot?'

'No, thanks. The platform seems level enough. I just need to get the circulation going again.' Esther flexed her knee joint, glad to have the space to stretch.

Dan swung the first of the bags out of the car. 'What do you think, then? Let's see inside, shall we?' He didn't wait for the answer to either question before striding off to open the huge door into the old ticket hall.

She followed him, curious to see the inside of their new home.

'Isn't it great?'

She thought his enthusiasm was misplaced. 'Dan, it's huge . . . even just getting it fit to live in . . .' She rubbed her forehead. 'Do you think we're up to this?'

He turned to her and put his hands on her shoulders. 'Don't worry. The buildings are sound. Once the new kitchen and bathrooms are in, most of the work is cosmetic. By the time the baby arrives, it'll be our little palace.'

'Maybe,' Esther said, her voice small against the sprawl of the buildings before her.

He seemed to sense her hesitation. 'Look, it's been a long journey and it's a lot to take in, I get it.'

She smiled. 'Give me a minute to get my bearings. It's very different seeing it now I'm here. The video you took didn't really give me the sense of size.'

'You should have come up with me. I did tell you to.'

She bit her tongue. 'Let's not, eh? I didn't know you were coming up here until two days before. You know how busy my work schedule is.' *Was.*

Dan patted her shoulder. She resisted the urge to shrug his hand away; she wasn't a fretful child.

'You'll love it here. You will. Smell how clean the air is and imagine what it will be like to raise our children here.'

'Children? Let's see how we get on with this one.' Esther patted her stomach, suppressing other responses that came to mind. *No more popping out for coffee with friends, no more nipping to the new deli on the corner, or the artisan bakery you love so much. No mobile phone signal either, wait until you cotton on to that fact.*

Dan went to fetch more bags from the car. They were finally here. How had he done that? How had he persuaded her? She'd tried to point out the things he'd miss when he started talk of moving away, but his enthusiasm turned her words into dandelion seeds and she watched them float away on the breeze. Maybe he was right and a new start was what they needed, she just wished it didn't feel so final. But there was another reason that tugged at the edge of her conscience. Tracking down her father would be so much more difficult without the resources available to her in Bristol, and keeping it from Dan would be impossible. A little voice niggled away at her. Why should she have to keep it a secret from Dan? Hadn't they had enough of secrets?

Not wanting to sour their arrival, she changed tack, opening her arms wide to take in the expanse of the land and buildings.

'We really own all this? There's so much space. I mean, it's a proper station, not a halt.'

He put the bags down. 'Yeah. I know. Over there is the station master's house. Then there's the ticket hall, waiting room, station master's office and storeroom.' He pointed to each area as he spoke. 'On the opposite side, the buildings are pretty much the same but without the cottage. We'll turn that waiting room and store room into our bedroom and a nursery. We'll get some privacy and can keep the guests over this side so they won't be disturbed by a crying baby.'

You mean the baby won't be disturbed by inconsiderate guests? Her question was left unspoken.

He pointed to the neat pile of wooden planks and beams, protected from the worst of the weather by a green tarpaulin, flanked by a large skip. 'Some of the building supplies have arrived.' He paused, a rare smile breaking cover. 'I have a surprise for you.' He took her hand in his. 'Come here.'

'What?' She followed him as he led her to the platform edge. She loved the way his smile seemed to add a quicksilver light to his slate eyes.

'Do you see where the track bed is?'

'Yes? The bit you want to turn into a performance space?'

'I changed my mind.'

His face was unreadable again and she had no idea where his train of thought was going. It was unlike him to be so changeable. After five years together, she thought she knew every mood, every expression, but his actions over the last year made her question her assumptions. She looked up at him, trying not to show the worry on her face.

'Oh?'

'It's going to be a surprise for you.'

She felt herself tense.

'I'm going to build you a swimming pool, because I know how much you love to swim.'

She exhaled, happiness filling the space vacated by the air. Her very own pool. It was the best gift he could have given her. In the water, she could fully relax, not having to go through the automatic risk assessment she carried out internally every time she had to move. Is the surface even? Is the flooring slippery? Are there hidden trip hazards? What did she have to do to avoid falling? Her eyes brimmed with tears that he would think to do this for her. In the water she was weightless. Some days the pain in her leg was so bad that the only relief she could get was from floating. But above all, being in water meant she was equal to everyone else.

'We'll put solar panels up and rig up an air-source heat pump so that you can swim all year round.'

'Really? Even in the winter? Can we afford it?'

He nodded. 'The coolant in the pump boils at very low temperatures, so even on chilly winter days it should be an efficient way to heat the water. It's an interesting challenge to get the best efficiency and sustainability ratio. And of course, it will be an added draw for the guests.'

With one sentence, he'd managed to tarnish her happiness. The pool wasn't for her. Not really. It was a business decision and a project for him. She realised he was still talking and she assembled her best smile before giving him her full attention again.

'. . . in its day, it was more important than a halt, but it was only a matter of time before stations like this closed.'

'I had no idea you'd become such an expert.' She raised an eyebrow. 'Don't you think it's odd that the station is so far away from the nearest town?'

'It didn't used to be. Weren't you listening?'

Esther circled her temple with her forefinger. 'Baby brain. I could forget my own name at times. Remind me.'

'You're Esther.' He laughed and dodged her playful swipe. 'This station served Rosgill village, but the village was abandoned and flooded to make the Invergill Reservoir. There was no need for the station after that.'

'It's a bit Twilight Zone knowing there's a village at the bottom of the reservoir, though.'

'I know. Creepy, right?' Dan wiggled his fingers in front of her face and made a moaning sound, the way a child would when pretending to be a ghost.

Esther batted him away. 'Actually, it's pretty cool that you know all of this stuff. When the business starts up, the guests will love all of that.'

'Well, little boys and train sets, you know. Now we own a piece of history. I'm a very, very lucky little boy.'

He reached out for her hand, but she stepped forward and put her arms around him. She felt him tense for a second, then he relaxed into her, holding her tight against him. He smelled of soap and his jumper was scratchy against her face. She breathed him in deeply, wishing she didn't feel like a thief stealing affection from him.

'When Bump arrives, I'm buying him the biggest train set we can afford.'

'And if Bump is a girl?'

'Then she'll have the biggest train set we can afford. Complete with pink carriages and people she can dress up.'

Esther landed a playful slap on his chest.

'Ow!'

'Well, don't be so sexist then. You aren't your fath—' she stopped, screwing her face up as she inwardly checked herself for being stupid enough to mention Eric.

Dan let go of her, stopping short of physically pushing her away. 'I'll check to see if the furniture got here.' Picking up the bags, he strode up the platform to the house.

Esther followed him, still cursing herself and trying to ignore the creaking of the canopy overhead. She hoped that she wouldn't be able to hear it from their bedroom.

She pushed the front door open and walked straight into the kitchen. It all felt unreal to her. She remembered childhood holidays in rented cottages, and the feeling they gave her, like they'd broken into someone else's life and would be caught.

To her right, another doorway led to the stairs and the sitting room. Although it was the station master's house, it was no grander than a large cottage with two main rooms downstairs, and two bedrooms upstairs. The old box room had been converted to a severe bathroom, but at least it had a separate shower cubicle. It would do for now, but she was looking forward to the day when the renovations were complete and most of the accommodation was on one level. The whole place needed modernising and the cottage seemed like an afterthought, tacked onto the station as it was, breaking the line of symmetry.

Feeling for the light switch, Esther surveyed the kitchen. On first sight, she hated it. The central strip light overhead dimmed and flickered, then steadied. The pine cupboards, darkened with time and grease, were brassy ginger instead of the blonde they had once been. She'd had in her mind that there was a range cooker but now, standing in front of the free-standing gas cooker with its eye-level grill, she felt deflated. The removal men had plumbed in their washing machine, but there was no space for the dishwasher, which they'd dumped in the corner. She was glad Dan had suggested remodelling the waiting room as the new kitchen, even though it would make a big hole in what was left of their savings. It would be at the heart of the new layout, making it a focal point where the guests could gather, and it seemed to lend a more natural flow of movement through the house.

For now, she was stuck with this kitchen and its lurid yellow and green floral wallpaper that fought for her attention. It seemed to be everywhere. In contrast, the tiled splash backs were oatmeal-brown, some with wheat sheaves in relief, but the majority were plain. She closed her eyes. The room shimmied and shifted, and she felt air rush past her as everything grew in size. The edge of the table was now at her eye-level and she had to stand on tip-toe to see over it. Her mother, Anthea, stood at the stove wearing a yellow, frilled apron, stirring something monstrous in a saucepan. Esther knew that the memory should have made her feel more relaxed, made her smile, but instead the little ball of unhappiness moved to her ribcage and pulsed in time with her heartbeat. The room shimmied again and, as everything around her shrank back to its normal size, she glanced upwards noticing the wood-chip paper on the ceiling, blooming yellow with age and grease. It would all have to go.

They had big plans to remodel the cottage to maximise guest accommodation. The downstairs was to become three single bedrooms with a shared bathroom. The two bedrooms upstairs were a generous size already, so it would be easier to partition them and double the number of rooms. She'd picked the furniture: simple wooden bed frames with good quality mattresses, a small desk or table, a chair, and a lamp in each. For a while, she'd toyed with the idea of painting each room a different colour, but Dan pointed out that they should aim to keep everything neutral and in the end, she'd agreed. She looked in her handbag for her diary, remembering to add blankets to the list of things to buy, but it wasn't there. She tutted to herself and looked for a piece of paper at the bottom of her bag. After a few moments of rummaging past the cough sweets, tissues, headache tablets, and lip balm, she pulled out a receipt from Waitrose. It was dated 17th September, the day before her 34th birthday. What had she bought? Toothpaste, tiger bread, brie, grapes, Prosecco, and a birthday cake. Her birthday cake.

She quickly wrote 'blankets' on the back of the receipt and tucked it back into her bag. It had been a good birthday, overall. Dan had been attentive and thoughtful. She pictured him chopping onions, peppers and garlic, humming along to the radio as he worked. That kitchen had been her triumph in the apartment. She'd had a difficult job persuading him to go with the glossy red lacquered doors and polished concrete worktops, but when it was finished, she knew it gave him as much pleasure as it did her. It would be so out of place here. Just like she was.

Despite its dated decor, Esther was puzzled by how clean the surfaces and cupboards were. She had steeled herself to scrub away years of dust and grime but, except for the years of grease on the ceiling, it looked like someone had beaten her to it. Dan must have arranged for someone to come in. It wasn't like him to be so thoughtful and she smiled to herself. Perhaps she'd been too hasty to judge his motives over the swimming pool. *Maybe he does mean it this time.*

Opening the drawer under the sink, she spotted a set of keys on a large metal loop. They were all old, mostly of a mortise type, but there were also three or four smaller brass keys – the kind that might open a desk. She closed the drawer again and pulled open the door to the nearest cupboard. It was empty, but there was a faint smell of bleach.

Dan appeared in the doorway carrying a box marked 'kitchen.' 'Where do you want this?'

She half-resented the inference that the kitchen was her domain, but pointed to the worktop anyway and started to unpack the provisions they'd brought with them. She opened a cupboard and was surprised to see it was stocked with tins of soup, beans, UHT milk, cereal, and jars of pasta sauce. The one next to it contained packets of pasta, rice, tea, coffee and a loaf of bread. Checking the labels, all of the food was in date. Curious, she crossed the room to the fridge and opened it to see it had been filled with milk, cheese, salad items, cold meats, a chicken, chops, mince and some vegetables.

Looking over her shoulder, Dan pointed to the contents of the fridge. 'What's this?'

'Didn't you organise it with the removal company? There must be a week's worth of shopping here.'

'I wish I'd thought of it, but the removal company wasn't exactly top end.' A shadow passed over his face and he looked like he wanted to say something else, but was silent.

'It's not just the food though. Have you seen how clean the cottage is?'

'The agent might have organised it for us, I guess. The cleaning at least. The food is a little over the top – unless, of course, they know something we don't.'

She wasn't sure if he was joking. Sometimes his deadpan delivery was hard for even her to read. 'I'm sure they'll re-charge us for it.'

'I'll check the contract in the morning.' Dan turned on the taps and began to wash his hands. 'I can't imagine I'd have agreed to that.'

No, I can't imagine either.

'The rest of the furniture is here and they've put the bed up. There are a load of boxes in the sitting room, along with our kitchen table and chairs.' Dan nodded over to the pine table in the middle of the kitchen. 'I think that'll be the first thing in the skip.'

'Indeed. This place is a museum to everything that was never hip. It's not even retro enough to be cool now. You know, it's very similar to a kitchen we had when I was little. I can picture Mum standing at that stove.' Esther rubbed at the small of her back. 'I could really do with a hot soak after that journey. My leg is aching fit to burn. I bet you're shattered after all that driving.'

'I'm not so bad just now, but I'll sleep well tonight. Did I see some towels and bedding in one of the boxes? I'll need to find the immersion switch if we want hot water tonight. Where did you stash the kettle?'

'Towels and bedding came up with the removal guys. Kettle's in the boot of the car. I'll get it.'

'No, stay here, I'll go. It's getting quite dark out now and you're bound to trip over.' Dan shut the door behind him and as he did so, the light overhead flickered and fizzed and the motor in the fridge coughed.

Esther listened to his footsteps echoing down the platform. She opened the fridge again, ignoring the sputtering lights in the cottage, and stared at the contents, trying to decide whether she was hungry enough to make a snack. Without warning, the hairs rose on the back of her neck and she had an acute feeling of being watched. She whipped around and looked out of the kitchen window, half-expecting to see someone looking in. There was no-one there. She laughed at herself, knowing her jitters came from the deep-rooted tiredness inside her.

Dan brought in another box and started to unpack the kettle, some cutlery, a selection of mugs and two plates. Then, with a flourish, he pulled out a bottle of Veuve Cliquot. 'Ta-da! We have to have it in mugs, but it'll still taste like a celebration.'

He was like a schoolboy showing off to a captive audience. She liked this version of him – it was a side she'd not seen much of in the last year.

'Just a drop for me, please. I don't want Bump hiccupping all night and getting a taste for booze before breast.'

He popped the cork, the way Esther had seen Eric teach him at their engagement party, holding the cork and turning the bottle. She hated being reminded that he was more like his father than she wanted to admit. She pushed the thoughts of Eric away, in case they led to thoughts about her own father. Nothing good ever came from dwelling on him and now wasn't the right time to raise the subject with Dan.

He poured the Champagne into the mugs and raised his.

'To our new baby, to our new life, to our new home . . . and to a new us.'

Esther clinked her mug against Dan's. At the mention of their new home, the ball of unhappiness dislodged from its hiding place behind her ribcage and rose upwards to nudge her heart. It would take a long time for Rosgill to feel like home.

'Evening.' A man-monolith stood in the doorway, blocking the fading remains of daylight.

Esther and Dan both jumped, startled. Esther glanced from the stranger to Dan, then back to the doorway. She thought she caught a flash of recognition in Dan's face and waited for him to speak first.

'Hi, I'm Dan and this is Esther.' In what seemed to her to be a flanking manoeuvre, he strode across the kitchen and shook hands with the stranger.

'Sorry to startle you both. I'm Michael – Mike – O'Rourke. I live up the glen; about two miles north-west. I'm probably your nearest neighbour as the crow flies,' he said, stooping so as not to bang his head on the lintel.

Dan, who had seemed to have been holding his breath, relaxed. Taking her cue from him, Esther motioned to Mike to sit down, pulling out a chair for him at the pine table. He crossed the kitchen with feline grace, folding his long legs under the table in a fluid movement. He glanced at her leg, the metal pylon plain to see, poking out from under her skirt.

In that moment, Esther could tell what kind of person he was. Over the years, she'd had the whole spectrum of reactions from people. Empathy, sympathy, embarrassment, condescension, curiosity. Almost everyone acted differently once they'd noticed her disability. Some people spoke to Dan instead, while others shuffled from foot to foot, unable to focus on anything except her missing limb. Most of the time it bypassed her as something other people needed to learn to deal with, but the worst people were the ones who wanted to know what had happened to her. Forcing her to relive the accident. No matter how kind their questioning, she was always left feeling sullied, invaded by their ghoulish desire for detail.

Mike's eyes locked on hers and she saw no judgement, no condescension or sympathy. She knew he saw her for who she was, not as a wounded creature to be cared for or pitied. His eyes were magnetic, drawing her in. She couldn't decide whether they were hazel or amber, and they seemed to shimmer as he returned her gaze. They were darker in the middle, reminding her of tiger-eye stones, fringed by long, black lashes. His whole expression implied mischief, of his own making, but also as though he was daring her to relive all her rebellions too. His dark hair curled just above his collar, longer on top, and he used both hands to push it back off his face, strong fingers raking through it. Dark stubble contoured his face and he gave off the scent of mountain forests as he moved.

Aware that she was staring, Esther felt heat radiating in her cheeks and, turning her back to them both, filled the kettle with water from the sink. She could see Dan and Mike reflected in the kitchen window and saw Mike reach a hand out towards Dan, before withdrawing it abruptly as the strip-light overhead dimmed and quivered. A tight silence fell over the men at the table.

'I hope you don't mind me dropping in on you like this? Did you have a good journey up?' Mike's soft Irish burr bent his words in the air.

'Well, it was a long journey, alright. We set off yesterday

and stayed in Edinburgh overnight.' Dan fiddled with his wedding ring as he spoke.

'You're not Scottish?' To her own ears, her question sounded shrill, accusatory.

'Neither are you.' He winked. 'I'm Irish, from County Clare, but I've lived a long time here, and other places. And where have you come up from? Bristol, is it?'

Dan reddened and nodded, but said nothing.

How could he know that? Esther couldn't put her finger on it, but something was out of kilter between the two men. She felt almost as though she was intruding onto a conversation that started some time ago. 'Have you two met each other before?'

Dan and Mike spoke at the same time.

'No.' Dan was emphatic.

'Yes.' Mike nodded.

Esther stood, hands on hips. 'Well, which is it?'

'I saw yer man up here when he was after looking to buy the place.' Mike's explanation seemed to trigger Dan's memory.

'Ah, right! You're the guy at the garage. I remember now.' Dan smiled as though he'd solved a mathematical puzzle. 'I was a bit full of myself – I'd just had the offer accepted on this place.'

'It was nice to see. I'm just glad someone has finally bought it and will put some life back into it. All of us are. We left a welcoming present for you, I hope you don't mind.' Mike gestured to the cupboards.

'All of you?' It was Dan's turn to look puzzled.

'The people living in the glen. It'll be nice to have some new life up here. No-one has lived here for . . . well, I don't know how long exactly, but it's been donkey's years.'

Esther shook her head at Dan's lack of manners. 'It was a lovely surprise, thank you. We were just wondering who'd been so kind. It was quite the mystery.'

'Well, you'll have noticed that we're quite remote. Not much in the way of shops between here and Invergill. Your arrival has caused some stirrings among the locals, right enough.' Mike's smile was economical. 'What are your plans?'

Dan answered him. 'We're setting up a writing centre, putting on short courses and the like, but if that doesn't take off, we're also toying with linking up to some of the outward-bound activities in the area. With these mountains around us, there must be a call for people wanting to go caving or climbing.'

Esther took up the theme. 'And if that doesn't work, we can always resort to just doing B&B.'

'Aye, well, you're maybe right. I'd say you've a lot of work to do before anyone comes, though.' Mike looked at Esther. 'And it won't be easy with a babby on the way.'

'How did you know?' Esther, puzzled, looked from him to Dan.

'Yer man here mentioned it.'

'Really?'

Dan cut in. 'So, what do you do up here, Mike?'

She tried to shake the feeling that there was something Dan wasn't saying, but it gnawed at her as she listened to the two men talking.

'In the winter I'm a ski instructor, but in the summer I do all manner of jobs. I'll take work wherever I can get it. I was kind of wondering . . . well, with summer approaching and with so much to do around here, you might want an extra pair of hands about the place?'

'We have builders coming on Monday.'

Esther glared at Dan, before turning to Mike. 'I'm sure there'll be something you can help with. Even if it's just clearing some of the jungle out there. You must know a lot about the area? Anything we need to be aware of?'

'I'd say you might find it a bit strange at first, being townies an' all. Just practical things like there's no Sunday opening or late night shopping here, so you'll need to plan ahead for things.' Mike spotted Dan's mobile phone on the counter. 'And you can forget a mobile signal unless you're in Invergill.'

'Really?' Dan raised an eyebrow.

'Aye. But you know, the glen is a beautiful place to live. I'm sure you'll both be spellbound before long.'

'Well, you wanted peace and quiet, Dan.' Esther laughed. 'It's a good job they're connecting the land line just after the Easter weekend – it's only a little over a week to wait. We'll have to go to Invergill tomorrow and let everyone know we've arrived safely.'

The lights sputtered again, then finally went out, plunging the kitchen into a murky half-light.

'Bloody electrics. Stay where you are, there's a torch in the car and I think I know where the fuse-board is.' Dan's chair scraped on the stone flags as he pushed it back.

Mike struck a match to light the gloom and, as he did, Esther saw the kitchen scene reflected at her in his amber eyes. The flame licked the air between them and the hairs on the back of her neck stood up again. Her reflection danced in the flame and then, as the match died, it was gone. They sat for a few moments in silence and Esther was relieved when Mike spoke.

'I'll go after him. Stay here, we'll soon have it fixed.' Mike stood up, leaving Esther alone in the darkness.

After a few minutes, the power came back on and Esther heard a car start and pull away. She assumed it was Mike leaving and waited for Dan to come back in, but when there was no sign of him, she wandered out onto the platform. Their silver Toyota was still at the bottom of the lane where Dan had parked it, and she couldn't see either man. She stood for a moment, annoyed that Dan would be so thoughtless as to leave her alone when everything was so unfamiliar to her. She spotted a bench further down the platform and sat on it, taking in her surroundings.

She shivered. The evening air had a bite to it as the inky dark consumed the twilight haze over the mountains. As the day became night, the shadows from the trees reached out towards her, fingers of darkness poised, as though ready to snatch her away. The moon poked out from behind a cloud and the light of the sun dipped, the transformation from day to night happening as Esther absorbed the landscape. She looked up at the sky, trying to see patterns in the stars, looking for things she could recognise. The glen, remote and brooding as the gods, felt different to when she'd arrived. A pair of bats flitted across the station to the mountain, leathery wings beating through the night. An owl screeched to announce its presence and she tried to ignore the rustling bushes behind the opposite platform. The night brought with it an energy that had been absent during the day. How would she ever settle? It all felt so ominous.

Sophie would have loved it here. A wave of grief hit Esther in the guts, threatening to rise up into her chest and break out through her ribs. She quickly pulled her thoughts back and placed them in the lead casket inside her heart. She wouldn't allow herself to think about Sophie. Not now.

She fetched her coat from the car, then went back to sit on the platform, waiting for Dan. She was grateful for the time to think, to be alone, but at the same time she was annoyed that Dan would just go off and leave her, without even saying where he was going or how long he would be. She didn't want their first night in their new home to be punctuated by a row, but he was making it difficult. She put her hand on her stomach, taking comfort from the fact that she wasn't alone.

Caught up in the romance of becoming a family and the prospect of happy times ahead, she'd purposefully avoided dwelling on the practicalities. Doctors, midwives, hospitals. She'd need a barrage of health services to call on, not only to care for her pregnancy, but for regular adjustments to her prosthetic as her body changed. Dan, usually so methodical and orderly, didn't provide her with any answers to her questions and she worried that they were too remote if something went wrong. There was a recognisable difference in Dan. His mood was lighter, he seemed unperturbed, as though every practicality she placed before him to scrutinise bore no more weight than gossamer.

Now that it was over, she could finally allow herself to admit that she'd been dreading the long journey up here, confined in a small space with him. It was hard to anticipate his mood these last few months, but as their moving day loomed, so his mood seemed to lift. She, on the other hand, had become more anxious – their roles had reversed, but when? What had caused this change in him? And wasn't this what she'd wanted all along? It seemed churlish to be complaining. He'd been light-hearted and affectionate on the journey up, like he'd been in the early days of their relationship when everything was new and there was still lots to discover about each other. His actions seemed to her to be much freer than she was used to from him. She knew she should be pleased, but the thought burrowed into her and gnawed away from inside: if only he hadn't lied to her for so long. If only she didn't feel like he was building a roof over them while she was still laying the foundations. They were moving at two different speeds and she was lagging behind. Even so, she felt optimistic that this new phase in their lives would lead to a closer and deeper emotional connection with him, and that this time it would truly be them against the world, just as he had promised many times before.

On days like today, it would be easy to forget the sadness and hurt that had permeated their marriage for the last year. She thought of stark days and savage nights when their bed was a shipwreck and they'd clung to the sides, praying for rescue. Although she was trying to put the past behind them, the icy touch of those memories stabbed at her heart, and she knew that while she had forgiven him, it would be a long time before she could forget.

Eric didn't help matters. The more time and distance between Dan and his father the better, as far as Esther was concerned. She hoped Eric's influence would recede and she'd finally learn who her husband was, away from Eric's mutterings and curses of eternal damnation for anyone who fell short of his impossible standards. It was only two days since they'd said goodbye to him, but she questioned whether the reason for Dan's brighter disposition was an unspoken recognition that he didn't have to live up to his father's expectations on a daily basis.

When they'd said goodbye, Eric had clutched at Esther's hand. Looking deeply into her eyes, as though trying to gauge the purity of her soul, he'd leaned forward to whisper in her ear, "Run, Rabbit. Run." His fingers, claw-like with arthritis, and his warm breath dank with age, made her want to recoil as he pressed on. "Blessed is the man who remains steadfast under trial."

She shook her head at the thought. Having long since stopped trying to decipher Eric's ramblings, she now wondered what he'd meant. Maybe she was being unfair and he was doing his best. After all, who has all the answers? Not her own father, certainly. The only answers he'd ever sought were at the bottom of a bottle. Patrick had occupied her thoughts more and more. She had questions only he could provide the answers to, but did she want to ask them?

Sophie would have known what to do. Another sucker-punch.

If she thought hard enough, she could hear Sophie's gravelly laugh and her terrible singing. She'd loved how Sophie took advantage of her ditzy manner and appearance to wrong foot people who could only think in stereotypes. She knew everything about Sophie – even how she'd been named after a character in a book. Sophie had been there for all of Esther's milestones. Graduating from university, meeting Dan, renovating their first house, moving to the waterside apartment, getting married. When she was pregnant the first time, it was Sophie Esther had told first. And Sophie had been with her when she started to miscarry.

Esther had become adept at compartmentalising her feelings, but too late, she realised she'd let one too many recollections slip past her. She tried to push the memories away, but they were taking shape, forcing her to replay the years of friendship. Random images flashed before her.

Sophie in a red dress, laughing.

Shots of vodka lined up on a bar.

The allergy rash on Sophie's neck from eating shellfish.

Sophie dressed as Wonder Woman for Halloween.

Dan's face as he took the phone call.

Before she could stop it, the memories cornered her, baying like a pack of wild dogs for her attention.

"Sit down," he'd said. "There's been an accident."

Over the last year, she'd grown a defensive crust over her grief, but underneath the scab, the wound was raw and inflamed. She couldn't stop the images and snatches of remembered conversation coming at her and she crossed her arms across her stomach, doubling over to brace herself against the pain that burst out from her heart into every cell in her body.

'It's Sophie. She's dead.'

Esther had heard the words and knew what they meant, knew the enormity of them, knew that Dan would never joke or get something so important so wrong, and yet she laughed at the absurdity of it. He made no sense. For the first time in their life together, she couldn't make out what he was saying. Sophie was on holiday in Rhodes, she'd had a text from her just that morning.

'Darling, I know this is hard to hear.' He knelt down beside her and took her hands in his. 'She was diving off a boat and hit her head on some rocks below the surface. They said it was instant.'

Esther remembered how time had slowed and how, when she'd looked at Dan, it was as though she was seeing him through cellophane. She could picture the cerulean sky, the golden sands, and the ant-like holiday makers against the backdrop of bland hotels, it was as though she'd been transported into a child's painting. It would have been idyllic were it not for the water blooming red, the shouts of the other people on the boat, the frantic efforts to save her friend.

Her thoughts tumbled over each other. What happens when a person stops living? What's left behind? There was evidence of Sophie everywhere. The photograph of her and Esther taken at a fancy-dress party. The DVD Esther had been meaning to return. Books they'd bought for each other. A touch of her hand, a shared look. And that was only a tiny fraction of all the thousands of points where their lives intersected, there were hundreds of thousands more. No-one would ever know all the things they'd said to each other, all the things they'd done together, all the things they didn't need to say. Most of it would be lost, distilled down to a few memories, postcards and photographs, and when Esther died, the remaining fragments would be lost forever. Her thoughts continued to pitch and spill.

'But who's going to feed her chickens?'

Dan had looked at her as though he'd never seen her before. And that was how she'd felt then – like she had to be a whole new person, a person who didn't have Sophie to prop her up.

And that was how she'd been since, moving through her life, getting on with things and making decisions she wasn't sure she'd have made if Sophie had still been alive. Like this move. Like staying with Dan and trying for another baby. It would have been easier to leave, but she was afraid. She knew that the move would herald a new chapter in their lives and there were so many things to look forward to. None of that mattered because when she was alone, she couldn't block out the voice telling her it was no use running away from her grief. It was bound to catch up with her.

The quietness of their new home thundered in her ears. In Bristol, she could hear the cars, buses, and sirens, even though their apartment looked over the river. She'd often hear drunken laughter as people walked the path along the riverfront on their way to that week's trendy opening. Bristol also harboured memories of Sophie everywhere Esther looked.

Her heart tightened and she looked at her watch. Dan had been gone for nearly an hour. She pulled her mobile out of her coat pocket. Still no signal, just as Mike had predicted. He was an odd one, she thought. Turning up like that, as though he had some prior claim. Esther was unsettled by the encounter and yet Mike had been pleasant in the brief exchange they'd had. There was something about his eyes that unnerved her. Maybe it was their unusual colour, or the intensity with which he looked at her.

She scrolled through her address book, deleting the numbers she'd never need again: hairdressers, doctors, dentists. All manner of people whose job it was to keep her well and make her beautiful. Sophie's name was next on the list. Esther's thumb hovered over the delete key. She pressed it, then when the confirmation message popped up, she pressed cancel. Esther was not ready to let go just yet. She stared at the phone, summoning all her will not to cry. She quickly scrolled to voicemail. Two saved messages, both from Sophie. Esther pressed 'play' and waited for the dial tone which didn't come.

The noise of a car approaching down the bumpy track broke her reverie. She put the phone back in her pocket and wiped her nose on the cuff of her coat sleeve, feeling the scratchy tweed rubbing against her skin. A Land Rover pulled up and Dan spilled out of the passenger side, bent double with laughter. Mike got out of the driver's side, also laughing, and clapped Dan on the back. The two men straightened up and opened the rear door of the vehicle. Mike lifted out a piece of machinery and Dan reached into the back, pulling out two large petrol cans.

'What's so funny?'

Both men stopped as though the sound of her voice had brought them back to reality.

'I was just telling Dan some stories about my Mammy. Killing me with kindness one minute and smacking my legs with a wooden spoon in the next breath. I asked her once whether God was her invisible friend and got the walloping of my life for it.' Mike spoke with a fondness at the memory.

It didn't seem that funny to Esther, particularly considering Dan's religious upbringing, and she didn't know how to respond.

Dan saved her. 'Mike has lent us a generator so we have a back-up power source. I'll set it up tomorrow, then on Monday, when the builders come, I'll get them to check the electrics over.'

Mike gestured to the two petrol cans. 'These'll see you right for a couple of days if the power goes off again. I'll be off now and leave you fine people to your bed. You'll no doubt be tired after your long journey.'

A look passed between the two men that she couldn't interpret.

'If you need anything, my croft is about two miles north of here. There's a sign for the reservoir, go past that and I'm the next turning on the left, about half a mile further on.' Mike leaned forward to kiss Esther on the cheek.

Surprised, she unconsciously put her hand to her face, as the air cooled her skin where his lips had brushed. Esther watched the Land Rover reverse and turn away from Rosgill. She decided to wait until morning to ask Dan more about Mike. She was too tired to think straight and the nagging pain in her leg was becoming difficult to ignore.

❧

The lights in the cottage went off one by one: first the kitchen, then the hallway, then the bathroom, landing and, a long while after, the bedroom. Darkness enveloped the building once more and a breeze lifted leaves and tossed them along the platform. The station canopy groaned, relaying news of their arrival through the shifting air. The stream took up the message, embellishing the details, and the trees, shrouded in the first kiss of mist, sighed.

2

SUNDAY

THE MOON GLOWERED in the velvet sky, peeping from behind steel-smoke clouds, inspecting the new arrivals and sending shadows to play on the mountainside. Phosphorescent stars bobbed and curtsied in a celestial chorus line, in a bid to outshine the moon.

Down below in the glen, fern fronds curled tight against the cold and the bracken branches spread, protecting the ground from the seeping damp. Snowdrops thrusting from the iron earth, folded in on themselves, impervious to the freezing air; the compulsion to survive hidden underneath each delicate petal shroud. Heralding the first glimmerings of a spring that threatened never to come.

As time and tide ebbed and flowed, so the moon gained in size and stature. Just a few more nights and the earth would once again feel the full force of her ambition; feel the silver light energising the darkness. The moon observed the scene below, satisfied with the unfolding events.

During the night, a limpid fog settled over the halt, haunting and smothering until the air was lifeless, dank and mute. Wheels of mist snared the station, suspending time and reaching far down the glen. Crystal cobwebs, dew-heavy, collapsed under the weight of the atmosphere and the black grouse halted the morning mating call. Red squirrel mothers, heavy with kittens, lazed in dreys built in the crooks of trees, waiting for the return of better weather. Squirrel fathers kept watch over their precious stockpiles of nuts, occasionally stripping bark to relieve the boredom. Nothing moved. Nothing sounded.

❦

The old station creaked and groaned, maybe no more than usual, but enough to stop Esther from sleeping deeply. When she did succumb, her dreams were haunted by a savage green forest, closing in all around her, the air fetid with rotting vegetation. Aware of her surroundings, in the hours between night and day, it seemed to her that the building was protesting at their presence and she was glad to see the watery first light through the gaps in the shutters.

She rolled over and studied Dan's face. By now, she knew every fine line: his sandy lashes and heavy eyelids, shutters over the flint-grey eyes she knew so well; the thousands of tiny bristles, some red, some blonde, some almost black, that punctured his skin during the night. Added together, they became all the recognisable signs of him, but gave nothing away about the man himself. Her living puzzle of flesh and bone and logic.

She blamed Eric for Dan's coldness, not allowing herself to admit that it might just be his nature. It was easier to blame Eric. If he was the cause, then she reasoned she could reverse the damage he'd done; that it was possible. By loving

Dan, she could chisel away at his facade, sculpting, moulding and polishing him, until he understood how to love her back. He just needed someone to understand him, to show him. In return, Dan let her in – just a little – behind the portcullis.

She thought about the sampler Dan's mother had stitched, which still hung in the porch of the vicarage.

My father's house has many rooms. John 14:2.

Esther knew it was a reference to the afterlife and wondered if Olivia had known she was dying as she sat and sewed. But it could equally apply to Dan. As she looked at her sleeping husband, she asked herself how many of his rooms were still locked to her.

She considered reaching out to him, to feel the ripples of his wiry body under her hand, but stopped herself. The schism in their marriage, so wide and so deep, yawned between them and she had to struggle to remember how it felt to be his wife, how to be herself again. Every look, every word, every action seemed so loaded with meaning. If he responded to her touch, would he think she'd forgiven him and that they could just go back to being normal again? If he didn't respond, would she simply chalk up this rejection and add it to the others? It was time they stopped for breath, to be themselves again and to hope that the events of the last year hadn't irrevocably changed them. The voice deep inside her head persisted. She had to let go of it or they'd never be able to put the past behind them and she felt the weight of her own expectations, pressing into the fabric of their marriage.

If she could just unravel her thoughts, like pulling a loose stitch on a jumper, perhaps she'd be able to unpick everything that had happened over the last year, starting with losing the baby, and she'd wake up to find herself in Bristol still. Then none of this, moving to Scotland and giving everything that was familiar up, would have to happen. Sophie would be looking forward to being an honorary aunt to Esther's child and wouldn't be dead. She looked at her watch – just coming up to half-past nine – and felt her stomach tighten at the thought of going to Invergill to ring Eric. He'd no doubt be worrying about them and wouldn't hesitate in letting them know how selfish they'd been not to call him when they'd arrived.

Edging herself out of bed, she ran her hands over her stump, checking to make sure her skin hadn't become irritated after the car journey. She'd only had to deal with a wound ulcer once and the thought of being bedridden for weeks while it healed made her pay careful attention to limb care. Satisfied, she pulled a sock over her stump. There was a slight puckering where the silvery scar welded her skin together, but for the most part, her residual limb was smooth and hairless. Fitting her leg was as natural now as cleaning her teeth. It hadn't always been like that though, and she thought about the weeks and months following the accident. All those physiotherapy sessions. Learning to sit, stand, walk. It was all so long ago but she couldn't easily forget the fire that raged through every nerve; the white-hot pain that had her begging the doctors to cut her whole leg off, just so she could be at peace. Teaching herself to get back into a car again though had taken much more than physiotherapy, and if she was honest with herself, it was the real reason she hadn't come up here with Dan before now. Sometimes the accident came back to her in her dreams and she'd waken, drenched in sweat, clawing at the sheets. In recent months though, there had been a subtle shift and her dreams were haunted by the shadowy figure of her father. Since she'd found out she was pregnant again, he'd been on her mind more and more.

She stood and tested her weight, stretching out her leg just as the physiotherapist advocated, all these years later reluctant to vary her routine, and went downstairs to the kitchen. She pulled her left trainer on, before the coldness from the stone flags seeped into her bones. As she opened the front door, the wall of white fog took her by surprise, adding to her disorientation. Esther paused and breathed in the icy air. Unable to see more than a few feet in front of her, she skirted along the platform, wary of tripping or stumbling, trying to get her bearings.

The platform canopy continued its creaking; its cawing the only sound she could hear. No cars, no road noise, no birds even. The noise overhead taunted her, and she looked up at the fretwork of faded white dagger boards, tiny upside-down tombstones, fringing the canopy roof. The fog bleached the remaining colour out of the building. To her right, she could just make out the shape of the old wooden bench she had sat on last night. The fog reduced the sage green paint to monochrome grey, along with the rest of the woodwork. The bench seemed to her to be rooted in the past, its cast iron supports anchored into the platform surface and the seat itself like the planking on a gangway, the bridge between land and the place people were travelling to. She wondered how it had had survived all these years, exposed to the weather and souvenir hunters.

She pulled her sleeve down over her hand and wiped part of the seat dry, before sitting down. Looking out across the platform and the abandoned track-bed, she tried to make out the shapes on the other side and thought she saw a movement, but the fog blanketed everything. She gave a wry smile, thinking how isolated they were. After all, she'd wanted it to be just her and Dan, somewhere remote. She could hear her mother admonishing her, "Be careful what you wish for."

It was so unnaturally quiet. The fog blanketed the landscape, clinging to its curves and hollows, hiding sound underneath its folds. Esther felt edgy after her poor sleep, no less unsettled by her surroundings now that it was daylight. Something nudged against her leg and she jumped, her expelled breath mingling with the mist. She looked down, but there was nothing there. A movement in her peripheral vision caught her attention and she turned her head sharply to see what it was. A dark shape leapt out of the blankness, jumping onto the bench beside her.

'Shit!'

She laughed with relief as a black cat nuzzled into the crook of her arm. 'You scared me, you daft thing. Where did you come from, eh?' She fussed the cat as her pulse returned to normal. The cat rasped back at her, nudging her hand when she stopped.

'Esther? Esther, are you out here?'

Even though he was only at the kitchen door, the fog bent the sound waves, making his voice seem further away.

'Yep.' Esther picked up the cat and took it back inside with her. 'And I've found a friend.'

'Who's this, then?' Dan ruffled the fur on the cat's head.

'Dunno, no collar or tag. She nearly frightened me to death jumping up at me out of the fog.' She looked up at Dan from under her fringe. 'I'm going to call her Misty.'

'Misty?'

'You know, because of the fog.' She searched Dan's face for any hint that he found her joke funny, but as usual, he stonewalled her.

'Typical of you to find something in need of rescuing. And in any case, she's a he.'

She bit her tongue. It was hardly worth picking him up on. Perhaps he was right when he said she tried too hard to please people, to keep everything on an even keel. But did it matter? Wasn't it that very quality in her that had appealed to him at the start? Besides, it stopped her thinking about her own fears.

Even so, his teasing of her compulsion to solve other people's problems had started to grate. For her, it was an important part of who she was, and if she could prevent suffering or make someone else's life a little easier, wasn't that a good thing? If only he'd allow her a small win every now and then without commenting. After all, he'd got his way by moving them up here, taking her away from her work at the refuge. He'd been scathing in the past about her attempts to help the women who, in his view, were doomed to repeat the same mistakes over and over. Futile, he'd called it. She'd tried reasoning with him, tried to point out that her own mother had been one of those women. He had pulled her tight to him and stroked her hair. "But you have me to look after you," he'd said. And it was true. He made her feel safe – and still did.

'Then I'll call him Major Tom.'

Dan shrugged. 'Don't encourage it. It clearly belongs to someone. Make sure you wash your hands properly after handling him, we don't want you contracting anything nasty.' He reached into his pocket and pulled out a small bottle of anti-bacterial hand gel. He poured a little onto his left palm, then rubbed the liquid over both hands, taking great care to ensure that he didn't miss any of the creases in his knuckles and massaging the liquid all around his nails. He offered the bottle to her.

Esther said nothing, but filled the kettle, and switched it on. She stared at the stainless-steel body, spattered with dried-out circles where water had splashed and dulled the shine, and weighed up her words.

'Dan, you know nothing is going to go wrong this time, don't you?'

'You can't say that, Es. We just don't know.'

'I'm trying to apply logic, like you're always asking me to. Think about it. Statistically, we have a good chance, I'm nearly twelve weeks gone now, out of the worst danger of miscarrying. I'm thirty-four and my health is good – apart from this stupid leg – and even then, I get around better than many people.' She reached out for his hands and held them in hers. 'Most importantly, I feel really well. I can't allow myself to think about last time. Okay?'

Her tone, which started off low and calm, changed pitch and her question was sharper than she intended. There weren't more than a few minutes of each day where she didn't fear losing this baby too, but she couldn't tell him that. She woke up terrified every morning in case she'd got it wrong and she wasn't pregnant at all, but she thought that voicing her fears would make the possibility real and he had no time for her superstitions.

He pulled his hands away from hers and recommenced the ritual cleansing with the hand gel. 'You'll be due a scan soon.'

She swallowed hard, the lump of anxiety back in her throat threatening to choke her. She couldn't believe he could talk about the scan so casually. Just thinking about it brought back all the memories she'd tried so hard to suppress; how her world had turned upside-down when she went for her last scan – the pregnancy ending in miscarriage. Surely he felt the same? Even if she had managed to keep the bulk of her anxiety from him, he couldn't be so insensitive as to think she wouldn't be concerned this time round. Her grip tightened on the teaspoon.

He seemed not to notice her struggle. 'How did you sleep?'

She paused before answering, deciding whether to accept his change of direction, or pursue the tails of yet another argument.

'Not the best of sleeps. The house had a lot to say for itself last night.'

'Yeah, it'll be a while yet before we get used to the bumps and bangs. It doesn't help that it's been empty so long. It needs a thorough warming through. That bathroom was arctic this morning.'

She put the two mugs of steaming coffee on the worktop. 'What's the plan of action for the day, then? Are we going to Invergill to let everyone know we got here safely?'

'I'd rather not chance the road in this fog, not until we are a bit more familiar with it.'

She smiled. She hadn't been looking forward to going out in the fog either.

'Eric will be worried.'

'No. I rang him last night from Mike's.'

'Oh. Okay.' She knew she should have been relieved not to have to speak to her father in law, yet at the same time couldn't help feeling excluded. Why hadn't Dan mentioned it last night?

'I vote we unload what's left in the car and get cracking on making this place home. We can sort through some of those boxes in the living room if you want?'

She nodded, circling the rim of her cup with her index finger. 'Maybe.'

Unpacking the boxes seemed so final. It meant they really were staying here and her skin contracted at the thought. Even without the fog, her surroundings seemed so hostile and alien to her and instead of feeling excited, the now familiar sense of dread tugged at her.

'I'd wanted to go up the glen and explore a bit before the builders arrive tomorrow, but I don't think that will happen, unless the fog lifts.' He took hold of her hand, his thumb rubbing the place where her wedding ring should be.

'This is the right thing you know, Essie. I know you loved our life in Bristol, but that's over now and we have to make the best of this.'

She pulled her hand away and picked up her coffee mug. 'I know.'

Esther carried a bucket of hot, soapy water to the waiting room, using cleaning as an excuse to avoid unpacking. This room was to be their new kitchen, in the heart of the building, so that the cottage could be turned over to guest bedrooms. She looked around her. The windows either side of the door were quarter-paned, running from dado height to the ceiling. The lower half of each window was frosted and etched with the letters L, M & S. A wooden plank bench ran around the room, at roughly knee height, attached to the panelling and painted to match the rest of the wood. The walls were painted a creamy colour, from above the panelling to the picture rail, but the intervening years had caused flaking and discolouration. Still, she thought, at least there's no damp to contend with.

She set to work on the wood panelling, the sponge exposing the untainted paint below, pushing particles of grime into loops and whorls, making colossal fingerprint patterns. She hoped it would be possible to strip the wood back and tried to chip off some paint with her thumbnail, but it had hardened so much over time that she didn't even dent it. She liked cleaning, liked the feeling that she was making something into a better version of itself. She had a memory of following her mother around as she wiped everything down with a weak solution of bleach. Whenever she smelled bleach, she'd be transported right back to those Saturday mornings at home.

Dan popped his head around the door. 'How are you getting on? Do you need a break?'

She ignored his fussing. 'Good, I think. This panelling is lovely. Do you think we'll be able to keep some of it?' She straightened up and surveyed her progress. 'What do you think?'

'Yeah, let's save on materials wherever we can. The money isn't going to last for ever and if there is stuff here we can use, then we should. I wonder if we can strip the floor back, too?' He scuffed at the floor with his walking boot.

Esther bent down and dipped a scrubbing brush into the bucket and began to scrub in a small circular motion on the floor. She whistled, softly. 'Well, will you look at that?'

Dan peered closer at the honey-coloured spot Esther had revealed. 'Parquet?'

'Looks like it. I thought it was just dark brown planking, but I think it's years and years of grime.' She stood upright again, a rueful smile playing on her lips. 'So genius, I now have even more cleaning to do.' She nodded at the windows. 'What's LM & S mean?'

'London, Midland and Scottish Railways. That was the company that operated the line before British Rail. I think this station was originally built and operated by Highland Railways though, I'm sure I saw it on the deeds.'

Her eye was drawn to a square of panelling on the wall next to the cast-iron fireplace. It stood a few millimetres proud of the rest of the wood detail.

Dan followed her gaze. 'What's up?'

She ran her fingers over the panel. 'This doesn't seem right, let me just . . . ah, there it is. It's a door, well, maybe door is the wrong word. I think there's probably a recess behind there, where they used to store the coal for the fire. I can just about make out the outline of a keyhole, but it's gunked up with paint.'

He leaned down to look closer.

'Hah! Curiouser and curiouser. Do you think there's some cake or a potion behind the door? I bet there is.' She giggled. 'Odds on, I'm right.' She held her hand out, ready for Dan to take the bet, but when he showed no signs of reciprocating, let her arm drop to her side.

'Betting is sinful.'

'Ah, come on, Dan!' Esther nudged him with her elbow. 'I was making a book joke. You know, Alice down the rabbit-hole? After all, you're a writer now.'

'Non-fiction.'

Esther's pulse quickened and her blood sang in her ears. An image of a clammy forest, the air stained with moss, flitted across her consciousness and was gone. She breathed in, deeply.

'Dan, it wasn't a criticism. As far as I'm concerned, you're a writer, that's why we are here. Why we've given up our jobs—'

'Your job.'

'Okay then, my job. I'd have to cut back on my hours anyway, what with Bump on the way. We're a team. In this together, okay?' She smiled when he nodded back at her.

She didn't say that since Sophie had died, she'd found it hard to be at the refuge. She spent long afternoons in her office, waiting to hear Sophie's footsteps down the corridor, all the while knowing she'd never hear them again. Even before Sophie's death, Esther knew her time there was coming to an end. Being apart from Dan made her anxiety worse. She didn't like not knowing where he was, or what he was doing, and didn't want to allow herself the time to wonder who he was with. Perhaps she should share these thoughts with him, but even as the thought occurred to her, she knew it would never happen. Dan had closed that chapter of their life and she wasn't strong enough to attempt a re-reading.

She felt a movement against her leg, just like on the platform. She looked down to where Major Tom sat, waiting for her to notice him. 'I'll see can I find something to feed him.'

'Why bother? You're just encouraging him.' Dan scowled at the cat, kicking out with his boot.

'And you're just a big bag of fun today.' She kissed him on the forehead and called the cat, who followed her out of the waiting room and up the platform to the cottage.

As she opened a tin of tuna and forked it out into a bowl, the quietness of her surroundings wreathed around her, igniting her nerves, until the air was perfumed with a heady mix of anxiety and doubt. Somewhere upstairs, a door slammed and she jumped. The noise pulled her back to another house, another kitchen, when she was five years old and unable to make sense of the things her parents did.

This time, it had all happened so quickly. Her mother, Anthea, standing at the stove, cooking dinner. Her father, Patrick, at the table reading the newspaper and listening to the racing results. The smell of the hot oil in the chip pan and the sound of the neighbour's cylinder mower growling through the grass.

'Come here,' he'd said and Anthea had laughed.

'No, I need to watch this pan.'

'Come here, I told you.' Her father laughing, her mother stone-faced.

Anthea signalled to Esther to leave, so she ran upstairs, away from the threats and the blows, and the shouting that would only end with the banging of the front door. It could have been minutes, or maybe hours, and he was gone. Esther heard her mother in the bathroom, splashing cold water on her face, washing away the salty tears that she didn't want anyone to see.

She had more memories like that one. Yet when she thought about her father, they weren't the first ones that came to mind.

Her favourite memory was of the day he took her to see the circus. She could remember how his leathery skin felt as she slipped her hand inside his. She hadn't liked the clowns, their painted faces were the fabric of her nightmares, and he'd held her tight against him, keeping her from harm. His woollen coat had smelled of tobacco and his aftershave, Old Spice. In the interval, he'd bought doughnuts for them both, and they had a competition to see who could eat a whole doughnut without licking their lips. He'd won.

Setting the dish on the floor for the cat, she smiled. He'd loved her, she was sure. So why didn't he ever try to see her again once he'd left? Was the weight of what he'd done to her too much to carry? She'd asked Anthea about him a few times over the years. Each time, her mother had shut the subject down, refusing to even utter his name. She wished she knew how to contact him, how to make it right between them. If he could see her now, grown, married, pregnant, maybe he'd be able to put the past behind him, the way she wanted to. Maybe he'd feel able to be part of their lives again. After all, he was going to be a grandfather. Anthea would take more thinking about. And Dan – she'd have to find a way of getting him onside too. After losing his own mother, Esther hoped he'd understand why she needed to find her father, but whenever she mentioned him, Dan went straight into protective mode. It was easier not to speak about her father, but it didn't stop her heart craving him.

Deciding there was no time like the present, that if he was serious about the fresh start he'd been plugging, she closed the kitchen door and made her way back up the platform, determined to make Dan listen to her this time.

Esther returned to the waiting room as Dan was trying to prise open the secret panel with a screwdriver. He swore softly under his breath, unable to get sufficient purchase to lever the door open. There was a sharp crack as the wood splintered and he stopped, as though fearful of breaking the panel completely.

'Here, let me.' Esther knelt as best she could beside him and put her hands on the panel. Leaning closer, with her ear to the wood, she thought she could make out a very faint rustling. 'Shh! I think I can hear something.' The noise stopped.

Esther listened for a short while, but there was no further sound. 'I must be hearing things. There's a bunch of keys in the kitchen drawer. I'm sure one of them will open this.'

He stood and reached down to help her up. 'A job for later, maybe.'

She took a deep breath, having rehearsed everything she wanted to say. 'Dan?'

'Hmm?'

'I want to look for my father.' She stilled, shoulders stiff, waiting for the objections to fall.

'Why?' He pulled her close and wrapped his arms around her.

'Because we're having a baby. Because he's going to be a granddad and I think he should have the chance to be part of that.'

She felt his chest rise and fall against her cheek. Heard his heart beat, solid, steady, strong.

'What does Anthea think about that?'

'She doesn't know. I haven't told her.'

'Because you think she'll be upset?'

'Yes. But what if he's changed? Doesn't he deserve a second chance?'

Dan smiled and kissed the top of her head. 'That's what I love about you. Your capacity to forgive.'

She swallowed hard. If she could forgive Patrick, why wasn't it so easy to forgive Dan?

'Is it really what you want? What if he doesn't want to see you?'

It was her deepest fear and in his usual way, he'd homed in on it.

'Then I'll know. Once and for all.'

Dan considered what she'd said. 'I'm not sure, Es. It's a big gamble and I need you here, with me. There's so much to do here and I don't want you getting hurt.'

He dropped his arms and stood away from her, the concern plain to see in his eyes. She decided to play her trump card.

'If you had the chance to spend more time with your mum, would you?'

'It's different. She was ill. You can't compare the two.'

'Alcoholism is an illness too, Dan. And anyway, maybe he's straightened up?'

He sighed. 'Yes, sure, let's look for him,' he paused, then shook his head. 'We'll do it together. All I ask is that you wait until after the baby is born. I don't want any added stress on you before then. We've got enough to contend with.'

'Do you mean that? You're not angry?'

'Angry? No, of course not. You are silly, sometimes. If it's what you really want, then we should do it. I can't promise it'll turn out how you want, but let's give it a go.' He squeezed her against him again. 'Let's go and have some lunch.'

In one short conversation, she felt they'd made more progress than in weeks. She'd been certain he would object to her plan, though she couldn't articulate why. Perhaps she should cut him some slack and trust him a bit more. Although she was keen to get on with the search, she understood his reasons for wanting to delay. The trouble was that while part of her was happy to put it off; it would give her more time to warm Anthea up to the idea – she knew she wouldn't be able to wait. She'd need to do things quietly, slowly, so as not to attract suspicion. Especially now that she had a lead.

After lunch, Dan locked himself away in the sitting room,

sorting through his books and doing some research. He couldn't get an internet connection on his laptop, but Esther thought this was probably a good thing. She'd half expected him to ask her to help with unpacking the boxes, but he made it clear he didn't want to be disturbed. Feeling guilty that she'd managed to get out of unpacking, she decided to explore the rest of the property instead, testing herself to see if any of it could ever feel like home.

She opened the door to the ticket hall. On one side, there was a connecting door to the waiting room, and on the other, a door to the store room. Dan had earmarked this space for meetings and classes, but Esther couldn't see how that would work without ripping out the counter and ticket windows. The walls in this room were part-tiled, the deep green ceramic tiles still glossy after all these years. The top row of Victorian tiles, moulded in relief, followed a geometric design. He'd told her once, on a visit to the V&A in London, that the style was called Islamic. The Islamic Ceramics. She'd giggled, but Dan had frowned at her, not sharing the joke. The tiling was beautiful, and she hoped he'd incorporated them into the room re-design.

The area behind the counter was crammed with an assortment of built-in shelves, heavy oak cupboards, and free-standing metal filing drawers. She pulled one of them open and was surprised to see an ink pad and date stamp, along with a supply of paper with the British Rail logo on the letterhead. Sure that the ink would have dried out, she slammed the stamp onto the pad, disturbing the dust on top of the cabinet. Then she stamped one of the sheets of paper. The imprint was faint, but just readable: 03 July 1964. What had happened to this place in the last fifty years? Why was it empty for so long?

Realising that she hadn't been interested enough to ask Dan about its more recent history, she felt ashamed of herself. He was the one putting all his faith into this project and she'd simply trotted along behind him, willing to go where he led. No wonder she felt such a disconnect between her old life and their new home.

She reappraised the room. It would make a good office for them once she'd managed to clear out all the clutter. She spotted a Bakelite telephone on the desk in the corner. Some of the items might even be worth keeping – she was sure she'd seen an article in a Sunday magazine about how old phones could be reconditioned to work on modern exchanges. For the first time, she could picture herself sitting at the old desk, with its embossed leather top, doing their accounts and planning courses and events.

With pleasure, she noted that the floor was stone-flagged, made to cope with the heavier foot traffic of a ticket office. Neither of the connecting doors to the other rooms would open and she hadn't thought to pick up the keys from the kitchen drawer. She decided to go back for them and to see if she could match the keys to any of the locks. As she passed the waiting room from the outside, she felt a sudden urge to go in. She stopped in the doorway, puzzled. The cupboard next to the fireplace was open.

Her first instinct was to call Dan, but checked her runaway imagination, assuming that he must have managed to open the door after all. She shook her head and pulled the cupboard door open wide. Her breath caught as she noticed the scratches on the inside of the door; they looked fresh. She paused before reaching in to the cupboard, steeling herself in case a mouse ran towards her, or worse, across her hand, and was relieved when she pulled out a pile of fusty newspapers and blocky railway timetables. Blowing off the dust, she wiped her hands on her jeans. The oldest timetable dated from 1912 and showed services to Perth, Inverness and Aberdeen. She inhaled their old-bookshop smell, then thought what Dan would have had to say had he seen her. He was right, she supposed, she did need to start taking more care of herself for the baby's sake.

The newspapers were a bit more interesting, though they mostly dated from the 1960s. At first glance, the stories didn't seem very eye-catching, but a couple of the papers referred to a typhoid outbreak in Aberdeen. Esther put them to one side, thinking that there might be articles she could frame or put into a scrapbook for visitors to read.

She was about to close the cupboard door when an object at the back caught her attention. She stretched in to reach it and pulled out a heavy wooden disc, about half an inch thick and four inches across, slightly larger than the palm of her hand. The disc was carved on one side with three hares, chasing each other round in a circle, their ears meeting at a point in the centre. She liked the substantial feel of it in her hand, the smooth grain of the wood in relief to the carving. She wondered if it had been used as a paperweight to keep the newspapers tidy, ready for the fire, though it didn't seem large enough or heavy enough for that purpose.

She traced the pattern of the carving with her fingertips and, though she was not sure whether the source was her or the carving, felt the tips of her fingers start to vibrate. The vibrations grew stronger and pulsed from her fingertips up through her hand. Wave after wave throbbed through her and she felt – no, heard – the rhythm of an arcane language rumbling through her bones. She tried to pinpoint the source, but it seemed to come from deep within the earth, using her body as a vessel.

Though she couldn't understand the voices, she was transported by their murmurings for a fleeting moment to the mossy forest. She smelled ferns and peaty earth, pine-needles, and pure water running over the gravel in the stream. Shafts of sunlight pierced the gloom and the noise of the forest assaulted her ears, a rising cacophony of insects, birds, creatures, all clamouring for her attention. It was spell-binding and the sound filled her head, pushing aside any rational thought.

Startled, she let go of the carving, sending it clattering to the floor. The vision stopped and she was once more in the waiting room. Trembling, she grabbed the bench seat to pull herself up and sat down, trying to figure out what had just happened. The carving lay at her feet and she was almost afraid to pick it up again. She looked at it, trying to decide what to do. She'd never be able to explain this to Dan in a way he would understand and she wasn't sure exactly what had happened herself. It was over so quickly, but the scent of the forest lingered in the air and as she turned to follow the last remnants, her eye once more fell on the open cupboard. She had only held the object for a short time, half a minute at the most, but she felt as though it had started a chain reaction deep inside her.

Needing to feel it in her hands again, she reached down and picked up the carving, feeling its warmth from where she'd been holding it. She sat still, focusing on the fleeting image of the forest, trying to conjure it up again, but this time there was no change, no sense of another world pushing at the periphery of her vision. She turned the carving over and over in her hands, trying to find an identifying mark, but couldn't see anything. Gradually, she became aware of something else, something more visceral and urgent. Her leg was nagging at her. She'd tried to ignore the discomfort since she'd woken up, but now it was more insistent. Two days of travel had taken their toll.

Without knowing why, she decided to find a safe place to hide the carving, somewhere Dan wouldn't find it. She didn't know how to put it into words, but she felt like the station had given her a gift and, for now, she wanted to keep it for herself. She put the object in her pocket and walked the few steps back to the cottage, trying to bear most of her weight onto her left leg, reaching out with her hand to touch the rough stone wall to steady herself, swearing under her breath at the stubbornness that prevented her from carrying her stick as a matter of course. Dan was in the kitchen, washing his hands as he waited for the kettle to boil.

'Thanks for opening the cupboard. Did you see what was inside?'

'Cupboard? Which one?

'The one in the waiting room.'

His eyes narrowed. 'I didn't open it.'

She stared at him. 'Why does everything have to be such a mystery? Are you trying to freak me out? First you went all weird about the groceries, now you're saying you didn't open the cupboard.'

'I wasn't "weird" over the groceries. It just seemed like an unlikely thing to happen. That's all. And it turns out I was right. I didn't open the cupboard. It might have just swung free on its own. I did try bloody hard to open it earlier, you know?'

Aware she'd snapped, the old Esther – the Esther from a

year ago – would have backed down, wanting to make amends and avoid yet another row, but as she put her hand into her pocket and felt the solid wooden carving, all her old resentments flared.

'And what's with Mike? Are you sure you don't know him? You seem awful pally with someone you've barely met. If I didn't know you better, I'd think you were hiding something.'

As she said it, the truth hit home. She did know better and he had hidden things from her. Big things. Perhaps he still was.

'Jesus, Esther. This again? What do I have to do to make you trust me?'

She stood in the kitchen doorway, trying to come up with an answer, but he shook his head and pushed roughly past her into the sitting room.

Dan had resumed unpacking his books when, about an hour later, Esther joined him. He pointed to a corner of the room, under the rear window which looked out onto a shed and a scrappy patch of hard-standing.

'I thought I might set up a temporary study here, while the renovations are taking place. What do you think?'

'Here's as good a place as any. What are you going to do with all the books?' She looked around, trying to work out where everything would fit.

'I'm not planning to unpack them all. I marked the box with the ones I really need.'

She picked up a book from a pile he'd unpacked. It was about steam on the Highland Line. She quickly cast her eyes down the spines of the other books. All of them were about trains.

Dan noticed, and his cheeks flushed.

'Okay, you caught me. I'm in two minds about the subject of my book.'

'Oh?'

'Well, it's something you said when we arrived and it's been playing on my mind a bit.' He reached into his back pocket for the bottle of hand gel and squirted some into his palm.

Esther watched as he performed the ritual cleansing of his hands. His hand-washing had increased in frequency since they arrived, but humping boxes about and unpacking their stuff was a grubby job. She'd tried not to read more into it, but an ever-present sense of dread in the pit of her stomach gnawed away at her.

'You said something about how I'd become an expert on the history of the area. You're right, I did a lot of research before buying this place and it's kind of lit something inside me, fired my imagination. I'm going to write about the history of the railway here.'

'But I thought you wanted to write about the wildlife and the woodland?'

'The railway is more me. I'm an engineer.' He put his hands in his pockets. 'I can't change who I am.'

She thought for a few moments. It made sense, but she couldn't help feeling excluded from his thought processes – again.

'What can you say that hasn't already been said before? There must be hundreds of railway history books.'

He didn't answer.

'You'd already decided, hadn't you? Before we even got here, I mean. You must have done to mark the box with the right books in.'

He turned away from her and straightened up the pile she'd rifled through.

'Write about what makes you happiest. I just don't understand why you didn't mention it to me. I've always supported all of your choices.' *I even let you drag me all the way up here.*

'I'm still going to be writing – just about a different subject.' His stare bordered on challenging. 'It's not important. It's just a detail. It's like you making a Victoria sponge instead of a chocolate cake. It's still a cake.'

She returned his gaze and considered his words. His logic was impeccable as always, but she wanted to explain how it felt different to her, how she so often felt left out, but the words wouldn't come. It wasn't just this decision, or the decision to move to Scotland, away from everything that was familiar to her. It went back further than that, right back to last year and the miscarriage and the unravelling of the life she thought they had. She spoke with care, knowing he would understand the subtext.

'It was important enough for you to move us all the way up here. I just don't understand why you'd let me go on believing something that isn't true.'

She turned away and opened the door leading onto the platform. He didn't follow her.

The fog had thinned in places, no longer the thick, choking blanket that had greeted her that morning. She shivered as the chill evening air found its way under each layer of clothing. Although she was tempted to go back inside, Esther was still too angry with Dan to want to make up with him. Part of her thought she might be over-reacting. Dan offered her security and she'd grabbed it with both hands, but in his attempt to set things right between them, to get back to how it was before, he was excluding her. She knew they had to talk about it. She had to tell him he didn't need to try so hard and that they had to work together as a couple to put the past behind them. She reached into her pocket, pulled out the carving and thought back to the incident in the waiting room, unsure now whether it had even happened. She tried to work out what type of wood it was. It was too yellow to be oak so she guessed it might be yew and made a mental note to look it up on the internet when they were connected. She'd meant to hide it in the sitting room, but he was still in there, and she wanted some distance between them. A circle of oak leaves ran around the edge of the disc, broken intermittently by a carved acorn. It gave the impression that each of the three interlocking hares was running across the floor of a forest.

She was charmed by the object and sat staring at it for many minutes until a vibration in her coat pocket interrupted her thoughts. She pulled out her phone. It was still vibrating and the caller display flashed off and on. She nearly dropped it, hardly believing what her eyes were telling her: Sophie.

Confusion jabbed at her as she struggled to collect her thoughts. *Sophie is alive!* The realisation that it wasn't possible collided with the hope she'd briefly felt, and her instinct was to hurl the phone far away from her, like it was cursed. Yet she held on to it, fearful of breaking the tenuous connection. The vibrating stopped and she sat, rigid, for some moments before she mustered the courage to look at the caller display again.

There were no missed calls. And yet, there had to be. She hadn't imagined it. She opened her list of recent calls, her hands shaking from cold and shock. Except for Dan, the only other recognisable number on the list was Anthea's. She pressed the button to call Dan, but the dial tone dropped out straight away. Still no signal. It couldn't have been Sophie. Esther didn't even know where Sophie's phone was now. Was it sent back to England with all of Sophie's other personal items? Perhaps it had been donated to charity with the rest of her possessions. *That's it. It's been sold and the new owner is trying out the random numbers stored on the phone.*

She put the carving back in her pocket and looked at her phone again. Her breath caught as she noticed there was one bar of signal strength and she quickly selected Sophie's number. She listened as the dial tone changed to ringing. Esther knew she'd have to make do with the voicemail message, but she needed to hear Sophie's voice again.

'I've missed you.'

Esther cried out and dropped the phone. Sophie's breathy voice rang out as clear as if they were sitting side by side. Esther scrambled to pick it up, but the screen was blank again. Even before she put it to her ear, she could hear the three-note tone and the pre-recorded voice telling her to hang up and try again. She ended the call and pressed redial. The hairs stood up along her arms. She knew she wasn't mistaken; it was Sophie's voice she'd heard. Come on. Come on. Dammit! She listened intently, but the line failed to connect over and over.

Shaking with frustration, she stared at the screen. No signal. As she sat in the freezing night, a single tear spilled down her cheek. Then another and another, until all of her pent-up tears threatened to engulf her and she was choking back huge, shattering sobs. Esther pulled her right leg up onto the bench and curled up on her side, cat-like, rocking to and fro as she sobbed. She didn't hear Dan join her on the platform. He crouched down beside her and reached out to brush a stray lock of dark hair from her face. She opened her eyes.

'Shh,' he said. 'It's okay.'

She sat up and put her arms around him, taking comfort from his warmth and the familiar smell of his neck – a mix of fabric softener and the bergamot notes of his cologne.

'What's up? What's got you so upset?' His eyes scanned her face for any clue he could recognise and process. 'It was just a silly argument.'

'No. Yes. I mean . . . Sophie. Sophie called me. She spoke to me. I heard her voice.'

He looked at her for several moments, unable to grasp what she was trying to tell him. 'What do you mean you heard her voice?'

'My phone rang. It was Sophie, but it rang off before I could answer it. I was so shocked. When I tried again, I couldn't get through, so I kept trying. Then I heard her voice.' Esther's speech was muffled as she spoke into his shoulder. In those short moments, she forgot about their quarrel and her disappointment with him and silently pleaded for him not to tell her to pull herself together.

When he did speak, his voice was low and soft and he was looking at her in the same way he had when he'd broken the news of Sophie's death to her.

'Darling, there's no signal here. You're exhausted and I guess your body is out of whack coping with the baby.' He pulled her tight into him and stroked her hair. 'Maybe you did hear something.'

She tensed against him. He wouldn't give in to her so easily, what was he going to say next?

'The mind is very powerful, you know. You'll have heard her voice because you wanted to so much.'

Esther didn't want to hear that it was all in her mind, or worse, that it was her hormones rampaging. For once, she needed him to believe that sometimes things happen that can't be explained, but that would be expecting the impossible. Her fingers brushed against the carving in her pocket and once again, the scent of pine surrounded her.

'Can you smell that?'

'What?'

'The smell of pine trees. You must be able to smell it?'

'I haven't noticed – besides, they are all around us now. Easy to acclimatise to.' He changed tack. 'You know, the atmospheric conditions here are a bit screwy. Maybe that has something to do with it?' He picked up the phone and looked at the call list. 'You've been calling your voice mail a lot recently, perhaps it was a message that you've already stored. I don't know what happened, I wish I could come up with something to convince you, but I can't explain it.' He stopped, as though he was going to say something else. Instead he pulled her closer to him. 'I'm worried about you. You don't seem to be coping very well with the move.'

She didn't respond, thinking instead about the previous evening, sitting on the platform and trying to listen to the voicemail messages Sophie had left. That must be the explanation, she'd somehow managed to listen to an old message. Yet at the same time, she knew that couldn't be the case. She knew every word of every message and none matched what she'd heard tonight. Sophie couldn't have called because she was dead. The one saving grace was that even Dan was sensitive enough not to point that out. Her thoughts made no sense and she let him comfort her as he led her back into the cottage and sat her down by the fire. She stared at the flames behind the glass door of the wood burner, turning things over in her mind, reaching no satisfying conclusions as he busied himself making a hot drink for them both.

Unusually for Dan, he kept up a stream of chatter from the kitchen, but she barely acknowledged it. She reached into her pocket and her fingers closed around the carving. She felt calmer now, her breathing more settled and her tears had abated. She closed her eyes, content to drift, carried by the river of her thoughts. Sleep came to her quickly.

❧

The chorus line of birches gossiped about the argument to each other as the shadows fell. The night scent rose upwards bringing with it the words the couple had said, and not said, and wished they'd said, until the air stank with their rancour. The pinhole stars glittered through the lace canopy of branches overhead and the peaty ground, trembling with anticipation, began to warm as an old magick stirred, deep in the earth. The trees that clung to the mountainside felt the excitement as the pine needles fringing their branches shivered in the breeze, while the soil shifted and settled, creating new hiding places and hollows.

The station exhaled and the hunter sank low into the undergrowth. Watching.

3

MONDAY

ESTHER WOKE ON a bed of bracken, the air quiet and cool and with the smell of waxen earth in her nostrils. She lay still for a moment, letting her mind catch up with her wakening body. There was no sign of the cheerless fog that had plagued the day and as her eyes adjusted, pinpoint stars flickered in the coal-black sky.

The moon lit the clearing from behind a gauzy cloud, just enough for her to make out the shelter of the hollow, nestled into the rise of the mountain. Sitting up, she looked down at her naked body and instinctively drew her long legs up under her chin, hugging her knees. The metal shaft of her right leg was cold against her skin. The breeze picked up and she shivered. Silver birches waxed and waned in the breeze, their shadows dancing on the forest floor like dryads.

All her senses on high alert, she looked around, trying to get her bearings and to make sense of what had happened. There was no sign of Dan or anyone else. Fear coursed through her; the tiny hairs on her neck standing proud of her skin and her pulse racing. This was bad. She had to get back home, back to Dan, back to safety, but nothing looked familiar to her and a growing dread burrowed into her stomach. She ran her hands over her body, checking for injuries as she stood up, hunching her shoulders and stooping low to the ground, conscious of her nakedness. Her mouth tasted of iron as the fear she felt fused with her blood. The trees loomed in towards her, closing ranks, surrounding her on every side.

There was no obvious path to take. She fought with brambles and branches that lashed out at her as she tried to pass, taking little nicks out of her skin. The terrain was pitted, rutted, too rough to gain any speed, so she focused on placing her feet carefully, all the time alert for the slightest movement nearby, her mouth set in a grim line of concentration.

Whatever had happened, whatever had caused her to be out here alone, she had to get back to Dan. Back to safety.

Picking her way through the trees, she found herself at the edge of a clearing. She had no idea which direction she was facing, which way was home. The sound of twigs snapping behind her made her whip around. The light from the moon emphasised the shadows and, moving slowly, she took refuge behind the nearest tree, eyes fixed on the edge of the clearing, trying to see where the sound had come from.

He materialised in the way the fog had. First, a tentative outline and then, as her eyes grew accustomed to the shapes in the forest, he became something more solid, more visceral, yet poised to vanish back into the ether.

Esther put her hand over her mouth to stop herself from crying out. Her heart battered against her ribs like it wanted to break free. Could he hear her?

He stayed at the edge of the clearing, partly obscured by the trees as though he was an extension of the dark shadows they cast. She took in his lean limbs, taut and ready to spring at the slightest sound. He wore a primitive brown tunic, belted at the waist, and the animal pelt draped over his shoulders clung to him like a second skin. She was unable to make out his features for his face was obscured by the shadows and the hood he wore. When he stepped back into the trees, she thought she glimpsed a dagger hanging in a sheath from his belt, moonlight flashing a warning off the curved edge of the blade as he stalked through the trees, moving away from her.

Instinctively, she crossed her arms in front of her belly to protect her child from harm. Although her head told her to flee, her intuition insisted she waited and watched to see whether he'd appear again. She hesitated for as long as she dared, hoping that he wasn't tracking around the clearing to circle up behind her.

The moon disappeared behind a cloud bank, taking with it the weak light, and in the next breath she took flight, her reflexes taking over. The forest closed in around her as she fled, with tree roots snaking out to catch her ankles, trying to trip her. She ran as best as she could, but her gait was uneven and sluggish. Twigs snapped underfoot, and as she pushed forward she was sure he would have heard her moving through the trees.

Esther knew he must be gaining ground on her all the time and didn't dare to look behind her. She imagined his hot breath on her shoulders, the cold dagger in his hand. The thought spurred her onwards as she imagined him reaching for the blade that would stop her heart. Dodging overhanging branches and exposed roots, slippery with lichen, she no longer cared that that she was naked; she moved as fast as she dared, as fast as her body would let her. The only thing that mattered now was reaching safety and protecting her baby.

She changed course, avoiding the patches where the moon lit the shadows, and paused behind a tree, trying to steady her breathing. Thinking quickly, she decided her best chance was to lie low; the only way to get out of this alive was to trick him and hope that he couldn't pick up her scent.

A shape to the left caught her attention. It was too uniform, too regular to occur naturally, and she squinted into the gloom, trembling with adrenalin, not trusting what her eyes were seeing. It was a doorway, about three feet high, carved into the trunk of a broad oak on the far bank of the stream. It looked familiar, just like the door in the wood-panelled waiting room back at Rosgill. Like that one, it had swung part way open. She had to try to make it to the doorway, to whatever lay on the other side.

The oaks whispered relentlessly, 'He is coming. He is coming.'

She doubled back towards the burn, hoping that the noise of the water would deaden the sound of her steps as she tried to reach the doorway. She side-stepped out of the way of the moonlight, but her leg was not built for such a manoeuvre and she lost her footing, rolling down the bank towards the river bed. Partially obscured by the overhanging tree roots, Esther lay among the rotting leaf mulch, scooping handfuls over her luminous skin as camouflage. She closed her eyes knowing that at any minute he could be upon her and it would all be over. She could hear him coming through the undergrowth, the relentless crashing of his footsteps through the dead leaves on the forest floor keeping time with her beating heart.

Far above her, the constellations pulsed to each other and Orion smiled in the knowledge that the hunt had begun.

❧

'Essie, Es? Wake up.' Dan shook her, gently at first, then harder when she didn't rouse.

'He's coming, he's coming!'

'Esther! Wake up!'

She opened her eyes and screamed, seeing Dan looming over her.

'Shh. Shh. It's okay.' Dan took her in his arms, her rabbit-heart fluttering against his. 'What was all that about?'

Esther closed her eyes, trying to picture her dream. The scene was in her grasp, but when she tried to articulate it, the images turned into eels and slipped away from her. With his help, she slowed her breathing and relaxed against him.

'I'm sorry, I'm sorry.' She sobbed into his chest.

'You've nothing to be sorry for. It was just a bad dream. Come on, let's try to go back to sleep. Snuggle in.' Dan stroked her hair and laid her back onto the pillow before getting back into bed himself. He curved his body round her. She lay awake listening to his breathing until it deepened and sleep once again took her husband. She knew it was just a dream, but she could smell the forest clinging to her skin and hair, and sleep would be a long time coming.

When daylight finally came, Dan brought her a tray in bed. Tea, toast and cereal. The dark circles under his eyes matched hers.

'How are you feeling now?' He sat on the edge of the bed, twisting his wedding ring round on his finger.

'I'm okay. A bit tired, but okay. I might just take it a bit easier today.'

He visibly relaxed. 'I thought I was going to have to argue with you about getting some rest. Stay there as long as you need to.' He walked over to the window, opening the shutters. 'We probably won't see the builders today. The fog is back – thicker than yesterday even. I've never seen anything like it.'

'Welcome to Scotland.' Esther raised her mug in a mock toast. 'You know, I don't mind if the builders don't come today. I'm not really up to it.'

He nodded. 'I think you're right. Any idea what caused the nightmare? Careful, you'll get jam on the duvet.'

It was probably something to do with the phone call from my dead friend.

She shook her head and laid the tray aside on the bed, the marshmallow expanse of duvet dimpling under the weight.

He came and sat by her side and took her hand. 'Essie, is everything okay? Are we okay? You just seem a bit . . . off.'

She paused, deciding whether now was the right time to voice her worries, or whether she risked putting a crease in their progress.

'I think it's all been more of a strain than I thought. The last six months . . . well, the last year really, have been hard. This is a big move for us.' She watched the shadow pass over his face, knowing he was thinking about the part he'd played in past events. She continued, trying to reassure him, trying to stave off another round of gunfire.

'I'm not complaining, where you go, I go. It's just a lot of change all at once. And we've been through such a lot already.'

'Moving was our best option.'

She nodded. 'I understand that. I want us to make a go of this. We're still feeling the ripples of the last twelve months.

It'll take time, that's all. Are you sure it's what you want – me and the baby?'

His expression softened as he reached out to touch her cheek. 'All I ever wanted was a family of my own. Having children together is the best thing that could happen. I just didn't want to go through another round of IVF. We couldn't afford it, even before the redundancy. Then, when you fell pregnant anyway, I was scared about the timing, knowing we were coming up here to start again.'

Her heart leapt, nudging away the depth-charge of anxiety. This was progress; he rarely mentioned his redundancy. It was his Achilles heel in the same way that the miscarriage was hers. She held her breath, scared to break the spell as she waited for him to continue, but the moment was over.

'There's plenty of food in the cupboards, what with the stuff we brought and Mikey's welcome gift, so we won't need to worry about supplies for a good few days yet. We may as well just hunker down and get used to the place.'

'Mikey, is it?'

Dan stood up and turned back towards the window. 'It just seems to suit him, is all. He's a friendly guy.'

Esther smiled. Despite her initial misgivings, Dan seemed to be quite taken with Mike and she thought it would do him good to have someone other than her to talk to.

'Did he say if he is single?'

'Who? Mikey?'

'Yes. I thought if he had a partner it might be nice to get to know her . . . or him.'

Dan scowled. 'He didn't say.'

'And of course, you didn't think to ask.' She sighed. 'Dan, if we are going to settle here, we need to really put roots down and be part of this community. That means making friends with people, no matter how uncomfortable that feels.' *And you have to realise not everyone shares your views on love and marriage.*

She patted the bed beside her, signalling him to come and sit down next to her. She knew he found social situations difficult, but it also seemed to her as though he didn't try. She wondered how much was Dan himself and how much was Eric's influence.

'Are you finished with that?' Dan picked up the tray and took it downstairs, ignoring her invitation.

She lay back, cursing Eric. As if it wasn't difficult enough to get Dan to try new things, she had to contend with the indoctrination that ran though his core. Her husband was an enigma. For a man of science, he held some very contrary views, particularly where the line between science and nature blurred.

There were though, some distinct benefits in moving from Bristol. Contact with Eric would now be much more limited and within her control. He didn't fit her idea of what it meant be to be a Christian man, with his constant use of the Old Testament to back up his narrow-mindedness. She hoped Dan would mellow and be more accepting of others now that he was out from under Eric's spell. She was aware she had no yardstick to measure Dan and Eric's relationship by and her thoughts inevitably turned to her own father. Her memories of him were fading, and she could only remember his face from the few photographs she kept in her diary. Patrick tall, imposing, dwarfing Anthea in their wedding photos. They looked young, carefree. When did things change?

Her last memory of him always began the same way, with

the bald noise of the burst tyre, then the juddering of the brakes as her father pumped his foot hard on them. The silence of slow motion as the world outside the car sped up while time stopped for the occupants. The swerving motion slamming her body across the back seat and into the door, then back across the seat, her 8-year-old body ricocheting into the other door before crumpling into the foot well. The pain lighting every nerve in her arms and legs and back. The washing-machine tumble as the car rolled onto its roof, then back over again – the time lines inside and outside of the car converging and colliding at a singularity. The smell of petrol and whisky and blood. She remembered how hard it was to stay awake, how she'd wanted to sleep but the man in the blue uniform kept waking her up, asking her name and flashing a light into her eyes. She remembered wondering whose leg it was that was sticking up from the floor of the car, its bloody, twisted foot folded back on itself. Her scream as she realised the leg belonged to her – the sound that still punctuated her nightmares. Then only darkness and silence.

She'd become very efficient at blocking out the endurance test that was the weeks she spent in hospital. Three operations, physiotherapy that set every nerve on fire, the endless round of faceless doctors and nurses, prodding, poking, analysing and measuring every secretion. That summer had been very hot. Indolent days and sweat-soaked nights. The unfairness of being stuck inside when everyone else was swimming and playing was branded onto her memory. But the worst of it was going back to school, some six months after the accident, only to find that her friends had formed new groups, and that being in a wheelchair meant she was different. And different was not cool.

Esther endured the taunts in the playground. Her classmates were curious at first about her leg, but then the whispering started and it was everywhere she went. Her mother told her to ignore the gossip – that it would go away. But she could still feel the burning shame firing inside her every Saturday morning, after the ritual cleansing of the house with bleach, when Anthea went out for a few hours and Mrs Gray came to sit with Esther. Her father had disappeared. All traces of him had been erased from their lives.

Anthea never said she was visiting Patrick in jail, but Esther knew. When the visits stopped, Esther wondered what had happened to her father, but her mother would never tell her. Soon, the only sign he'd ever existed was Esther's broken body.

Finding him was the only way she'd ever know the answers to all the questions she had. She knew it was a combination of things. Her own circle was getting smaller. Sophie was gone, Anthea lived in America with her new husband. All she had now was Dan, and the baby. Now that she was going to be a parent, she saw things differently. She wondered where he was, whether he thought about her, whether he felt any guilt at maiming his child. Esther couldn't imagine how she'd survive hurting her own child. Was it the same for him? Or did he not think about her at all, except for Christmas and birthdays – and maybe not even then.

She wanted something better for her own child, no matter the personal cost to herself. Her child would have two parents and a stable home. Resting her hand on her stomach, she let the doubt trickle into her mind. What if she lost this baby too? Or maybe she wasn't pregnant at all? Maybe she'd imagined it. The worst of the morning sickness had passed and she had very little sign of a bump. It could be weeks yet until she felt the baby move. There were few physical signs she could pinpoint to give her reassurance. Her breasts were a little more tender than normal. Were they getting bigger? She smoothed the flat of her hand over them, enjoying the sensation. She couldn't be sure.

Aware that she was spooking herself and even though she already knew the answer, she swung herself out of bed and shuffled down it until she could reach the chest of drawers. She picked up her pink leather jewellery box. It had been a present from her mother; a replacement for the jewellery box she'd had as a child, the one with the ballerina in. The one that had been smashed in another argument between her parents. She opened the box and lifted out the ring tray, smiling as the ballerina pirouetted to the tinkling tune. Nestling into the tangle of necklaces and bracelets at the bottom, she pulled out the pregnancy test wand and looked at it again. The reassuring blue line plain to see, she mouthed a silent prayer of thanks.

She put the test back and picked up the ring tray. As she did so, her wedding ring, a simple polished D-shaped band, blinked back at her. She picked it up and looked at it, holding it up to the light. The inscription inside showed some signs of wear. 'You. Me. Us.' She slipped the hoop of gold onto her ring finger, the metal cold against her skin. She splayed her hand out, looking at the ring, trying to shake the dog-with-a-new-collar feeling.

It had been nearly a year since she'd last worn it.

In all that time, Dan had never said anything, but she knew he'd noticed. Perhaps it was time to get used to wearing it again.

While Dan was in the shower, Esther decided to explore the other side of the station. She sat on the platform edge, then dropped down onto the old track-bed, taking care to test the ground. The rails and sleepers were long-gone and the track-bed was pitted where the sleepers had lain for so long. A tangle of weeds and thistles snapped at her ankles as she picked her way through. She thought of her nightmare and the ease with which she'd fled through the forest. Esther didn't believe in feeling sorry for herself. She had to make the best of what she'd been given, but she allowed herself to acknowledge that sometimes it would be nice to feel the ground with both feet again.

She hauled herself up onto the opposite platform and looked back at the station. The fog obscured much of the detail of the building, but she could make out enough of its form to gauge its presence. The creaking dagger-boards were not as noticeable now that the fog had smothered the breeze. Turning away from the station, she surveyed the squat building in front of her. Originally part waiting room, part store room, Dan wanted this to be their bedroom and nursery, away from the main house for privacy. It was the first thing the builders were meant to start on, somewhere they could escape from the noise and the dust in the main house.

Esther opened the door into the waiting room, a mirror image of the one on the other platform. The windows faced north and weak daylight filtered through the filmy deposits left on the glass. She rubbed a spot clean on the low wooden bench, wiping her hands on her jeans and sat, mentally furnishing the room. The Moses basket could go under the window, next to her side of the bed. They'd paint the panelling in this room, white probably, to reflect more light. With her hands folded in her lap, she was content to sit and think.

Although the terror of miscarrying was a constant companion, every so often she allowed herself to think about what the future might look like. She wondered whether the baby would be a girl or a boy and whether it was unlucky to allow such thoughts to form.

She pictured Dan's reaction if he could see inside her head and smiled, knowing he'd have a clever answer about her superstitions. After her nightmare last night, he'd been so tender and careful with her, just like he was when they'd first met. Now she was a little more comfortable in their new surroundings, she realised that it was just as much her responsibility to put things right as his. It was easier in many ways to stay angry with him, as it allowed her to avoid all the things she wanted to ask. She didn't want this baby to feel her anger, or hurt, or sorrow, and resolved to break the routine. Esther knew she had to forgive him, had to find a way. Perhaps she should start attending church with him again, cementing her faith with his. Showing her faith in him, in them as a couple. It would be Easter in a few days, the symbolic start of new beginnings. She'd suggest it to him later.

The door opened a little wider, hinges screaking. Major Tom nosed his way in and trotted over, jumping up on the seat beside her. She tried the handle of the connecting door to the store room, expecting it to be locked, but it opened as she pushed against it. The room was gloomier than the other, with fewer windows. Racks of shelving covered one wall, eating into the floor space. Dan wanted to partition this room, making an en-suite for them and a nursery for the baby. Shooing the cat away, she closed the door between the two rooms and, with one final look around, stepped back onto the platform. The cat ran off into the fog.

Esther climbed up onto the main platform, thinking that she'd be grateful when the builders came so they could start on the wooden bridge Dan had drawn up plans for to connect both sides of the station. Although they now owned a lot of land, she was beginning to feel fettered by the renovations needed, not to mention the fog which kept them - and her in particular - tethered to Rosgill. She opened the door to the cottage and was surprised to see Mike sitting at the table. Dan had his back to her, hands in the sink. He turned around as she came in.

'There you are.' He smiled at her and the effect changed the steel in his eyes to a softer, pewter colour.

'Hello. Hi, Mike.' She pulled out a chair and sat opposite him at the table. 'I didn't hear your Land Rover? Is that a pot of tea on the go, Dan?'

'Yep, here.' Dan held out a steaming mug for her. 'Mikey has some news.'

'I walked down, I don't trust the roads in this fog. In fact, that's why I'm here. I think we're going to be cut off for a few days.'

'Cut off? What do you mean?' Esther, puzzled, looked from Mike to Dan.

'There's been an accident further down the glen. A construction lorry going up to the reservoir has come off the Invergill Viaduct and damaged one of the spans.'

'Oh, no! Was anyone hurt?'

'No, the driver is okay. He was travelling too fast in this fog and not used to how treacherous that road can be. It's caused a hell of a mess down there, though. They're having to get an engineer down from Aberdeen.'

'Oh, Dan! What a shame you can't help.'

His back and shoulders tensed and he turned back towards the sink, away from Esther.

'Yes, what a shame. What a shame I'm an aviation engineer. What a shame there is no call for my speciality and how lucky I am that I was made redundant, just so I could start all over again.'

'Dan, I—' She started to speak, but he raised his hand to cut her off, avoiding her eye.

'I know what you meant, Esther. I know, okay? Come on, Mike. I'll show you round the rest of the place.'

Mike squeezed her hand in a gesture of solidarity, then picked up his mug and followed Dan. She sat at the table, the rebuke leaving a raw, stinging welt across her heart.

She listened to the two men as they walked from room to room; Dan explaining his vision for each one. Following them would only make Dan angrier, so she remained at the table, feeling excluded in her own home, quietly resentful that Dan had made this all about him, without thinking for one second how much she'd given up. He was so like Eric in that respect. Only ten minutes ago hadn't she been thinking about making more of an effort? Having Mikey here so often wasn't helping. He monopolised Dan, and while she was happy that Dan had made a friend, she couldn't help feeling put out.

She glanced down at her wedding ring. For better for worse. She softened. It had been her lack of judgement, her poor choice of words that had upset him. *I really should know better by now.* The two men started down the stairs, boots clumping on the wooden treads.

She called out to them: 'I'm going to start dinner. Mike, will you stay and have something with us?'

Mike looked to Dan, who gave the slightest of nods.

‘Thanks. That’d be grand.’

She saw her reflection in Mike’s topaz eyes. She shivered and turned away.

‘I’m going to walk up the track a bit with Mikey – try to see what else is around us. Do you need us for anything?’

‘No, dinner will be a while yet, take your time.’

Esther nodded and watched the two men leave the cottage. She busied herself preparing dinner and tried to ignore an insistent cawing from the canopy, but it was pervasive. She called out to the cat, but there was no sign of him, so she switched the radio on, glad of the newsreader’s company. The reception was patchy, but she welcomed the sound as it filled the emptiness of the kitchen. It was the first sound from the world outside Rosgill she’d heard for days and it was a welcome relief. She gathered up the minced beef, some potatoes and a couple of carrots and set about making a cottage pie, humming to herself as she peeled the potatoes.

‘It’s six-thirty. And now on 4, a change to our advertised programme. Instead of the News Quiz, *we have a short story, ‘The Dinner Party’.’* The continuity announcer broke into her thoughts as she browned the mince with a stock cube and some onion. The narrator’s voice was familiar – smooth and coaxing – the voice of a hundred TV adverts.

‘Picture the scene, dear listener. A young couple hosting Sunday lunch for an aged parent. A parent who engenders fear into them both, but for different reasons. A cruel parent, given to manipulating people through the word of God.’

Esther snorted. *This should be good.* She stabbed at a potato with the tip of a knife, but it was still too hard to mash.

‘The young couple have something to tell the old man, but they don’t know how to broach the subject. Soon, they will have

missed their opportunity as even now, his taxi is wending its way through the Bristol traffic to collect him.'

The mince was starting to catch. She turned down the flame and gave it a final stir, standing over the water bubbling in the pan.

'Esther stood to clear the dinner plates and looked at the clock. She took the plates through to the kitchen, then signalled her husband to help her. "You are going to have to tell him." Esther lowered her voice. "Do it now, so he has time to talk to you about it."'

The knife dropped with a clatter to the floor as she stood, rigid. She looked around her. Was this a joke? The narrator paused, as though waiting to regain her attention.

'Esther, will you please sit and listen?' He boomed at her. 'It's a very good story. Where was I? Yes . . . that's it . . .' He resumed the narrative.

'Dan nodded his head briefly. "I'll make some coffee. Can you pour him a nip of brandy?"

Esther had never seen her father-in-law drink spirits and raised an eyebrow, but reached for the brandy bottle at the back of the cupboard. She found a balloon glass and poured out two fingers of the amber liquid. She set the glass on the tray as Dan laid out the coffee cups in a straight line, making sure that all of the handles faced to the right.'

Esther sat at the table, unmoving and oblivious to the pan of potatoes boiling over on the stove. Still the narrator pushed on, recounting the story of how they broke the news of their move to Eric.

'It was tempting to move one of the cups, just to see what Dan would do, but Esther checked herself. She was being needlessly mean. She carried the tray through to where Eric reclined

on one of the bright orange sofas and set it down on the low table. Taking a seat opposite him, she waited for Dan to appear with the coffee pot.

"No sign of another baby, then?" Eric's red-rimmed eyes scalded her. "I'll pray to God for you."

She sat on her hands to stop herself from throwing his brandy all over him. Eric dropped his gaze, as though already deep in prayer. She stood and went over to the window, a vast expanse of glass set into a steel frame. As she looked down onto the quayside below, she saw life going on all around her. From her vantage point, she counted four couples with children in buggies, on reins or tottering along, bending to inspect leaves or insects or other mysteries. A group of white-haired ladies sat outside one of the cafes, enjoying a coffee and a natter. Lycra-clad joggers and cyclists flashed along the quayside, enjoying the first sunny day of the year. For a moment, she hated the apartment and her hermetically-sealed lifestyle. She longed to run through fields and forests, following the breeze as it led her past waterfalls, crags and woods full of bluebells. And, even if she could only manage to walk, that would be enough for her. Scotland would be good for them. For the first time, she tasted anticipation about the move.

"Dad, we have some news." Dan set the coffee pot down on the tray and sat on the sofa, next to his father.

Eric stared hard at his son, appraising him.

"You know things have been difficult at work? Well, the company has lost a lot of contracts and I've been made redundant."

Esther exhaled, she knew how difficult it was for her husband to admit this, especially to his father. She knew he'd never go as far as admitting the full extent of the problem though. Maybe he never would and it would always sit between them, silently.

"I see," Eric said, nodding slowly.

"I'm . . . we're . . . going to use the redundancy money to start again, somewhere else."

"Somewhere else." Eric's intonation was not a question.

Esther shifted in her seat, unsure of where Eric's train of thought was going.

"And where is this 'somewhere else', then?"

"Scotland, Dad. We're moving to Scotland."'

Esther was transported back to that moment, the moment where Scotland had stopped being a plan and become something concrete, something inevitable. She could see the shadows they cast on the terrifying white terrazzo floor tiles. She felt the warmth of the sun on her face as it moved around to the west and the dappled water danced in the dock below. She realised she'd never have to worry about slipping over on those tiles again. It seemed like it was another lifetime away. She stared as the disembodied voice continued.

'Eric said nothing and Dan rushed to fill the silence. "There's no work for me here, Dad. The aerospace industry is tied up by the Americans. The best I can hope for is a fixed-term contract – probably six months at a time. There's no security in that. With my pay-off, our savings, and the equity in this place, we'll be sitting pretty for a while."

Still, Eric said nothing and Esther wanted to hug Dan tightly to her, to tell him he'd said enough and could stop now. More than anything, she wanted him to stop prodding the wasps' nest of Eric's emotions. He was too calm and his quietness unnerved her.

"What will you do in Scotland? What about your job,

Esther? I can't see you giving that up easily." Eric's attention turned to Esther, eyes misting.

Esther, thinking Eric was on the verge of tears, softened her voice. "It's been a tough decision – for both of us – but I think this is a good opportunity. The Writers Centre will be a new adventure."

"Writers Centre?"

"Yes." She set her chin in defiance. "We are creating a centre for writers to come up on courses or retreats. Dan's found the perfect place for us, just south of Inverness."

"And what will you be doing, Daniel?" Eric's stare returned to Dan, who looked uncomfortable under the scrutiny.

"I'm going to write, Dad. Non-fiction. Manuals, handbooks, guidebooks – whatever comes my way. And when I am not writing, I'll be helping Essie and playing host to other writers."

It took a little time for Esther to figure out why there was such tension in the room. Too late, she realised that Eric was incapable of any sentiment and that his eyes were brimming with bile, not tears.

With his gnarly fingers pointing at Dan, Eric quoted from his beloved Proverbs, "Whoever works his land will have plenty of bread, but he who follows worthless pursuits lacks sense."

"Eric! That's unfair. You know how hard Dan worked. It's not his fault he's been made redundant, and he's not the only one."

She couldn't bear to see the defeated look on her husband's face and, although she knew Dan would be annoyed that she'd faced Eric down, she wasn't going to stand by and watch him demolish her husband.

Eric stared at her.

"Eric, Dan is doing the best he can in a bad situation. Can you, for once, put yourself in his shoes? All those years of study. All those years working on MoD contracts and for what? To have them shit all over him?"

"You are a child of God, Esther. A wholesome tongue is a tree of life: but perverseness therein is a breach in the spirit. Watch your filthy language."

"Dad!"

Eric stood and turned to his son. "I'll wait downstairs for my taxi. Call round to the house tomorrow night, Daniel, and we will talk more. In the meantime, I will be praying for you both."

As Eric let himself out of the apartment, Esther felt ashamed of herself for feeling resentful. Dan was doing his best. She couldn't claim to be completely on board with all the decisions he made, but she knew he was putting her first. She resolved to be a good wife, to listen to her husband and to support him more than she had done so far. Isn't that right, Esther?'

The stove hissed as the boiling water splashed over. Esther stared at the radio. She couldn't begin to explain what had just happened, or why.

'It's six-thirty. And now on 4, it's Sandi Toksvig with the *News Quiz*.'

She shivered, despite the warmth in the kitchen from the stove. She wondered if she was going mad – there were too many things happening that she just couldn't explain. Was Dan right? Could it be weird atmospheric conditions? Or was it hormonal? Was she losing her mind? No matter how hard she tried to shrug it all off, the thought persisted that there was something else at work, something other-worldly

– something that she'd never be able to make Dan accept. Even just thinking it seemed absurd.

Once the phone line was connected, she was sure she'd feel less isolated. If only she could speak to her mother, she wouldn't feel so foolish. Anthea would understand. Esther gave a small smile at the thought of the pile of books at Anthea's bedside. Books about mediums, astrology, hauntings and mind-reading. The kind of books Dan openly sneered at. When she thought about it, she realised that she had stopped reading books on the paranormal not long after she'd met Dan. Listening to him talk about his ideas, she was seduced and she was an easy convert, putting her faith in science, the way he showed her.

There were almost no recognisable signs of the life they'd led in Bristol and it hadn't really sunk in that this was their new home; their new life. It still felt as though they were on holiday, inhabiting someone else's cottage for a few days. If the builders ever turned up, she'd probably start to feel more a part of things, more like she was shaping her environment. Little by little, brick by brick, they'd make the changes together and build their future. Maybe then she'd be able to make sense of the world around her.

Esther was quiet as she served up, reflecting on both the memory of that last dinner with Eric and the strange day-dream she'd had about it.

Dan poured the drinks: wine for him and Mike, and apple juice for Esther. 'Let's have a toast,' he said. 'To our new home, and new friends.'

'Ah, come on now. You can do better than that.' Mike stood, glass in hand, filling the room with his personality.

She tensed. Dan wasn't used to being challenged or teased, but instead of the stony look she'd expected to see on his face, he laughed.

'You're right. That was pathetic. Come on then, if you think you can do better.'

Mike bowed and began speaking, his voice low, careful to give each word the attention it deserved.

'In the shadow of each idea, in the liminal space between beginning and end, that's where your Kingdom lies. May it shape you and keep you safe.'

Esther put her glass down and stared openly. Her amazement showed in her voice. 'You wrote that?'

'I'm not just a culchie, you know. I've an education on me.' He laughed at her obvious discomfort.

'Yes. Yes, of course. I didn't mean—'

'No harm now, Esther. I'm taking the mickey. I've a huge appetite for everything. Food, wine, poetry, art . . . ' He paused, leaving them hanging to see what was next on his list. 'Sex. Life is for living and I want to experience as much as I can. Mammy says "You're a long time dead" and all good boys listen to their Mammy.'

'Come on, let's eat.' Dan covered her hand briefly with his, then reached behind him onto the kitchen counter for the hand gel.

Mike glanced at Esther and she pretended not to notice, moving peas around on her plate. Even though she hardly knew Mike, she was glad he was there, and as the evening wore on, he regaled them with his wild tales. It was a relief not having to think, to have someone else do the entertaining, not to have to second-guess Dan's mood.

'. . . so, when it came to the end of the job – and I sweated my guts out cleaning that hen-house down, mind – can you imagine how pleased I was to be offered my wages in chickens?' Mike's eyes crinkled at the corners and he pulled a face in mock affront. 'I lived on chicken curry for a month after that!'

They all laughed at the idea. Esther hadn't seen her husband so relaxed since before the redundancy. She reached out to play with the short hairs on the back of his neck and he leaned in to her touch. She wanted to blow a bubble around this moment, to preserve the memory. She allowed herself to wonder if this was the real Mike, or whether it was an intricate cabaret act that he dusted off from time to time as he seemed so rehearsed, trotting out story after story. *Keep 'em laughing, then they won't ask questions.* And she had so very many questions about Mike.

The anecdotes kept coming. 'I could tell you a thing or two. I've seen plenty in my time.' Mike continued. 'Like when I was seventeen and had just finished my Leaving Cert. The summer was hot and the days long. It was good to be outside after being cooped up all year in classrooms. I started work on a farm in Roscommon, it was harvest time and the hay needed to be brought in quickly before the weather turned. It was hard work, back-breaking.' Mike paused, remembering.

'Every day, we'd stop around midday for soup and sandwiches brought down from the farmhouse by Clodagh, the eldest daughter. She was a grand girl. Big . . .'

Dan snorted, and Esther wondered what Mike was going to say next. She was learning quickly that he had no filter; whatever came into his head came out of his mouth.

'. . . doorstops of soda bread and home-made cheese.' He winked, as though he could read their minds and indicated the thickness of the bread between the spread of his thumb and forefinger.

'Then, about two days before we were due to finish, the youngest daughter brought lunch instead of Clodagh. She was the finest girl I'd ever seen, with her long, red curls and olive eyes. Her name was Cara. Well, one thing led to another and I got Cara to agree to meet me after we'd finished work for the day.'

'Oh yeah?' Dan smirked.

'I shared the caravan with three other fellas. Her virtue was safe. Well, as safe as anyone's around me.' Mike laughed.

Esther shifted uncomfortably in her chair. There was an undercurrent, something in his intonation that seemed off, like he was only telling the parts of the story that made him look good.

Mike continued, 'So we got talking and she said she wanted to do something wild. I had some mushrooms in my pocket from my early morning walk and we decided to make tea with them. She put on the water to boil and I chopped them up and added them to the boiling water. Now, I don't know if you've ever had mushroom tea, but it's godawful tasting.'

Esther and Dan both shook their heads. She was intrigued at the thought of it, and oddly pleased that Mike thought it might be something she'd do, but the reality was that she was too straight to ever see it through. She wasn't so sure about Dan. She could imagine him experimenting, but he'd see it as a scientific venture, recording the sensation meticulously and it would most definitely be a one-off.

'So we threw a coupla teabags in, brewed it a bit longer and strained it. I didn't know how Cara was going to be after drinking it, so we went to the barn and shimmied up the ladder to the hayloft. The hit comes quicker if you drink it and I wanted to be somewhere safe. When it came, it was magical. Colours whirled and spun from my fingertips and I was like a human paintbrush: everywhere I pointed, I left a trail of colour. We lay on the bales of hay and I watched as they formed two columns, rising to fight each other, like Roman legions. Then it seemed like a good idea to take our clothes off, so we did.'

Esther tried to rid herself of the image of a younger Mike, naked and supple, with perfect skin and athletic limbs that he'd not quite grown into. She shifted in her chair, uncomfortable at the direction her thoughts were taking her. The only man she'd seen naked was Dan and she had never thought about anyone else that way.

'Cara was the most beautiful girl I'd ever met. Her skin felt like rose petals and I'll never forget the way she bit her bottom lip, it was such a come-on. I left trails of colour all over her body as I traced patterns with my fingertips.'

Dan and Esther sat spellbound listening to Mike as he talked.

'I can't tell you how beautiful this girl was. And the effect of the mushrooms just intensified her beauty. It was like I'd never seen her before, like she'd only been as real as a photograph of herself. As you'd expect, I was quite worked up.' He shrugged as though gently embarrassed. 'I wanted every part of this girl, to taste her, smell her, feel her body rising up to meet mine. God, the effect she had on me.'

Esther looked at Dan out of the corner of her eye, wondering if he ever thought about her like that.

'Just as the world was beginning to slow down around us and we started kissing, Cara got a terrible stomach cramp.

She sat bolt upright, and looked at me, horrified. Then she kind of crawled away from me and into the corner of the hayloft, where she let out the most enormous fart. The girl was mortified and I, being green and high, just laughed. Then I got a cramp too. That straightened me up quick enough, just in time to hear Cara fart again, only this time it wasn't just a fart.'

Dan's mouth was twitching with amusement. Esther relaxed. She'd felt sure he'd object or show some sign of disgust at all this talk of bodily functions.

'There was a commotion down below, Cara's father was out looking for her. She was crouching in the corner, naked, and the stench was eye-watering. Still the cramps were coming and I knew it was only a matter of time before I succumbed too. I tried to keep as still as I could but a huge cramp wracked through me gut and I let out the mother of all farts.

Cara whispered "Holy Jaysus, me Da'll kill us." But there was nothing I could do.'

They giggled at the scene Mike had painted. Dan refilled Mike's glass, before tipping the last of the bottle into his own.

'Sure enough, he heard us alright and climbed the ladder. The last thing I remember was seeing the barrel of his gun pointed right at me little fella, if you get me, and beautiful, beautiful Cara crouching naked in the corner covered in her own shite. I was out of there; I jumped down, it must have been a good fifteen feet, and I just ran. I never did go back for me wages, but I do think of Cara from time to time.'

Mike took a huge gulp of wine and Dan snorted, unable to suppress his laughter any longer. Caught in a spiral, when one stopped laughing the other started again, until both were convulsed.

Esther watched the two men, a spike of jealousy shooting through her. Dan never laughed like that with her.

Eventually, they both calmed sufficiently for Mike to push his plate away and pat his stomach.

'Esther, darling, that was grand. I'll be back tomorrow, about the same time, now I know what a good cook you are.'

Dan laughed. 'Didn't I tell you how lucky I am?'

She felt herself blushing, unused to the compliments, and stood to clear the plates.

'Here, let me help you. Leave the clearing to me. It's the least I can do.' Mike stood also.

'I'll go and set the burner.' Dan carried his drink through to the sitting room, leaving Esther and Mike alone in the kitchen.

'You wash, I'll dry.' Mike pulled the tea towel from the back of the kitchen chair.

Esther felt like she ought to resent the easy way with which he had settled in, had taken command. She plunged her hands into the hot water. It was hotter than she expected, but she didn't want to make a fuss in case he thought her feeble.

'So then, do you think you'll like it here?' Mike rubbed at a plate, soapy water dripping onto the floor.

Torn between being truthful and making the best of things, Esther hesitated a fraction too long, her hands submerged in the water as she spoke. He pounced on the silence.

'I see. That bad. Why did you come all the way up here? I mean, you didn't even see the place first – am I right?' His questioning was gentle, his tone soothing, like he was coaxing a frightened animal out of hiding.

'It's complicated.'

He laughed. 'It always is.'

He handed her the crockery in a haphazard manner, with no thought to a logical order. Glasses followed saucepans. Cutlery followed plates. Dan would always wash the cleanest items first, to get the best use of the water and prevent the glasses from smearing. She was about to say as much, then stopped herself. It felt good to break the rules, just once.

Faint strains of music came from the sitting room. It sounded old-fashioned and it took a moment for her to recognise it. 'Moonlight Serenade' by the Glen Miller orchestra. Mike hummed the tune, softly, and without realising it, they both started to sway gently in time to the music as they stood at the sink. The tune ended and the programme host took over.

Mike was the first to break the silence. 'I'll just go and see if Himself wants some coffee.'

Esther poured the water into from the bowl into the sink and ran some more, adding a glug of washing liquid to the mix. *Those glasses need another wash. They'll never get past Dan.*

Mike busied himself with the coffee as Esther washed the glasses again, running them under the hot tap to clean off the suds.

'We can't be having smeary glasses now, can we? The very fabric of the universe would collapse.' He flicked the tea towel at her and she giggled.

Mimicking a BBC announcer, she held one of the glasses to the light. 'I am an only child, therefore I was also the family dishwasher and I have standards to uphold.' She blew an imaginary mote of dust away and polished the stem of the glass, then sniffed as though it was to be inspected by the Queen.

He nudged her sideways with his body, gently enough so that she didn't overbalance. 'An only child, eh?'

'I always wanted brothers and sisters. I'm hoping for a big family.' Esther glanced down, at her stomach. 'When you're part of a big family, there are other people to rely on. You're never alone. There were twins my age a few doors away from where we lived and we'd often play together. I was very jealous of them each having a ready-made best friend. The whole family would bundle into the car on Sundays and go out for the day. Sometimes they'd take me along too. Before the accident . . . ' Her voice trailed off and she realised she was dangerously close to crying. She shook her head and continued, 'Then after, I'd watch them from the bedroom window, but they never looked up at me.'

She smiled brightly at Mike, not wanting him to see the cracks in her veneer. But she knew he'd noticed; had glimpsed how she'd been let down by the people who should have cared more about her.

'I come from a big family.' He opened his arms out to emphasise his point, then lowered his voice to a whisper, as though he was speaking to a co-conspirator. 'We never did anything together either, except go to Mass.'

Esther laughed. She couldn't tell whether he was just trying to make her feel better or whether it was true.

'You'd have hated it,' he said, nodding at her. 'The house was always noisy and messy – clean, mind you; Mammy waged a one-woman war on germs and dirt. It's a wonder I've any skin left on my neck after all the scrubbing she did. I still hate the smell of Imperial Leather.'

'I'm not a fan either, it reminds me of my granny's

bathroom.' Such a little thing to have in common, silly really, but Esther felt the first fluttering of a new friendship when he rewarded her with a smile that started with his mouth and ended with his eyes.

'I've eight brothers and sisters. I'm in the middle, so there are four older and three younger than me. It was kinda hard to make yourself heard in our house, always a door slamming somewhere, or herds of children and various friends tramping up and down the stairs. I've come to appreciate the solitude of this place.' He held her gaze for a second too long and she began to fidget.

'Eight children. That's a lot. How did she keep track of you all?'

'In truth, she didn't – but don't let her hear anyone say that. We were all a little wild and I'm sure she was sick to the back teeth of the Guards turning up at the house to bring one of us back – usually me.'

Esther considered what he'd said. Her own mother knew the sound of the police at the door too well. Something else they had in common, but the reasons couldn't have been more different.

She put the last of the glasses on the draining board and got a fresh tea towel out of the drawer, handing it to Mike.

'Oh-ho! So, you think I can meet your impossible standards?'

'You have to start somewhere.' She grinned back at him, enjoying the banter. Perhaps this was what having a brother felt like. And yet, she couldn't work out why, but her shoulders were tense and her spine rigid.

'Mike? I know you said you're probably our nearest neighbour, but are you sure there's no one closer? There's a black cat hanging around and it looks well-cared for. I was just wondering who it belongs to?'

He thought for a moment. 'Dunno. Maybe it's come from the estate. They keep them up in the stables, fearsome ratters. But you know, cats don't really ever belong to anyone.'

'Estate?'

'Pretty much all the land around here belongs to the Strathgill Estate. It's the kind of place that used to have a laird, but is now in private hands.'

'Ugh. So, pheasant shoots and deer-stalking for wealthy Americans and bankers? That sort of thing?'

'Yes, but don't be so hard on them. They do much more too. They've a great conservation record and are the largest employer around here. As well as being my landlord.' He winked.

'Oh, I assumed you owned the cottage?'

'Nope. Moved in about 6 months ago.' Mike set the coffee pot onto the tray. 'Come on, coffee's done.'

Esther noticed how he'd arranged the coffee cups, handles all facing the same way and the spoons at the same angle, and shivered.

The three of them sat around the fire, nursing their drinks. A warm fug settled over them and Esther looked at her husband. Dan seemed relaxed, happy, all the tension in his body had gone. Not for the first time, she thought Mike was a good influence on him. She'd just have to keep her opinions to herself, learn to choke back the resentment. A wall of tiredness rushed up on her and she reluctantly broke the silence.

'I'm sorry, I need my bed. Don't mind me though, stay and finish your wine, Mike. Hell, stay on the sofa if you want to.

It's too late to be stumbling around in the dark.' Esther kissed the top of Dan's head.

'Sure, stay – there's plenty of room and that sofa is far comfier than it looks. I can find you a pillow and some blankets.' Dan was insistent.

'Okay, then. I'll finish my wine and decide if I am too drunk to make it back.'

'Good. That's settled, then.' Esther put her hand on Mike's shoulder as she passed him. An image of Dan and Mike, entwined on the forest floor, rushed at her. Mike was running his hand up and down the length of Dan's back, leaving trails of colour: orange, ochre, rust, on his naked body. Mike's mouth sought out Dan's who willingly submitted to him. She jerked her hand off Mike's shoulder.

'Are you okay?' Dan asked.

'Static shock,' said Mike and as he looked at her, she felt the heat of her heart, burning her from within.

She took the stairs carefully, holding onto the banister as though it was the only thing keeping her tethered to the earth. She sat on the edge of the bed for a long time, wondering if Mike had felt it too and whether she'd be able to sleep, knowing he'd be sleeping downstairs.

❧

The stream gurgled to the stone bed and the long grasses swished and murmured, pulsing the developments through the glen into the dense forest. The moon silvered the clouds and the owls sat in judgement on the proceedings at the station below. The earth, warming through in readiness for spring, stirred and settled, making the start of new hollows and forms.

Higher up, a stag pawed the ground, beating out an ancient imprint with its hooves. The rhythm of the glen, the rhythm of new life, in the language of the old ones.

4

TUESDAY

THIS NIGHT WAS no different. The forest called to Esther and she was unable to resist, terrified though she was of what might be lurking there. She woke in the same place, naked and with no sign of Dan or anything familiar. None of it made any sense to her, but there was no time to lose. She knew what was coming, that she was being hunted and that he'd be here soon.

With only her instincts to guide her, she made her way through the dense trees, her steps heavy and hesitant, placing her feet carefully, conscious that her leg was slowing her down. As her eyes adjusted to the dim light, she stopped and leaned against a nearby tree, looking up at the interlocking branches overhead.

The moon filtered through the lacy canopy, dappling the forest floor. The forest seemed to beckon her, to coax her in. All around her, the stink of rotting vegetation rose up to meet the mountain air, in a counterpoint of decay and putrefaction. Black shadows lingered between the sentinel oaks standing guard, waiting for him to appear.

She forced herself to slow her breathing, replacing her

shallow pant for deep lungfuls of the mountain air. She wondered how close she could get to him. Whether she'd be able to make out his features. Who was he? And why was he pursuing her?

Nearby, on a crop of boulders, a puddle of white caught her eye. She made her way over to the rocks, taking care all the while to listen for the hunter. The white object that had drawn her eye was a garment of some kind. She picked it up and was astonished to see that it was a gown so finely woven that it could have been made of cobwebs. She'd never seen anything so beautiful. Was it for her? Who had left it there? Glad of something to cover her nakedness, she gathered up the fabric, light as snow, and let it cascade over her head and shoulders. The gown skimmed her body, spilling to the floor like a waterfall. The white fur trim on the collar tickled her neck and as she put her hand to her throat, her fingers brushed against a small, oval gemstone brooch. She looked down at the amber stone and the colour reminded her of Mike's eyes.

At the same moment, the familiar sound of a twig snapping pulled the thread of her thoughts from her. She stepped behind a tree, out of the moonlight, and observed the hunter as he made his way to the rocks where she'd picked up the garment. He put his hand down on the rock, as though he was making sure that the gown wasn't there. Moonlight peppered the place where he stood and he turned to face her direction. Milk-white spirals of mist wreathed around him as he scanned the shadows.

Esther held her breath, but kept her eyes on the hunter, ready to flee if he made one move towards her. As he turned, the moonlight lit his face and she finally understood why she'd not been able to make out his features. A mask covered his eyes and nose, giving him the appearance of an animal, but it was too dark to make out the features clearly. Perhaps a fox, or a cat. Maybe a wolf.

She stared at him for several minutes, unsure whether he could see her. Her fingers rested on the tree, tracing the deep, vertical welts of the gnarled bark. The hunter moved forwards, and she stepped back, further into the shadows, so as not to give her hiding position away. The dress snagged on a low holly bush and as she reached down, she felt a prickle as the pad of her right forefinger dragged across the spiny holly leaf. She looked at the wound, a drop of blood pooling at the tip, and raised it to her lips. The earth slowed and she closed her eyes. The blood tasted of musky leaves, of iron, of urgent velvet kisses. The image of Dan and Mike, entwined on the forest floor, pushed into her mind, assaulting her senses. Limbs locked in urgency, the smell of wood-smoke and leather hanging in the air.

A sound nearby broke the illusion and she snapped her head towards the direction it had come from, expecting to see the hunter bearing down.

❧

'Esther, sweetheart. There's a cup of tea here for you.' Dan set the mug down beside the bed. 'It's nearly half past ten.'

She opened her eyes and smiled. 'I was dreaming about the forest again. I was wearing a beautiful white dress.'

'What do you mean?'

'I . . . I don't know.' She paused, trying to collect her thoughts. 'I'm not making sense, am I?' She laughed.

'Have you bitten your lip? That looks like blood.' He ran

his thumb across her lower lip, to wipe away the smudge. 'I don't go in for all of this dream interpretation stuff, but I'd say the forest is a manifestation of you being uprooted.' He looked pleased with himself.

'Really?' She raised herself onto one elbow.

He snorted. 'No, of course not! You dreamed about the forest because that's where we live now. It's on your mind. That's all. Honestly, I do wonder about what goes on in your head sometimes.'

Esther sank bank onto the pillows. 'Is Mike still here?'

'No, he left early this morning. It was very late when I came up to bed, but I gave him a pillow and some blankets and made sure the wood burner was well stocked.'

'Will he have got home alright, d'you think?' She kept her tone light, casual.

'I wouldn't worry about that one. He's well used to finding his way around, fog or no fog. You heard his stories for yourself.'

She got out of bed and opened the curtains. The familiar wall of white greeted her and she sighed. 'I'm losing track of days. What day is it?'

'Tuesday. This bloody fog has been down since Sunday – another day we won't see the builders. Mind you, I guess the bridge is still out, anyway.'

'Well, we can't go on like this. Let's crack on with the jobs we can do around the place. It might save us some money too, if we do some of the prep ourselves.'

He thought for a moment. 'Sure. We'll be a bit hampered for tools, but Mikey might be able to sort something out.'

'Mike?'

'Yes. Remember he's looking for odd jobs to do? I spoke

to him about it last night. There's plenty he can make a start on and he has a whole barn full of tools.'

Still not fully awake, she sat on the edge of the bed, looking pensive as she drank her tea, remembering the image of Dan and Mike entwined. What did it mean? Was she reading too much into it? Her heart thudded against her ribcage. Shouldn't she be feeling concerned? He'd come into their lives and was monopolising her husband and they knew so little about him.

Dan misunderstood her silence. 'Remember, on Saturday night he lent us the generator? I was up at his place. He's got a good set-up going there and we may as well pass some of the work his way.'

'Yeah, sure. Good idea. How will we get in touch with him though?'

The bedroom door creaked open and Esther's stomach lurched. Major Tom jumped up onto the bed, snuggling into Esther's side and settled, purring, while fixing Dan with a baleful stare.

'Mikey won't be too far away. That one has a sixth sense.' Dan could barely contain his irritation with the cat and raised his hand to sweep it away. 'Bloody thing.'

'Oh he's fine – leave him be. It's nice having him about the place, even if we don't know who he belongs to. Anyway, I thought you don't believe in things like the sixth sense?'

'It's all relative,' he said and grinned. His mobile bleeped and he pulled it out of his back pocket, scrolling down the screen.

She watched him carefully as his expression changed. The edge of his mouth turned upwards. The flicker of his eyes as he scanned the words on the screen.

'Is that a text? Who's it from?'

'No, just a low battery warning. Still no signal. I think we have to face it, until this fog lifts, we aren't going anywhere. Do you want to crack on with some of the admin stuff?'

'What, because I'm a woman and women do admin?' She was only half teasing.

'No. Because you are far more organised than I am. I'm a hindrance. A giant, horny hindrance and I'm coming for you.' He threw the covers back, scattering the cat to the floor and lunged at her. Esther squealed with surprise and allowed herself to be caught.

Esther could hear Dan humming to himself as he swept out the storeroom next door to the waiting room. She could picture exactly how he'd approach the task, dipping his broom into a mop bucket to dampen the dust and prevent it clouding the air, a tip he'd learned from his gran. He'd passed the same tip onto her when they were renovating their first house together.

She liked listening to the noise of him working. It was comforting. For the first time since they'd arrived, she felt as though they were pulling together. She tried to think back to the last time he'd made the first move on her and realised with a spark of sadness that it had been months. In fact, it was the night she'd conceived; the night she'd finally decided she would join him in Scotland after all. Sex between them had always been a minefield of misunderstandings and missed chances. Esther blamed her physical condition, and their lack of experience didn't help. Dan was her first lover and she suspected she was his, though he wouldn't be drawn on the subject. She'd spent her teenage years mooning after boys who weren't interested in her, and just as many subsequent years fending off the weirdos that got off on dating an amputee.

'Stump fiends.' Sophie whispered in her ear, as clear as if she'd been standing there.

Esther, unthinking, replied out loud with her standard response, 'Stump suckers.'

'Did you say something?' Dan stood in the doorway, holding a broom.

'No – sorry, was just thinking out loud.'

He gave her a quizzical look then went back into the storeroom.

Esther smiled at the memory. Sophie had a range of names for the guys who were fascinated more by Esther's accident than by Esther herself. They were the detail hunters, collecting gory stories to wear like badges of honour, and Sophie despised them. Over the years, both girls had learned to spot them before they'd even opened their mouths.

Dan was different. She'd met him through a dating website and from the start he was interested in her opinions and dreams. He was different to the others. But even so, before they met, she'd told him about her disability, so he'd had time to arrange his features into a neutral expression when he saw her for the first time.

In the early days he'd been curious, asking lots of questions about the mechanics of the prosthetic. He never asked her for the details of the accident, but she sometimes felt like she was the subject of an experiment, particularly when he started making suggestions about small improvements to her leg. Sophie had asked her which was worse: the gore tourists, or Dan who wanted to make things easier for her.

Most importantly, Dan accepted that her disability was just part of who she was. After years of feeling self-conscious about her body, Esther recognised that acceptance might be as good as it was going to get for her and she latched onto it. His attitude hadn't changed in all the time she'd known him. When her skin was rubbed raw from the suction collar, it was Dan who helped her, tending to it with antiseptic cream and bandages. Her lover was forced to be her carer, and although he told her over and over that he didn't mind, it wasn't the point. She minded.

Unless he was dressing her skin, he avoided touching her legs at all. She'd asked him about it once, but he'd replied that he didn't touch her elbows or her thumbs either. She couldn't make him see that he only ever complimented her appearance when she wore jeans or trousers; the metal pylon hidden beneath dark blue denim. She'd bought several synthetic skins to cover the pylon – one of them even had a tattoo of a butterfly on the inside of the ankle. They'd made her feel like a Barbie doll, with rubberised legs and flexible knees that would only lock in two positions. The blancmange-pink limb sticking out from under her dress or skirt looked absurd in her eyes, so she rarely bothered with it.

She rubbed her hand over her stomach. Since she announced she was pregnant, it was almost like Dan had given up on their sex life completely, like his job was done. She put her hand to her neck, tracing the path his mouth had taken, and shivered with the remembered pleasure. He'd been so tender, so caring, not the perfunctory performance she was used to. Perhaps there was something in the air.

Even the persistent fog couldn't dampen her mood. She looked around the waiting room. She'd ask Dan to cut back the vine that had broken through the quarter pane. Maybe he could also board the windows up and clean them too, as she didn't want to risk standing on a step ladder. She'd ended up in a heap on the floor the last time. After all those years without her leg, she still sometimes just forgot and would step off with Peggy leading the way. Her and Dan had both laughed at the time, but now with Bump to consider, she had to be more careful. At a push, the windows could wait until the kitchen had been fitted. No sense making it spotless for the builders.

She eyed the closed cupboard door. It stared back. Running her fingers over the panel, it swung free with no trouble, the inside now empty. She'd had boxed up all the timetables and papers, putting them aside to sort them out once she got too big to move around so much and the days yawned before her.

Putting her hand on her belly, she wondered how long it would be before she felt the baby move. The books said any time from seventeen weeks, but she'd read online that it could be much earlier. She was coming into her twelfth week now. She sat as still as she could, focusing all her attention on her stomach. She still couldn't feel anything different and the old, familiar panic took hold, creeping along her veins, snaking around her heart.

Despite knowing the answer already, Esther hauled herself up the stairs to the bathroom and ripped open a new pregnancy test – the one she kept in her wash bag as a backup. Fingers fumbling with the wrapper, she nearly dropped it on the floor. She squatted over the toilet, but when she got herself into position, she could hardly squeeze out any urine.

Esther washed her hands and sat on the edge of the bath, staring at the plastic wand. The black and white wall tiles closed in around her and a draught from the small window made her shiver. The wait was interminable. She'd never understood the women on the TV shows who looked away for the whole of the two minutes whilst the test developed. On one level, she knew it was to heighten the drama, but she didn't think it could be any more dramatic than it already was, or that any woman would behave in such a way. She wanted to note every second, how quickly the line appeared, whether it was dark or faint, and then spend hours online comparing notes with other mums-to-be.

Time hung like the fog while she willed the line to appear. She closed her eyes and threw her head back in a silent prayer of thanks when it winked at her through the little window after no more than thirty seconds, solid and reassuring. After the last time, she wasn't taking any chances. She wrapped the stick in toilet paper and threw it in the waste bin, then thought better of it and retrieved it, throwing away just the tissue. She took it into the bedroom and put it with the other test, at the bottom of her jewellery box, so that when the next bout of anxiety erupted, she would be sure.

Her eye caught something nestling underneath all the tangled necklaces. She pushed everything else aside to see it better. *Shit!* The amber brooch from her dreams stared back at her. *What the fuck is going on? Where did this brooch come from?* There was a subtle shift inside her, a ratchet clicking into place, but the puzzle wasn't quite complete enough for her to make sense of it. She was starting to believe that there was some other force at work, that someone or something was sending her a message. Or maybe Dan was right after all and she just had an overactive imagination. As she reached out to pick up the brooch, Dan shouted up the stairs.

'Esther, come and see this!'

She snapped the lid of the jewellery box shut and carefully

took the stairs, tutting to herself as she realised she still hadn't sorted the keys out for the internal doors. The fog seemed to be thinning and she could see a bit further than before. Major Tom trotted along beside her, seeming to know not to wind round her ankles, and she bent down to tickle the top of his head.

'Es? Where are you?'

'Coming,' she replied and opened the storeroom door.

'Look at this, it seems the wildlife want to share the Halt with us.' He pointed to the floor.

'What am I looking at?' She squinted, scrunching up her nose and mouth at the same time.

'These, look. Paw prints.' He crouched down next to them.

'Major Tom is outside. They'll be his, surely?'

'No, Es. Look again. These aren't cat prints. A rabbit or maybe a hare made these, see the longer marks at the back?'

'Oh, yeah.' Esther raised an eyebrow. 'I wonder how they got there?'

'Cheeky little sods, they are. You wait, once the fog lifts, it'll be like something out of Snow White with all the wildlife for miles popping in.'

'So long as the bluebirds help with the washing up, I won't mind,' she laughed. 'Do you think the fog is beginning to lift? It doesn't seem to be as thick as before.'

'Let's hope so, eh? If it does, I'll take the car out later and see if I can find a shop. I could do with getting to a phone to find out what's going on with the builders and the bridge.'

She left him to it and wandered back to the cottage. Major Tom followed her, tail in the air.

Later that morning, Esther sat at the kitchen table, making

lists in her plain, round handwriting. Spread out on the table before her was a list of menu ideas for when the centre opened and a list of things to buy for each bedroom. She got up and started rooting through the boxes in the sitting room, passing over items or nudging them out of the way. She couldn't find the diary she'd made her haphazard notes in. It should have been in her handbag, but at the last minute she'd put it in another box. Now she couldn't find it, or remember what the box looked like.

For a few seconds she doubted herself. Had she packed it away after all? She'd tucked the photograph of her parents on their wedding day between its pages, along with the remaining links to her father – a note of his prison number and the address he was released to. It wasn't much and the information was at least fifteen years old, but at least she had somewhere to start.

She looked around at all the unopened boxes, trying to remember which one it was. *What if it was a box that went to storage?* She drummed her fingers on the windowsill, trying to quell the sick feeling that threatened to engulf her as she realised she may have lost the diary. *Think! Where was it?*

The idea of rummaging through the boxes wasn't very appealing. Dan had organised the move and done most of the packing. She wouldn't know where to begin and he'd have already decided which order to unpack in. Her fingers brushed the laptop on the windowsill, where Dan had left it charging. *That's it!* She opened it up and searched through the recently-opened Excel files and spotted one called 'House Move.' Her hunch was right, Dan had not only numbered the boxes from his study, but had listed the contents on the spreadsheet. There were times his pernickety ways proved to be useful. She scanned through the list quickly, but couldn't see an entry for her diary. As she looked around the room again, she spotted a blue shoe box that she didn't remember packing, sealed with several lengths of parcel tape. It didn't seem to be numbered, so it was unlikely to be Dan's. She started hunting for the scissors.

Dan interrupted her rummaging.

'Did you make a list?'

'I made several.' She grinned. 'I'm beginning to get a feel now for how this place might work. Have you seen my diary anywhere?'

He kissed the top of her head. 'Nope, sorry. I'm glad you seem more settled. I know it was a leap of faith, but trust me, this place was too good to pass up.' He paused, and when he spoke again there was a slight catch in his voice. 'Using the redundancy money this way makes me feel like I have a contribution to make.'

Esther wanted to hug him. It was the first time she'd heard him be anything other than negative about his redundancy. It was another land mine in the path of their happiness. She knew however they still had a long way to go. He'd never told her exactly how he'd spent his days after he'd lost his job; the days where he pretended to go to work. The shock that he could deceive her, combined with the depth and extent of it, made her question how well she knew her husband, even now. More than that, she felt sadness that he didn't trust her enough to open up to her, that he felt he had to pretend everything was normal. That realisation was the real weakness in their marriage and she didn't see any way of making it better.

'Dan?'

'Hmm?'

'Do you think there is something strange about this place?'

'Strange?'

'Yes. Think about it, have you ever known fog to last this long? It's so silent here during the day and there was that phone call from Sophie . . .'

Just voicing her concerns to Dan made her realise how bizarre they sounded. Even so, she knew better than to mention the daydream about the radio to him. And she'd never get him to understand the feeling the carving had given her.

'All of these things have a rational explanation. Are you feeling okay? You've been a bit distracted lately, like you're in a trance.'

'Don't you feel cut off? Anything could have happened. The rest of Scotland could have been annihilated in a nuclear attack. Aliens could have landed. Zombies might be roaming the streets of Inverness. I don't think I've ever felt so remote before.'

'Are you regretting coming here?' Dan looked down, avoiding eye contact with her.

She thought for a moment before answering. 'No, of course not. I think I had a romantic view of what it would be like, just you and me but with a bit less civilisation and convenience than we were used to.'

'You hate it here, don't you?'

Esther paused and sighed. 'Dan. You have to stop doubting, it's caustic. It's just not what I pictured. Can't you just accept that we are here, together?'

He hesitated before speaking. 'I wake up every day and think how lucky I am. You could have left me, Es. I wouldn't have blamed you.'

She chewed the inside of her cheek, thinking how to respond. 'I thought about it, Dan. You must know that. It was hard enough losing the baby. I couldn't face losing everything else too.'

'I know. I'm glad you stayed.' He placed a hand on her shoulder.

A streak of pain coursed through her leg and she winced.

'What's up?'

'Phantom leg pains.' She didn't look at him, didn't want to see the momentary irritation flicker across his eyes. She knew he didn't believe her about the pains, but they were very real. Sometimes in bed at night she wanted to scratch her skin off to make the burning sensation stop, but of course, there was nothing for her to scratch.

'Can I do anything?' His question was a reflex.

Esther shook her head. Another reflex.

'Right, I'm going to see if I can find a shop. Have you seen my keys?' He patted his coat pockets.

'They're on the side in the kitchen.'

'You don't want to come?' He raised an eyebrow at her. 'Explore the area a bit?'

She was torn. The chance to get out of the cottage appealed, but it would mean getting into the car and she couldn't face it. Not so soon after their arduous journey up here.

'No, I'm tired. I'll light the fire and read for a bit. Be careful, it's still really foggy out there.'

He nodded and she felt the change in temperature as he went out onto the platform, letting cold air in. A few moments later, she heard the car pull away up the lane. She busied herself setting the fire by twisting up sheets of newspaper, then piling kindling on top. The fire caught first time and she sat by the stove, feeding logs into the iron maw, feeling something approaching contentment.

As she handled the wood, she remembered the carving. She'd hidden it underneath one of the seat cushions on the sofa, not wanting to share it with Dan just yet. Lifting the cushion, she felt around until her fingers closed over it, happy to make contact with it again. She sank back into the seat and turned the disc over in her hands. There were no marks on it that she could use to identify how old it was or where it came from. Her fingers traced the outline of the hares and she noticed that they were carved as an optical illusion. Each hare had two ears, but one ear also formed half of the next pair.

She sat, stroking the carving, deep in thought. As she relaxed, the walls and floor of the sitting room seemed to flex and curve, moving around her as she half slept, taking her back to a time she'd tried to forget, but which was imprinted on her subconscious.

The overhead strip light hummed. Esther focused all her attention on it to distract herself from her nagging bladder. Outside the room, she could hear shoes squeaking on linoleum and curtains swishing on metal rails. Somewhere down the corridor, a phone rang and rang. Still Esther looked at the ceiling. There were 108 ceiling tiles, arranged in twelve rows of nine. She began to count them again. Something about this room wasn't right. She'd been here before, but last time the door was on the left. And hadn't the bed been on the other wall?

After what felt like hours, but could only have been minutes, the sonographer came back, bringing with her the corridor smell of overcooked food and disinfectant. Her smile reached her quick, hazel eyes, bright with just the right balance of efficiency and kindness. Esther looked at the sonographer's name badge. Belinda Button. The kind of name a sonographer should have. The kind of name that made wishes come true.

Belinda Button asked Esther to lift her top and push her trousers down, past her hips. Then she smeared the icy jelly over Esther's stomach. Her skin contracted in protest. Esther scanned the monitor next to her bed. She could hear a pulsing, whooshing sound as Belinda pressed the transducer into her abdomen. Dan held her hand and smiled down at her.

Belinda peered closer at the monitor and said, in a rounded Bristolian accent, 'Hmm. One second, my love, I'm just going to see can I move things round a bit.' She turned the monitor away from Esther and Dan and moved the transducer around, pressing harder than was comfortable.

'What's wrong? There's something wrong, isn't there?' Dan's voice, piano-wire tight, sliced across the room. Belinda Button didn't answer.

'Tell us what's wrong!' he demanded.

Esther stayed quiet; in her own way she'd known that this would happen. Her body began to dissolve as she sank further into the thin foam of the bed.

Belinda, fiddling with a setting on the monitor, clapped her hands. 'Ah, there we go.' She turned the monitor back around to face the bed.

'Well now, Esther. That's just grand. The heartbeat's very strong. Will you have a look at this lovely picture? Can you see your baby?'

Esther and Dan looked at Martian static on the screen. 'I think so,' Esther replied, not certain what she was seeing.

'Here, look. This is the body.' She pointed to the screen. 'And this is the head.'

Esther relaxed and Dan bent down to kiss her forehead. This time it was all going to be just fine.

'And you can just make out the tail here, see?'

'The . . . the tail?' Esther's eyes widened in horror and her mouth followed suit.

'Why, yes dear. And look, you can just make out the others behind him.' The sonographer pointed to six dark dots on the screen. 'I count seven little leverets in total, though there could be more hiding. They're tricksy little blighters at this stage.'

Dan let go of her hand. Esther fell through the bed, through the floor and onto the sofa in the cottage.

Dan slammed the front door, the sudden noise jolting Esther from her sleep. It took her a few seconds to gather her thoughts and she looked around her, puzzled. The antiseptic hospital smell hung in the air and she couldn't shake the feeling that it was more than just a dream. The carving had fallen out of her hand and onto the floor, and Esther quickly scooted it under the sofa, out of Dan's vision.

'Un-fucking-believable.' He threw his keys onto the kitchen table, pacing between the kitchen and sitting room, paying no attention to Esther, who sat watching him, not daring to speak.

'The fucking car has a fucking puncture and no fucking spare.' His features twisted into a Francis Bacon image. 'I got about three quarters of a mile up the main road and had to pull over. I've had to walk all the way back. And the fucking fog is as bad as before. There's no way out of here.'

Esther stayed quiet. She'd witnessed too many heated rows when she was a little girl to try to intervene now. She made herself as small as possible and burrowed into the corner of the sofa, hoping her stillness would shield her from his temper.

'For fuck's sake! Still no fucking signal and still we have this . . .' He waved his hand in the general direction of the fog.

Her stomach lurched. The fog seemed to be rolling towards them, pushing in at the window. She imagined the glass shattering, covering them in deadly diamond shards. She closed her eyes in silent prayer. *Please let his mood lift. Please.*

'I'm sick to death of this weather and not being able to get hold of anyone. FUCK!' He thumped both hands on the wall, then turned and started pacing in the other direction around the room.

She glanced at her watch. He'd been gone more than three hours.

'Wait. What did you say happened?' His story didn't add up.

'I said.' He paused, before emphasising every word. 'The car has a puncture and no spare. I had to leave it a mile up the road and walk back. Why?'

'Because you've been over three hours, that's why. Three hours! Where have you been?' Even as she spoke, she knew she'd lost any chance of keeping him onside. He hated being challenged and she'd just backed him into a corner.

'Who the fuck do you think you are talking to? Since when did I have to answer to you? His face was contorted with anger and as he spoke, little flecks of spit landed on her cheek.

She felt a column of acrimony rising through her body to her mouth where it spilled out of her.

'Since you decided to be so fucking economical with the truth. Since YOU decided not to tell me you'd lost your job and pretended to go to work anyway. Since the day I couldn't get hold of you to tell you I was losing OUR child and had to face the shame and confusion of calling your office to be told you lost your job two months earlier. That's when.'

There was a small part of her that knew she'd gone too far, but it felt good to say the words that she'd held onto for so long, to let them loose, to hear how they sounded and to see the impact as each one struck home.

'Jesus, Esther. You're a sanctimonious bitch sometimes.'

'And you're a fucking automaton.'

They stood facing each other, each surveying their wounds. The intensity of their savagery shocking them both into silence. For a moment, it seemed like it could go either way with their relationship shattering into a million shards. Esther shifted her weight to spread it more evenly and in the process, took a small step towards him. The atmosphere shifted and they both spoke at the same time.

'Dan, we can't carry on like this.'

'Essie. We have to stop this.'

He reached out and cupped her cheek with his hand, wincing as she flinched from his touch.

'I'm sorry. I didn't mean it. You have every right to be angry, every right to want to know where I am. I know I took your trust for granted, but I will win it back.'

Esther, wary, allowed herself to relax a little. He seemed genuinely contrite and she decided that it was time she was honest with him. There were too many unspoken thoughts between them, stopping any real progress.

'I felt so let down. I don't care about you losing your job – not in the way you think I do. But it pulls me up short sometimes – that something so big happened and you didn't turn to me. It made me feel . . . redundant.'

She watched him recoil as the word fizzled and died, wanting to wound him just one more time.

He hung his head, avoiding her eye. 'I'll never make you feel that way again. All of this,' he gestured, 'all of this is for us. Me, you, the baby.' He reached out to pull her close to him.

'I'm sorry too,' she said, his shoulder half-muffling her words. 'So many strange things have happened since we've been here. I feel jittery and on edge. Haven't you noticed anything weird about this place?'

'Just that it's all new for us and this odd weather is making it that much harder to adjust. By now we should have explored the area a bit, been on walks, got to know the place a bit better. We've got cabin fever, that's all.'

She didn't reply.

'Let's be a bit kinder to each other. You are so important to me and I want our child to be happy and secure, with two parents who love him.'

'Or her.'

'Or her.' Dan smiled and kissed the top of her head. 'I know it could be a girl or a boy and I'd be just as pleased with either, but I can't help thinking it's a boy.'

And I'm equally sure she's a girl. 'You're right. This should be a happy time for us. We've got so much to look forward to – maybe more than we ever did in Bristol.'

'Come on, to prove how much of a new man I am, I'll make dinner tonight.'

Despite herself, she laughed at him. It felt good to be in his arms, talking about the future and he was trying, she had to credit him for that. Even so, she was half-conscious of the jagged thought burrowing into her mind.

He didn't actually tell me what had taken so long, or where he'd been.

'I've been thinking about what you said earlier.'

Dan stopped stirring the gravy and turned towards Esther. 'What?'

'You know, about being kinder to each other and making sure our child is happy and secure.' She paused, uncertain how to continue. She didn't want to risk a repeat of their earlier row, but wanted to capitalise on Dan's apparent willingness to talk.

He turned the gas off and waited for her to speak again, pulling out the pocket-sized bottle of hand gel from his jeans and squirting some onto his hands.

'I know we don't talk about it much, but we never had that, did we? We never had the security we want to give to our child. Neither of us can really remember what it was like to have two parents.' She pulled out a chair and sat down at the table, the chair legs shrieking across the stone floor. 'It's one of the things we had in common at the beginning.'

Dan finished cleaning his hands and pulled up a chair opposite her, careful to lift the legs so they didn't scrape across the floor. 'Yeah, I guess. I have very specific memories from childhood, like getting a pair of roller skates when I wanted a bike. Or the time I cut my foot in the sea on a shell. I know mum was there and she must have tended to the cut, but she's more like a shadow at the edge of my vision.'

Esther nodded. 'Go on.'

'I would be hard pushed to remember a conversation with her and sometimes I struggle to recall what she looked like. But it's her perfume I remember most vividly

– Shalimar – and the softness of her cheek against mine.'

'Perfume?' A note of disbelief crept into her voice. Knowing how Eric was, perfume seemed rather worldly, especially such a heavy-hitting fragrance. She surprised herself at how easy it was to slip into Eric's closed-minded ways.

Dan didn't seem to have noticed her tone, or at least, hadn't noticed the implied criticism.

'Yes. She always wore a dab of it behind her ears and on her wrists. No matter where she was going or what she was doing. So Dad says, anyway.'

'Do you think he misses her?'

'Oh, Es. He does. I know it. Every night before bed, he says a prayer then kisses their wedding photograph. He thinks no-one else knows, but I've seen him. She meant the world to him, the way you do to me.'

She reached out across the table, placing her hand over Dan's. 'I didn't know that about him.'

'I get it, Essie. You look at him and see a resentful, angry man. But to me, he's just someone who has forgotten how to be at peace.'

Esther looked at her husband and saw him more clearly than she had for months. It was as though they'd been separated for a long time and now he was coming back to her. His eyes had softened to the colour of mountain slate and all the tension, so evident in recent months, had left his body.

'But you're right. Neither of us had the kind of upbringing we want for our own child. You might not have had your dad, but you at least had your mum.'

She gave a low whistle. 'Yes, that's true, but it still wasn't easy. She did the best she could for me – but she didn't leave him, even when she had chance to.'

'Do you blame Anthea for the accident?'

'No! Is that how it sounded? No. Dad was to blame. He was drinking, he was out of control. He should never have been behind the wheel.' *And I should never have been in the car with him.*

'Logically though, if Anthea had left him, the accident wouldn't have happened. Therefore, she must shoulder some responsibility?'

Esther started fidgeting. The kitchen felt very warm and she pulled the collar of her jumper away from her neck. This wasn't how the conversation was supposed to go. She could feel the man she wanted slipping away from her again.

'What could she have done? She had a small child and nowhere to go.'

'But she lied to you.'

'She lied about Dad, yes. I might have done the same in her shoes. I was eight years old and horribly maimed. I nearly died. I can't imagine how she must have felt seeing me go through all that pain. She didn't want me to know he was in prison for what he'd done to me, or that woman and her children, so in her mind telling me he'd left was kinder. She didn't want me to feel any guilt about what had happened to Dad.'

The steel returned to Dan's eyes. 'But she still lied.'

Esther bridled at his insistence, knowing he was testing her somehow. 'What's your point, Dan?'

'Just that sometimes we lie to protect the ones we love.' He moved his hand from under hers and reached for the hand gel.

The kitchen table had become Esther's makeshift work space. Dan had commandeered the desk in the sitting room and although he never said anything, she knew him well enough to understand he liked to keep his desk neat and tidy and she would be an unwelcome intrusion. The sheaf of papers on the table could probably wait, but she needed something to fill her time; the endless fog sapped her energy and purpose. Pulling the paperwork towards her, she shuffled through the various documents, sorting them into three piles as she went: legal, business, personal. The legal pile mostly comprised of letters backwards and forwards from their solicitor about the sale of the apartment and the purchase of Rosgill. There wasn't much for her to do, so she set about putting them in date order, ready for filing. Dan would approve.

The sound of hammering from the living room made her jump. Not realising Dan had come back into the cottage, she followed the sound and saw him hanging a rectangular mirror on the wall next to the window.

'Is it level?'

Esther stood back, squinting. 'Er . . . yeah. I think so. Where'd you find it?'

'It was propped up against the wall in the store room. D'you like it?'

It was hideous. She didn't know what to say. The dark, heavily carved frame looked clumsy and fussy compared to the other furniture in the room. Panels of carved leaves ran along each edge of the frame, linked at the corners by a trefoil design. It looked vaguely religious, like it would be more at home in a gothic pile than in her sitting room. There was no way he'd have allowed such an ugly object in their previous home.

'Maybe we can paint the frame? It's a bit chunky.'

'I like it. Look at the craftsmanship in that carving. And it looks good there.' He stood back and surveyed the wall. He tutted but avoided looking at her as he stepped forward again, making tiny adjustments to the mirror's position, running his fingers over the carved leaves. 'There. That's better.'

'It's such a departure from your usual style, Dan. I never thought you'd go for the country cottage look. What's next, horse brasses?'

'It's a mirror. You're over-thinking it.'

Her eyes widened a fraction – the type of micro-expression that a poker player would pounce on, but he continued.

'We're in a different place now. Besides, it's just a mirror.' His voice softened. 'Come here.'

She stood next to him and looked into the mirror at the two people gazing back. Dan, taller than her and rangy with it. He had the body of a distance runner, angular and without padding. He'd started to wear his hair differently, running gel through it so that it was messier, spikier, and the stubble on his chin seemed more groomed, curated. She wondered if others could see past his spiky outer casing, whether they thought it was worth getting to the seed inside. As much as she loved him, she had her doubts. He wasn't easy to live with and made it hard for people to get to know him. She couldn't remember him ever having a close friend before; she'd been that for him. But now there was Mike. How had he managed to win Dan's trust so easily?

Dan put his arm around her shoulders, still staring at his own reflection in the mirror, seemingly unwilling to meet her eye.

'What do you see in the mirror, Dan?'

'Hmm?'

'When you look at our reflection, what do you see?'

'I see the two of us, here in our new home, ready to face

our new life together.' He smiled and kissed the top of her head, like he was pleased he'd given her the right answer.

Esther smiled back, all the time willing him to recognise that there were three of them standing in front of the mirror, and feeling a spike of sadness when he didn't mention the baby.

The boxes seemed to be multiplying. As fast as they unpacked one, another seemed to appear. Most of their belongings had gone into storage while the refurbishments were taking place, but they'd agreed that having a few non-essential things around them would help them to settle in. For both of them, that meant books. They'd tried to whittle them down to the bare minimum, aware that they'd simply have to repack and move anything they brought with them, but Esther found it so hard to choose.

There were shelves already built into the alcoves either side of the wood burner. Dan had wanted to claim one side for his books, allocating the other side to Esther. In turn, she wanted to mix the books together. They couldn't even agree on how to set out their possessions. Esther capitulated without putting up much resistance. Some battles just weren't worth the victory. Besides, it meant she could organise her shelves how she wanted to. By genre, alphabetical by author, alphabetical by title, by the colour of their spines. She was completely free. In the end, she decided to group her books by genre because it meant she'd be able to find a suitable book according to her mood.

As she put the books on the shelves, she thought about how each reminded her of a period in her life. Some were from her time at university. Most had been sent to storage – being an English Literature student meant she'd collected a huge number of titles. But she kept her favourites close: *The Inheritors*, Eliot's poems; Shakespeare's sonnets.

She unpacked a hardbacked translation of Ovid's *Metamorphoses*, covered in red linen that had been glued so tightly to the backing board that the edges were beginning to fray. She'd struggled with the work to begin with, but over time had fallen for the rich tapestry of characters and events. All human life was within these pages as he wove tales of sex, death, love, revenge and war around the gods and mortals.

She read the first line from the prologue, out loud: "I intend to speak of forms changed into new entities. You, gods, since you are the ones who alter these, and all other things, inspire my attempt, and spin out a continuous thread of words, from the world's first origins to my own time."

At once, she was taken back to sun-dappled days spent reading aloud to her study group about how Daphne turned into an olive tree to escape Apollo's attention; of Ceyx and Alcyone who both turned into kingfishers so that they could spend eternity together after Ceyx was killed. These myths had filled the gap left behind when fairy tales no longer satisfied her. If she could only persuade Dan to read fiction, she was sure he'd enjoy Ovid. The scientist in him would recognise the order resulting from the chaos at the beginning of time and the separation of the elements when the universe began its transformation. The adherent in him would recognise the parallels with the Bible, though he'd struggle with the idea that the gods may be vengeful. Perhaps she could read it aloud to him, or they could take turns as they prepared the evening meal. They could even extend the readings beyond the two of them and make it a feature of the retreats, selecting texts themed to inspire each group as they prepared dinner in the evening. Pleased with herself, she set the book to one side, promising herself that she would start that very evening.

She unpicked the last of the parcel tape, flattening the box and putting it behind the sofa out of the way. As she turned to go into the kitchen to wash her hands, the ugly mirror caught her eye. She stood in front of it, trying to fathom why Dan liked it so much. Everything about it was crude: from the carving, to the slapdash way the staining had been applied. She'd never understand him and the thought made her smile. There was always something new to learn.

She studied her reflection. Dark shadows settled under her eyes and haunted her cheeks. The mirror made it worse than it was, she was sure of it. Major Tom jumped up onto the windowsill, making her look away from the mirror. She turned her attention once more to her reflection. Ovid slipped from her hand onto the floor, pages splayed as she cried out. For a split second, instead of seeing her face, she saw a hare staring back at her.

Later that night, Esther lay in bed, listening to Dan brushing his teeth in the bathroom. They'd come here for a fresh start, to leave behind the mistakes of the past, but it was having the opposite effect. The silence and isolation were forcing her to think about things that should have remained buried. Sophie was here with her at every turn. Hardly a day went by when Esther didn't feel a fresh wave of loss. And it was all so complicated, coming on top of losing the baby and finding out about Dan's lies. She wore each sadness like a necklace that choked her, biting into her skin. It was hard to untangle one sadness from another, to smooth it out, to lay it flat and bare. And now Dan was forcing her hand by making her talk about her parents. She stopped herself in mid-thought. She was being unfair – after all, hadn't she brought things to a head by saying she wanted to find Patrick? She knew Dan had given in too easily. This was his way of needling her, making his point.

Esther was resolute though. She'd given it too much thought over the past few months to let go now. Even though she knew she wouldn't be able to wait until after the baby was born to start her search in earnest, she didn't want to rush headlong into it either, not without considering all of the possible outcomes. She wanted to test out her own feelings first, to try them on, parade about, in much the way she might do if she was buying a new coat. Searching for her father would throw up a number of hurdles along the way, not least in respect of the loyalty she felt to Anthea. But that was assuming she decided to go ahead. Her head told her she should leave things be, there was no sense scouring through the past. If Patrick had wanted to contact her, he'd had plenty of opportunity.

But in truth, in the small, dark hours of the night, she allowed herself to admit that her father was always there, just under the surface, waiting for her to call him home.

❧

The oaks and birches understood loss. They mourned each passing season, weeping bronze and gold tears until they could weep no more, and then the spruce took up the lamentation, the song of sadness chiming through needles dense with frost and ice.

Esther's thoughts floated out into the night, catching on roots and branches, snared by the spruce, adding a new harmony to their crystal song. The last remaining hazel trees woke from their meditation and listened in communion.

The forest fell silent, waiting for the hazels to impart their wisdom, and when they finally spoke, the forest leaned in to listen.

5

WEDNESDAY

FROM TIME TO time, the forest floor was flecked with silvered moonlight and she began to recognise the pattern of the trees. Each night, the forest brought her back to the same place. She knew that in a few moments she'd hear the twig snap heralding the hunter's presence, and for the first time, she felt a new emotion stirring. Her suspicion, deeply-rooted, was now tinted by a reluctant curiosity. She wanted to know who he was, why she kept coming back to this place. Each night, she felt she was getting closer to the answer.

The stars pulsed through the trees, sending a Morse code from the universe. A thousand pairs of eyes watched her from the shadows and branches, from under bushes and rocks, waiting to see what she'd do next. Tonight, the earth would reveal more to her than before and she shivered, anticipating the subtle change as a new layer began to show itself. She was stronger, suppler, more agile. She moved faster through the forest, but was completely unprepared for the magnitude of the change that she was presented with on this night. She stared at her legs, both of them, her right leg the mirror image of her left. She ran her hands over her knee, calf, shin, ankle.

Her hands flexed and curved around the muscles, bone, skin. In answer, her leg welcomed her hands, responding with the slightest shiver, the new skin unused to being worn and touched, but seeking more.

She'd forgotten what it felt like to have two symmetrical legs, and for a fleeting moment thought about Peg, lying somewhere, abandoned. But she couldn't deny the lick of pleasure from feeling the earth beneath both feet; couldn't refute how good it felt to have the solid ground beneath her, pushing her forwards. There was a balance, a harmony within her, that she didn't know she'd missed. Her legs were long and lean, her thighs powerful and graceful. Her moon-rounded belly hinted at more to come. Her body was a tuning fork, ready to pick up vibrations from the ground underfoot.

She coursed through the trees, ducking to avoid the low-hanging branches, embedding the memory in her muscles. The white gown was waiting for her on the mossy boulders. The darkness between the trees shrouded her and scent from the shadows weaved through her dark hair. The moon, almost at its fullest point, flaunted its ample promise as she shrugged the gown over her head and shoulders. The garment whispered over her skin, sending trails of pleasure through her. Taking care to stay out of the moonlight and keeping the shadows close, she twirled around, feeling the freedom that came from unfettered movement.

There was no sign of the hunter. Was she disappointed? She still didn't know anything about him, or what he represented. Why was he pursuing her? She was no closer to knowing. Each night he was gaining ground, but she was running further. What would happen when he caught her? She was sure he would. Lost in her thoughts, she plucked at the delicate fabric of the gown. Glancing down, the amber brooch winked back at her and she thought about that first night at Rosgill when the lights went out and she'd seen herself reflected in Mike's eyes. He'd unsettled her then, as he had every time she'd seen him since. Or was it this place? She'd never been so far from other people before, so far away from everything that was familiar to her. Nothing here was easy.

How had the brooch turned up in her jewellery box? She had so many questions and she was no nearer any answers. Maybe she was losing her mind. That's what Dan would say. That she was overtired, overwrought – hormonal. That she was being silly, or these things never happened. He'd be wrong. She knew it was something deeper inside her, something she'd never be able to explain to him. If she had to put it in terms he'd understand, she'd say the shift was spiritual; that the connection she was starting to feel with the natural world was similar to his faith in God.

Anticipating the sound of the twig snapping, she turned to face the direction he would appear from. She watched him materialise, the air around him flexing and curving as he pushed through. For a second, their eyes met and every muscle in her body tensed, every hair bristled.

No longer lulled by the sensual forest, instinct took over and Esther fled. With two legs, her stride was confident, purposeful. It was as though she knew every rock, every tree root and, as she ran, she was able to use them as a springboard to jump from, breaking her tracks. Her ears filled with the sounds of the night. Bark cracked and settled as the cool night wound round each tree. Ferns, curled up for the night, released their scent as she brushed past. Her footprints left the barest indentations on the mossy rocks and river bank. Her feet sighed over the forest floor, more gentle than the night breeze that stirred up eddies of leaves and twigs. She was able to side-step and back track easily, her new leg affording her an agility that her prosthetic denied. The ground beneath her urged her forward, and the blood in her veins pulsed with the euphoria that came from her speed over the terrain. This was how freedom felt.

She slowed and hid deep in the sulky shadows, away from the moonlight that would give her away, trembling as she tried to slow her breathing. She heard him long before she saw him. He was close, but not as close as before. She knew he would catch her, but it wouldn't be tonight. Tonight, she was enjoying the chase; he followed where she led and she enjoyed the power the hunt gave her. She wanted to know why he pursued her relentlessly, but more than that, she couldn't shake the feeling that she knew him. Had always known him.

❧

She woke to the sound of an alarm ringing close by. Groggy from her dream, it took a few moments for her to work out where she was and she felt a fleeting disappointment that she was no longer in the forest. The space beside her, where Dan should have been, was empty and still the alarm insisted she woke up. Disoriented, she reached out for her phone from the bedside table, nudging a glass of water against the bedside lamp. It was 8 o'clock. Still no signal. She rolled onto Dan's side of the bed and grabbed for his phone to stop the alarm.
'Dan?'

There was no answer.

Where is he? Why did he set the alarm? The soft pillows

and duvet called to her and she briefly considered rolling over and going back asleep, but her bladder was nagging away. She pulled on her dressing gown and reached for her crutch, not wanting to be bothered with fitting her leg.

Inspecting herself in the bathroom mirror, Esther posed and turned, smoothing the fabric of her jersey nightshirt over her stomach. She thought she could detect a rounding. It seemed fuller than usual under the palm of her hand. She noted with pleasure that the dark circles under her eyes had disappeared and her skin looked clearer. Tucking her dark hair behind her ears, she splashed cold water on her face, enjoying the fresh feeling, even as the skin on her scalp contracted in shock.

She half-expected to see Dan in the kitchen, making breakfast, the noise of the radio drowning out her calls from upstairs. There was no sign of him either in the kitchen or sitting room. She felt a mixture of irritation and worry. Although they'd made an uneasy peace last night after their row, why would he go off and leave her without saying anything? Surely he knew how she felt? Using her crutch, she swung her way over to the kettle and switched it on. There was nothing for it but to wait for him to come back. Perhaps he'd gone to see if Mike could tow the Toyota.

The endless fog peered in at the window, showing no sign of abating. Esther spooned a sugar into her tea. Dan wouldn't approve but he wasn't around to have an opinion. She relished the small rebellion, then chastised herself as she remembered their agreement. She'd brought his phone down from the bedroom as a reminder to ask him to disable the alarm, and she could feel the slim shape in her pocket, nudging her hip and her conscience. How bad would it be to look at his messages? The thought tugged at the hem of her dressing gown. *Bad, Esther. It would be bad.* She mentally shrugged, pulling the phone out of her pocket and swiped her finger across the screen. It was locked. It was a sign, she told herself, and put the phone back on the table.

As she sat in the warm kitchen, waiting for Dan to return, the phone taunted her from the corner of her eye. He rarely let it out of his sight. If she could work out what the code was to unlock the screen, he'd never know and it would set her mind at rest to know he wasn't hiding anything from her. If anything, she thought, she would be able to relax and they'd both benefit from that. Besides, she might not get another chance to have such unencumbered access to it. How easy it was to convince herself she was doing the right thing. The thought didn't sit comfortably at all with her, and yet she continued.

Keeping an ear out for footsteps up the platform, she tried the first 4 digits of his birthday, then hers. Nothing. She tried various combinations of their wedding anniversary without success. Staring around the kitchen for inspiration, she tried to put herself into his mindset. What other sequence of numbers might he choose? She tried the first four prime numbers, 2, 3, 5, 7 but again was frustrated when the phone refused to unlock. Then she remembered the quotation he used as a screensaver.

"God is faithful, and he will not let you be tempted beyond your ability, but with the temptation he will also provide the way of escape, that you may be able to endure it." Corinthians 10:13

1013. The phone unlocked. Without hesitation, she searched

the messages menu. She hadn't realised she'd been holding her breath and exhaled deeply when she looked at the list of messages. There were no names she didn't recognise, nothing to confirm her suspicions. She was about to lock the phone again, when her eye caught Sophie's name on the list.

Curious and nostalgic, she clicked onto the message string, scrolling back as far as she could. There were a handful of messages going back and forth between them, mostly general chat about cinema times, whether she should bring wine for dinner, or the odd link to something Sophie thought he'd find funny. Esther's emotions were mixed. She immediately felt sorrow, but it was different to the loss she felt every day when she thought of her friend; it stemmed from a recognition that Dan must have been grieving too. She'd been so wrapped up in her own sorrow that she hadn't stopped to consider how Dan must have been feeling. And he'd never said anything to her about it. She should have realised, should have known. He'd had his own friendship with Sophie and it was every bit as special and important as hers was. Her stomach lurched as she realised she was just as guilty of excluding him as he had been with her, and it was uncomfortable being faced with her own shortcomings. How could she have been so selfish? With a further sting of discomfort, she allowed herself to acknowledge that his emotional blankness was both enabling and convenient for her. Selfishness was a trait she despised in others, so why hadn't she recognised it in herself?

Still alert to any sounds of Dan coming back, she continued scrolling through the texts from and to Sophie. Her eye caught the date of the last message – 26th September. The day before Sophie had died. What was so important that she was contacting Dan whilst she was on holiday?

From: Sophie J
Have you thought any more about what I said? xx

From: Dan C
Yes.

From: Sophie J
Find a way to tell her. It's not fair, Dan.

Esther puzzled over the messages. What did they mean? What did Sophie want her to know? What was Dan keeping from her? She cursed herself for being stupid enough to go through his phone. She could hear her mother's voice, telling her no good would come from snooping. Now she was stuck, unable to admit to Dan that she'd hacked into his phone and read his messages, but the thought that there was another secret, so tantalisingly close, would not let her rest. She pondered all the different scenarios where she could raise it with Dan, and rejected every one. Reaching for her tea, she found it was cold. How long had she been sitting there, turning the phone over and over in her hands while she thought?

Hearing footsteps along the platform, she swiped across the screen to lock the phone again and put it on the table in front of her, willing the screen to switch off before he guessed what she'd done, and readying her excuses.

The cottage door opened, bringing with it a glimpse of the freezing fog. Dan stepped inside, looking sheepish and holding something behind his back.

Her first instinct was to berate him, to ask him where he'd been, but she didn't want a repetition of the previous day and, mindful of her promise and the need to keep him on side if she was ever to find out what Sophie had been talking about, smiled at him instead.

'Morning.'

'Hi. I didn't think you'd be up yet.'

'I wouldn't have been, but the alarm went off on your phone.' She felt the heat rising in her cheeks, at the mention of the phone and hoped he didn't notice.

'Really? Odd. I don't remember setting it.' He picked it up from the table and glanced at Esther. He looked as though he was about to say something, but stopped.

'Is it any clearer out there?' It wasn't the question she wanted to ask, but she had to break the silence between them.

'A little. I couldn't sleep, so I got up and went for a walk. I saw these and thought you'd like them.' He pulled his arm from behind his back and offered her a bunch of daffodils. 'I hoped you'd still be asleep, so I could bring them up to you. I thought they'd look pretty on the dressing table.'

She felt tears forming in her eyes. 'First daffodils. They're lovely.' She breathed them in deeply, smelling their soapy scent.

Dan smiled and pulled a mug out of the cupboard, half-filling it with water. He arranged the flowers and took them upstairs.

A few moments later, the cottage door opened again and Mike entered, carrying a plastic bag and a large Tupperware container. Esther stared at him, wrong-footed that he'd be so forward to just come in without knocking. Modesty made her pull the lapels of her dressing gown tighter across her chest, even though she was wearing her nightshirt underneath.

Again, the difference between their new home and their old was brought into stark relief for her. Friends didn't just drop by in Bristol. They phoned in advance, made plans, met for coffee. Calling in unannounced wasn't something she was used to at all. In Bristol, they'd had an entry phone with CCTV, and the 4th floor apartment gave them an extra degree of separation from all the lives playing out at ground level. When she thought about it though, she'd have preferred a townhouse in Redlands, with its rows of terraced houses teeming with life. The kind of place where people felt comfortable dropping in. She realised it was the flat that made them inaccessible to others, she was a princess sealed away in a tower. She'd wanted to hear children's feet running on pavements, car doors slamming, and pizza delivery drivers working late into the night. Their apartment, with its triple glazing, was sealed off from noise and disturbance. A huge glass box from which to view the world. A place where she could observe life and join in, on her terms.

'I brought you some bread.' He held out the container to her.

The loaf was still warm and he offered it so tenderly, as though he was giving her a sleeping animal to look after. She took the bread and put the kettle on. He pulled a carton of milk from the plastic bag he was holding and put it in the fridge.

'I thought you might want some fresh milk. Healthy teeth and bones, you know?' He nodded towards her stomach.

'Thanks, that's very thoughtful. I'm not sure I have any change in my purse. One sec . . .'

He held his hand up. 'Come away, now. None of that.'

An uneasy silence fell over them.

'So, how are you settling in?'

From out of nowhere and to her dismay, Esther started

crying and the more she tried to hold back the tears, the faster and thicker they came.

'I'm sorry,' she said, 'Just give me a minute, will you?' She dried her eyes on the tea towel. She could hear Dan's footsteps overhead in the bathroom and willed him to come down so she wouldn't have to explain herself. She heard the shower door sliding across.

Wordlessly, Mike took her hand and sat her down at the table. He fished in the cupboards for two mugs and a jar of coffee.

She watched him as he finished making the drinks, trying to work out why she felt so agitated around him. She thought it might have something to do with the way he moved. Each movement flowed one into the other, but there was a precision – a deliberateness – to each one. She was reminded of the way a cat places its paws, silent and delicate, ready to spring away at the slightest hint of danger. When she moved, she was also deliberate and precise, but her movements didn't flow. There was a vague mechanical edge to her walk, though over the years she'd incorporated the motion as best she could. She didn't have the range of movements, or degree of agility she needed to move with the kind of gracefulness Mike possessed.

'So, let's try that again.' He smiled as he put the coffee in front of her. 'How are you settling in?'

Her tears threatened to reappear, but she was in control of them this time. There were so many answers to the question. She wanted to say that things were going well, she loved Rosgill and was excited about opening it up to visitors. It was true, on some level, she did feel all of those things and yet, when she opened her mouth to speak, it all eluded her.

'I feel a bit lost.' It felt good to her to admit it.

'Well, now. That's hardly a surprise. It's such a big change for you. Once this fog lifts and we are over the threat of snow, you'll get to meet the folks that live around here. Maybe you'll feel less isolated then.'

He's right. The fog is making things much harder and we're both bubbling around in a pressure cooker. No wonder we've been at each other's throats.

'Yes,' she said. 'And when will that be?'

'Oh, August, I'd reckon.'

For a split second, panic clawed at her, then he winked at her and she relaxed enough to laugh at his teasing.

'I don't think I realised quite how far from everything we'd be. Or how dependent we'd be on the weather and basic communication.'

'This weather isn't really typical, but when we get a fog like this, it can take days to lift. Higher up in the glen, the air is quite clear. It's like looking down onto a blanket of cotton wool.'

He gulped his coffee down. Esther brought her mug to her lips and flinched as she touched the scalding liquid.

'You've missed the worst of the winter. We've had some heavy snows and you'll need to be prepared for it next year. I can give Dan a hand cutting enough wood to see you through the rest of the winter, so you'll have heat at least. They usually clear the top road with the snow plough, but Dan'll need to clear up to the road from the station. Even then, it can sometimes take a couple of days for them to clear the top road if the snow has been particularly heavy.'

'I bet it's beautiful when it snows.'

'It's enchanting, right enough.' He sipped his coffee, eyes

focused on Esther over the rim of the mug. 'We may get some more before spring finally takes hold.'

They sat in silence for a few moments and Esther heard the shower door sliding back across. She felt like she'd stolen this time with Mike and was about to be found out. She tried to think of something to say, something to prolong the conversation which would keep his focus on her, but she couldn't think of anything interesting enough. He made her feel gauche and unworldly. When he'd been talking the other evening about his antics, she'd had to listen to the detail carefully to follow the drift of the conversation. He was so open about drugs and petty crime and it shouldn't have come as a surprise to her, given her work at the refuge. Yet there was still a part of Esther that believed people were basically good; that the local bobby was a paragon of virtue and trust; and that drugs, alcohol addiction, and crime happened to other people. She refused to accept that she had more in common with the women at Helen House than she liked to admit. Patrick's drunkenness was not the same at all. Definitely not the same.

'Dan will be down in a few minutes,' she said, finally.

'How far can you walk?'

His question seemed to come from nowhere and she was unsure of the intent behind it.

'It depends on the ground conditions. If it's reasonably flat, I can manage a couple of miles. Hills are okay too if I can set the pace. I struggle with mud and off-road. Why?'

'Maybe we'll go for a walk, me and you. You might feel better if you can make sense of your surroundings.'

Esther didn't get chance to answer him as Dan jogged down the stairs.

'Mikey! Hey – good to see you.' Dan clasped Mike's shoulder in welcome. 'Any coffee left?'

'Sorry, no. I made instant.'

Esther watched the two men as their conversation went back and forth and she was reduced to playing a bit part again. There was an easiness between the two of them that felt both natural and, at the same time, at odds with what she knew about Dan. Perhaps this was how it had been with Sophie, except Dan was the one on the periphery. Their burgeoning friendship underlined what she'd lost, scoring red marks through her grief. She recognised the signs of jealousy that she harboured but, with a stab of bewilderment, realised she didn't know whether she was jealous that Dan had a new friend, or because his new friend was Mike.

Neither man seemed to notice when she got up from the table.

'I'm going for a bath.'

Dan raised a hand in acknowledgement and Mike inclined his head in her direction. She stood for a moment, waiting for one of them to say something else, and when they didn't, she turned away and climbed the stairs.

Esther added a few drops of the neroli perfume oil she kept for best to the bath. The flowers from Dan had chased away the remnants of any bad feeling and she felt more relaxed than she had when they'd arrived at Rosgill, just five days ago. She smoothed her hands over her stomach. It was lovely to be pregnant in the springtime, with the promise of new life burgeoning all around her. She thought about what Mike had said about the weather and hoped the hard winter was behind them. Snow, so treacherous underfoot, would hold her to ransom just as much as the fog. She had to find a way of coming to terms with her new environment; to find a way of making peace with it.

His words could apply equally to her marriage. It had felt like the longest of winters, with not even a glimpse of the sun. Although things weren't quite how they used to be, perhaps it was no bad thing. They'd come through together and now had to learn to adjust to their new life and new understanding of each other. She loved Dan, she was as sure of that as she could be, but now she felt secure enough within her own thoughts to allow herself to admit that she didn't always like him.

The scars of the previous year ran deep. They were always there, puckering and pinching her thoughts. The long-suppressed resentments she harboured were never very far from the surface. Dan was always so difficult to read. Part of her suspected he enjoyed being unreasonable, that it was a way for him to categorise the people who would make the effort to get to know him. A year ago, she'd have overlooked these aggravations, but not now. She'd expected marriage, while not necessarily the happy ending of a fairy tale, to be easier. How hard could it be if two people loved each other?

Perhaps she was being unfair. The first three years had been good. They'd done a lot of things together, pulled in the same direction. He pushed her to try new things. At first, she'd been sceptical when he wanted to buy a house so they could do it up and sell it on. But she'd given in to him and renovating the house together was more fun than she'd imagined. She'd been sad to see that little house go on the market, wanting to keep it to live in. A world they'd created. But Dan had his eye on bigger things and the profits from the house paid the deposit on the apartment. Life had been full of promise for them. They were unstoppable – with one exception. They were having difficulty conceiving.

Month after month, they faced the disappointment with just a little less stoicism each time. They tiptoed around each other, said a thousand words with a single glance. Dan broke first and suggested they consider IVF. She could have cried with relief. Initially Esther was concerned about the decision and the pressure it would put them under, but she needn't have worried. Dan made it easy for her to relax and feel confident. He seemed to take it all in his stride, drawing up a list of pros and cons, estimating their chances of success. He was diligent about dispensing her medication and injections – in fact, he'd been more positive about it than she was, approaching it as an experiment. In the two-week period while they waited to see had the pregnancy taken, he'd arranged treats for her and Sophie, trips to the theatre, meals out, film nights in – all to keep her occupied and to take her mind off the slow crawl of the minute hand.

She'd rewarded him with the news that the pregnancy was viable, and he'd punched the air with happiness, before kneeling in front of her, his head in her lap. It was only when he stood up again that she realised he'd been crying and the moment was preserved forever in her memory. That's the man she wanted, the caring man, the man who planned and thought about her and their future together. Even though he'd disappointed her when she needed him most, the memories of that golden time were strong enough for her to put her trust in this move. She'd been willing to follow him because she recognised that same spark of enthusiasm when he talked about starting again, in a new place, and it was seductive.

Esther inhaled deeply. With the memories of her first

pregnancy came sadness and anger. As soon as she noticed the blood spots on her knickers, she knew what the outcome was going to be. The dragging pains in her stomach told their own story. She'd rung Sophie, then the clinic who told her to go straight in. Finally, she'd rung Dan, torn between wanting to put off telling him, and needing him by her side. After leaving several messages on his mobile, she tried his office number. There was no answer there, either.

The bleeding worsened and cramps wracked her body. Frightened, angry, and worried that she couldn't reach Dan, she asked Sophie to take her phone and ring one of his colleagues.

"I think you need to hear this," Sophie said, her face pale as she handed Esther the phone.

"Esther, is that you? Hi, yes, it's Paul Lloyd," he paused, a note of embarrassment in his voice. "Listen, I don't know what's going on, but Dan doesn't work here any more."

'What? What did you say?"

Esther couldn't believe she'd heard him right and Sophie wouldn't meet her eye.

"Sorry to have to break it to you, but he was made redundant about two months ago. We've not seen him since."

"You're sure you mean Dan? Daniel Carr?"

"Yes."

There was a long silence while Esther came to terms that there was nothing else she wanted to say, not to Paul, not to Sophie, and not to Dan. After handing the phone back to Sophie, she rolled over on the hospital bed as her body rejected their baby, while her heart started to reject her husband. Nothing would ever be the same again. She'd be Esther, who'd had a miscarriage. Dan would be the husband who'd lied to her. She had so many questions and when he did eventually turn up at the hospital, he evaded every single one, remaining quiet in the face of her despair. She hadn't let him comfort her, not let him see how raw her grief was or how much he'd let her down, but it was always there, just under the surface.

Esther sighed to herself. She had too much time on her hands here and it led her to memories that hurt. Even though she'd felt a sense of relief at leaving her job, it had been a good displacement activity. She had to face the fact that this was her home now and she knew that the feeling of being in limbo would disappear, like the disorientation of the few days between Christmas and New Year when she didn't have to set her alarm and every day dragged like the Sundays of her childhood.

I must find a way of asking him about the text messages. What did Sophie want me to know? Oh, God! Were they having an affair?

Her guts twisted in a mixture of grief and betrayal, but even as the thought occurred to her, she dismissed it. *Sophie wouldn't do that to me.* Her breathing slowed again and another thought trickled through to taunt her, but her instincts told her to be silent and not raise the subject with Dan.

The temperature was cooling, so she drew some more water, feeling the heat diffusing as she lay there. She let her wet fingers trail over her body, enjoying the sensation as the warm water met the cooler air, leaving a trail of goose pimples on her skin. Her breasts were fuller, she could tell from the way they filled her palms as she cupped them, enjoying the intimacy of her own hands. With one hand below the waterline, she caressed her stomach, letting her fingers explore lower, lower,

lower. Seeking. Searching. Probing. She shivered with pleasure and closed her eyes.

The door creaked open and Major Tom jumped up on the side of the bath. He walked the length of the tub, then turned and came back, settling on the widest part, near Esther's head. He cast a haughty eye over the scene.

'Jesus!'

She sat up, guilty and embarrassed, her heart pounding. Water splashed over the side of the bath onto the tiles and the cat jumped up onto the windowsill, sending a bottle of shampoo clattering to the floor.

'Bloody stupid animal. You're walking a tightrope there.'

Her fingers had started to wrinkle and she speculated how she might look when she was old. She was at Rosgill and it was summer time. In what might be a rare break from seeing to guests, she imagined two large cane chairs on the platform with her pouring tea from a china pot. She knew it was a cliché, but she allowed the daydream to continue to take shape, comforted by the thought that she would eventually feel settled here and that she'd think of Rosgill as home. She pictured herself reading out snippets from the paper to Mike. Mike! What was she thinking? She laughed at the absurdity of it. She'd meant Dan, of course she'd meant Dan.

'Give me a couple of minutes and I'll give you a hand to get out of the bath,' Dan called up from the bottom of the stairs.

'Seems like bath time is over, Puss.'

When Esther made her way back downstairs, the two men were in the sitting room, poring over plans for the buildings. She felt a rush of affection for Dan, seeing him with his head bowed over the various pieces of paper, deep in conversation.

Having Mike around broke up the days. She made her way over to Dan and kissed the top of his head, ignoring his almost imperceptible flinch at her touch. She looked across at Mike. He'd noticed.

'What'cha doon?' she asked.

'Just looking through these plans to see if there is something we can easily make a start on.' Dan didn't look up as he spoke.

'And is there?' A note of irritation crept into her question. Was he trying to keep her at arm's length on purpose, or did he just not realise how off-hand his manner was?

Mike answered. 'There's plenty of painting we can be getting on with. Fancy giving us a hand?'

'Do we have all the stuff we need?' She remembered Dan pointing out a tarpaulin covering timber and bags of sand on the first night they'd arrived, but couldn't remember seeing anything like paint or brushes.

'Mikey has brought some brushes and some left-over paint, mostly white, so we can use it as undercoat at least. There's plenty of sanding to be done as well.'

Has he now? Well, how utterly thoughtful of him.

'Okay. Where d'you want me to start?' She relished the thought of doing something other than sitting around and waiting. The days were dragging and she had too much time to think. It wasn't helpful or productive to brood.

'We could have a go at undercoating the old ticket hall, if you like? That is, if you and your gammy leg are up to it.'

There it was again, that note of teasing in Mike's voice. Her instinct was to be outraged at his irreverence, but she laughed in spite of herself. His attitude towards her was refreshing.

'We are.' She stuck out her tongue at him.

'Come on, then. Let's get the stuff out of the Land Rover.'

'Oh, Dan! Maybe Mike can tow our car back with the Land Rover? Mike, you must have passed it on the way here?'

'I told you, there's no spare.' A muscle twitched at the side of Dan's mouth.

'Yes. Sorry. I forgot.'

Although there had been nothing in Dan's tone to suggest it, she couldn't help but feel she'd been rebuked and her cheeks smarted with the unfairness of it. She was only trying to help, to show him she was capable of solving problems too.

Dan held his hand out to her. 'I know. And it was a good idea.'

She allowed herself a small smile. He was in such an odd mood – or maybe she was reading too much into what he said. Mike went to fetch the paint from the Land Rover. She squeezed his hand and waited for him to reach for the hand gel. When he didn't, she felt relieved. Perhaps she had nothing to worry about after all.

Esther and Mike worked side-by-side in the old ticket hall. She was glad she'd managed to clean beforehand, it made the preparation easier. Mike had brought sheets of sandpaper with him for the woodwork and busied himself sanding down the door frame. Meanwhile, Esther was concentrating on brushing the walls to get rid of the flaking paint. It wasn't as bad as she'd first thought and once she'd applied some filler, the walls would be ready for paint – no need for expensive and messy plasterers. The profit from the sale of the flat would be eaten up by the renovations and borrowing from the bank was a distinct possibility.

They worked in silence and it made her feel uncomfortable.

Her stomach lurched and her tongue turned to dough in her mouth when she tried to strike up a conversation with him. Mike perplexed her, invading their lives with his wild tales and easy manner. Dan was so different here. Was it this place? Or was it Mike's influence? She couldn't push away the gnawing suspicion that was taking hold.

She wished she'd thought of bringing the radio from the kitchen with her and was half-way to suggesting going back for it when Mike yelped in pain.

'What's the matter? What's happened?'

'Feckin splinter, that's what. Ow!'

'Here. Let me see.' She took his hand in hers, feeling the warm, dry skin. His fingernails were blunt and square and his skin softer than she expected. There was strength behind that grip matching his size, and she imagined he'd have a powerful handshake, firm and uncompromising.

The splinter was sticking out, just proud of the pad of his thumb. She couldn't remember where the tweezers were, or even if she'd unpacked them. Unthinking, she put his hand to her mouth, in an attempt to catch the tail of the splinter between her teeth. With a little manoeuvring, she tugged it free. She held the splinter up for them both to examine and although it was quite large, the damage was superficial.

'Oh! I'm sorry – I wasn't thinking,' she said. 'That wasn't very hygienic, was it?' Her laugh wobbled in her throat.

'Ah, don't you worry about that. I've dealt with worse. Besides, if I need any anti-septic, I can always ask Dan, right?'

He winked at her and it felt good to share the moment with him, a small joke that was theirs alone.

'Why does he do that?'

'The hand-gel? Dunno. I used to worry about it, but he's better than he was.'

Esther didn't tell Mike how, not long after she'd miscarried, she'd seen Dan washing his mouth out with the gel. It was the first real sign of mental distress she remembered him showing and her attitude towards him softened a little as a result. How bad must he have felt to do that?

'You're not married then?' Her curiosity got the better of her and she cringed inwardly at how inane her question seemed.

Mike chuckled to himself and continued sanding. 'Me? No. I'm not the marrying kind.'

'And what is the "marrying kind"?' she asked.

He stopped sanding and as he looked at her she thought she saw a hint of a challenge aimed in her direction.

'Someone like you, I guess. Someone who wants to settle down, have children, build a life with someone, grow old together. That's not me.'

'And yet you think it's me?'

'Well, you're married, aren't you? And pregnant. And you've just relocated here with your husband.'

She couldn't tell if he was still teasing her. *There's more to me than that, though.* She put the wire brush down. She didn't want him to think of her that way.

He took a step towards her. 'I know,' he said.

She shook her head slightly, looking everywhere but at him. Had she voiced her thought?

'I know.' He reached out and touched her hair, feeling it between his fingers.

She met his gaze, mesmerised by his eyes, feeling as though she was falling inwards into herself.

Her body trembled as he stroked her hair, smoothing it down, like he was quieting a nervous animal. His hand brushed her ear and she was lost to the sounds of the forest, the birds clamouring for her attention, the trees whispering their secrets. The forest smelled like desire, earthy, raw and musky. She closed her eyes and he followed the contours of her eye socket with his thumb. The forest floor had been transformed by a carpet of daffodils, their scent rising into the air, soapy and fresh. Sunlight dappled the clearing and there was another smell, of wood smoke and leather, deeper and more intense than in her dreams.

'Let me show you,' he whispered, his mouth so close to her ear that she could feel his warm breath caressing the landscape of her neck.

She wanted him to kiss her. She pictured his mouth on hers, the peaty taste of his breath rooting her to the spot. If she allowed him to kiss her, he'd take her heart and turn it into fire and she was afraid. She opened her eyes. The forest was gone and she was back in the ticket office. Mike was sanding the door frame. He saw her looking at him and stopped, a quizzical expression on his face.

'Everything okay there, Esther? You look a bit pale. Want to come and sit down?'

'Did we . . . did you . . . ?' She didn't know what was real. What had just happened? She sat down on the bench seat.

'What? Did we what?' He squatted down in front of her. 'Tell me.'

She couldn't bring herself to say the words out loud.

'I just feel a little faint.'

'Okay, I'll go and make a cup of tea – hot and strong, with

a sugar in. Then maybe we can go and get some fresh air once you are feeling a bit better.'

Esther watched him open the door and saw his shape ease past the etched windows. She leaned forward, elbows on her knees and her head in her hands. What was it about him that caused so much unease in her? Dan would say she was hormonal – and he was probably right. Or, and she scarcely dared give light to the thought, maybe it really was all in her mind. If he was giving her signals, then she ought to be relieved that there was no foundation to her concerns about his closeness with Dan. She had no idea what on earth she was thinking, but wished more than ever before that she could talk to Sophie.

She pulled out her mobile phone and dialled Sophie's number. As before, the call dropped out straight away. She was about to put the phone back in her pocket when she decided to try something else. Tapping out the words on the keypad, she sent Sophie a text message:

To: Soph
I need you. Come back xx

'Still no signal?' Mike set the mug of tea down beside her.

Esther shook her head.

'There won't be, the mountains block it. If you want to call someone, you're welcome up at my place.'

'Thanks, but it's okay. I was just checking something.'

He nodded and they sat in silence for a few moments.

'Tell me about your leg.'

'What? What do you mean?' Her heart sank. He was a gore tourist – a stump-fiend after all.

'Tell me something you think I'll find interesting.'

'And if I don't want to talk about it?' She fidgeted, unnerved by his calm insistence.

'But you do. You want me to understand you, but I can't if I don't know. So tell me something about your leg.'

She thought about what he'd said. She did want him to understand her, but she'd never expressed those thoughts. It was ridiculous, Dan was emotionally immune and Mike seemed hyper-intuitive, like he could read her mind. She knew she'd have to be careful around him, she didn't want him picking up on the confusion he caused inside her.

'My foot was crushed when I was—'

'No. Don't tell me the medical details. Don't tell me about the accident. Tell me something else.'

'No-one ever asks me that. I don't know what to say.'

'I'm asking. And I'm interested in the answer.'

Esther breathed in deeply, then exhaled and it was as though the answer to the question found release with her outward breath.

'I don't know how to explain it. It's all to do with touch. When you touch your – oh, I don't know, let's say arm – the skin on your hand feels the skin on your arm, and in turn the skin on your arm feels the pressure from your hand. Touch is a two-way thing.' She paused, trying to assess whether he was following her or not.

He nodded, but didn't say anything.

Warming to her theme, she continued, 'I can touch the metal shaft of my leg and feel the metal with my fingertips. It's cold and hard and unyielding – just what I'd expect. I don't hate the metal for being metal, but I hate that the metal can't feel my fingertips, the gentle pressure, the thinnest film of grease or perspiration from the pads of my fingers.'

She looked down at the floor. Mike stayed silent.

'It extends beyond touch, of course.'

'Explain?'

'It's about connection. I stand on the ground, whatever the surface, but I will only ever feel it through one foot. It's easier to show you what I mean.' She stood and beckoned him to follow her.

When they arrived back at the cottage, Esther pulled out a chair from around the kitchen table and motioned for him to sit down.

'Take off one of your boots.'

Mike crossed his right foot over his left thigh and unlaced his boot, applying pressure to pull it over his heel. 'Now what?'

She looked at his sock and stifled a giggle. Rainbow-striped socks were the last thing she expected to see. She'd had him down as more of a navy sock guy.

'Colourful, eh?' He grinned at her. 'I'm full of surprises.'

I'm sure.

'Okay, so now I want you to stand up, and go upstairs.'

She watched his retreating back as he climbed the wooden stairs. When he got to the top, he turned to face her.

'I get it, I think. Having a prosthetic leg is like going around with just one shoe on? Like your steps are muffled and there's no connection with the ground?'

'Exactly!' She knew he'd understand. 'Now, take your sock off too.'

He did as he was asked, then walked down the stairs towards her.

'You see, I can't do that – well, not regularly. I have to wear something on my left foot so that the weight is evenly balanced, or it puts too much pressure onto the prosthetic and everything pops out of line.'

'Touch is a two-way thing. I get it.'

She pictured the vision Dan and Mike entwined in the forest, and shivered. 'Yes,' she said. And the moment was lost.

'Ready for that walk? Let's go.' He picked her jacket off the peg and held it out for her.

The peaty air clung to them as they wreathed their way off the end of the platform, following the track bed up the glen. Mike hadn't asked Dan if he'd wanted to join them and Esther felt a mixture of relief that she wouldn't have to try to second guess his mood, and disquiet that it was just her and Mike.

She found the terrain hard going. Shorter than Mike, she had to increase the frequency of her strides to keep up. He seemed to understand without her saying anything and slowed his stride to compensate. Even after five years together, she still had to remind Dan to slow down for her.

'I don't think I'd be able to find my way round, even without the fog. All these pine trees look the same.' She indicated to the trees around them.

'Spruce.' Mike replied.

'What?'

'They're spruce – Sitka Spruce in fact – not pines. Well, okay, some of them are pines, but these here, the ones that form the very dense canopy, they're Sitka Spruce. They grow tall, straight and provide protection for deer and other smaller animals.' He pulled one of the lower hanging branches downwards for her to inspect. 'You can always tell the difference between pine and spruce by looking at the needles, these are flat on one side, with a woody tip. Spruce.'

‘How do you know that?’

‘I take work where I can get it and there’s plenty of forestry work around. Planted a few thousand of these in my time up here, along with Larch where the soil is a bit poorer on the southern slopes of the mountains. Felled quite a few too.’

‘See, I’d never have known that.’ She knew she ought to take more interest in her surroundings. It was the kind of thing guests would expect them to know.

‘This one here, this is a Scots Pine. It’s a different shape altogether from the spruce. See how the branches curl outwards?’

Now he’d pointed it out, she could see the difference. And felt a little stupid for not making the distinction herself.

The fog pervaded every movement, constant, clinging, ethereal. The atmosphere in the cottage was suffocating as Esther and Dan skirted around each other’s mood, but being outside was almost worse. She felt light-headed, disoriented, struggling to breath in the vapour-clogged air. Stumbling over the uneven ground, she tensed up, ready to protect herself if she fell.

Mike offered her his hand, but she declined. If she couldn’t limit the amount of time she spent with Mike, then she’d at least limit the amount of physical contact. Besides, holding hands would throw her further off-balance. Dan wouldn’t have understood, would have seen it as some kind of slight or distancing between them, but Mike accepted her refusal without recrimination.

They walked for about twenty minutes, in silence. Esther listened to the sound of their feet splintering through the gorse, reminding her of the sounds the hunter made in her dreams. It was the only sound she could hear. She thought back to the first morning, sitting on the platform bench.

'Mike? Is it always so quiet here? I haven't heard any birds since the fog came down. Everything is so still, like it's been suspended in time almost. And yes, I know how stupid that sounds.'

He chuckled, his eyes lighting up as he did so. 'There are plenty of creatures around here. The fog's just made them nervous is all. You'll see and hear plenty when it lifts. It's winter still. Some of the birds are away to warmer parts and some of the animals are hibernating.'

'I don't think I expected it to be so silent. It's quite eerie. I feel like my thoughts are too loud even. It's like the fog is amplifying the silence.' They continued walking.

'Are you regretting your decision to come here?'

There it was. Your decision. It wasn't her decision, it was Dan's, but to pick Mike up on it seemed both churlish and somehow disloyal to Dan.

'No, of course not.' She stopped and faced him. 'I think I had a romantic view of what it would be like, just Dan and me and the empty space where we could breathe and reconnect.'

'And the reality disappoints you?'

'No. It's just different. Harder. Like I said, the fog is amplifying things. I don't just mean the silence, but I can't get away from my thoughts. I'd hoped it might be easier here, but everything is so out of whack.'

When he didn't pick up her cue, her disappointment felt like a papercut, stinging and deeper than she expected. She wanted to ask him about all of the strange things she'd experienced. Dan would never understand, would never take her seriously, but there was something about Mike that suggested he might be more open to her theories, no matter how outlandish they might seem.

She followed him along the deeply rutted path, concentrating on where she placed her feet, risking only momentary glances at his form. He leaned into the sullen fog as he walked, as though he could push it aside and make a path for them. Mike was much broader than the more athletic Dan. There was something of the mountains about him, something that made Esther think he'd established his place in the landscape. As she considered the thought, the germ of an idea began to root. She'd been fighting everything since she arrived. The cottage, Dan, the fog, the isolation. All of the problems they'd had in Bristol had been packed away in boxes and moved with them. For the first time, she felt she was closer to understanding what she had to do to feel settled.

'You're quiet.' Mike's voice, butter-soft, coaxed her out of her reflections.

'I was just thinking about the past.'

'And how's that working out for you?'

He knows how to ask the money questions.

'I think I have to let go. I think – somehow – I need to give myself up to this place, make peace with it. I have to put the past behind me and really mean it. Not hang on to arguments we've rehearsed over and over. Not cling on to the words that we've used to hurt each other.'

She felt her cheeks warming and knew she must be blushing. It felt odd, but not unpleasant, to be talking to him in such an intimate yet abstract way about her marriage. It was the kind of conversation she used to have with Sophie.

'We've come up here with all of these expectations and yes, I admit, I have been resentful about being uprooted from almost everything I know, everywhere I feel safe. The ghosts that haunted me haven't gone away, it's their voices I hear in the silence.'

'What are they trying to tell you?' He stopped again, waiting for her to answer.

'That I need to let go. That if I can't move beyond what's happened, I'll be forever stuck in some sort of loop, clinging onto recriminations.'

'I'd say listen to those voices. The past belongs where it is. It's now that matters.' His gaze held hers. 'I only want to know about now. About what can happen. About the possibilities.'

He put his hands on her shoulders, fingers squeezing into the quilted material of her jacket, bruising through her skin and biting into her bones.

'Do you want that, Esther?'

An image of the hunter, standing over her with his spear raised, flashed before her eyes. She imagined launching herself at him, landing blow after blow, fighting him off until he was knocked to the ground and she could escape. She fought the urge to pull away, her feelings of suffocation heightened by Mike's tight hold on her. She tensed up and he released her.

'Are you okay?'

'Yes. Yes, sorry. Just a bit hot. The baby is generating more heat than a nuclear reactor, I can't get my temperature right,' she joked. 'How far have we walked, do you think?'

Mike frowned. 'Maybe a mile. Possibly a bit more. Do you want to go back?

'No.' The answer surprised her.

They slowed down, moving in unison. Esther chewed the inside of her cheek, while she contemplated the contrariness of her thoughts and actions. She wanted to stay away from Mike, but he was magnetic. She wanted to be close to her husband, but he was always just out of reach. The scent of pine needles and moss laced the dank haze. They walked in silence. Worried that they would get lost in the forest, Esther tried to remember individual trees so that they could find their way back. As she stared into the mist, a movement caught her eye and she gasped, her scalp tightening with fear. She thought she glimpsed someone watching them, but when she looked closer, there was nothing there. The clearing was familiar to her; she recognised it from her dreams. How could she dream about a place she'd never been to?

'You okay, there? You look kind of spacey again.'

She wanted to tell him about the carving and the strange visions she'd been having, but something deeper inside her cautioned against it. He'd talk to Dan and Dan wouldn't understand.

'Yeah. Sorry. I'm okay. Deja vu, I think.' She thought she glimpsed a half-smile forming, but he turned his face away from hers before she could be sure.

There was something in the slope of his shoulders, the shape of his back, the curve of his legs that made her think she'd met him before, long before they'd ever come to Scotland. And as soon as the thought took shape, the gnawing suspicion in her gut returned.

'Mike? Did you ever live in Bristol?'

'No. I know the city pretty well, but I've never lived there. Why?'

She noticed he'd reddened, almost imperceptibly, and a hint of defensiveness had crept into his tone.

'There's something very familiar about you. I thought

maybe we'd met before, you know, had friends in common or something.'

'No, you're wrong. Come on, let's head back.'

What are you hiding?

The evening closed in quickly and they returned to the cottage having walked in a loop around the station. Dan was reading a book, the soft-glow of the table lamp casting shadows on the landscape of his face. Tempting smells wafted from the kitchen.

'Something smells good.' Esther steadied herself with one hand on the banisters as a streak of pain jolted through her body. Neither Dan nor Mike noticed.

Dan looked pleased with himself. 'I made a casserole. Good, solid nourishment for the little one. I expect you'll be tired after your walk?'

Esther shrugged her coat off and hung it on the peg. 'I am. Is there enough for three?'

Dan raised an eyebrow at Mike. 'Want to stay? There's plenty and we have that bread you baked still.'

Mike hesitated. 'Er, yeah. Sure. I'm not going to be in the way?'

Esther and Dan both shook their heads to reassure him.

'Dan, would you mind if I took a tray upstairs? I'm beat and want to get horizontal.' She didn't want to admit in front of Mike that for the last twenty minutes of their walk, the pain from the suction collar had been white-hot and she was worried she'd rubbed the skin raw.

'No, silly. Why would I? Go and get some rest. I'll bring the tray up in a bit.'

Gingerly, she climbed the stairs. She shouldn't have tried to hide the fact that she was limping, but she didn't want Mike to think of her as weaker, someone who needed constant looking after. She knew it shouldn't matter, but it was important to her that other people saw her first and not her disability. What was it her mother always said? Pride comes before a fall? She might have a point, Esther was fit to drop from tiredness and pain – and all too aware that she could have called a halt to it before it got so bad.

She undressed, put on her nightshirt and sat on the edge of the bed as she applied cleansing lotion with cotton wool pads to her face. Snatches of chatter from the kitchen drifted up the stairs.

'. . . walked round in a loop . . .' Mike's voice.

'. . . yeah, that's the route I take too when I go for a run . . .' Dan's voice.

'She asked me whether I'd ever lived in Bristol.'

Esther sat up straight, knocking the cleanser off the edge of the bed onto the floor, the noise muffling Dan's response. Why would he mention that?

Using a cotton-wool pad, she mopped up the few drops of cleanser that had spilled and left the used pad at the side of the bed. She was in too much pain to make it to the bathroom tonight. She eased herself into bed, her dark hair contrasting with the crisp whiteness of the pillowcases. Her thoughts clattered against each other – the teeth of a misaligned cog. They were definitely hiding something from her – but what? She felt like she was floating and within a few moments of closing her eyes, Esther was fast asleep.

❧

The fog, illuminated by the moon, left a phosphorescent trail along the glen. All around, insects tunnelled and burrowed, churning the earth, exposing it to the air like the secrets Esther would soon uncover.

Deep within the soil, the primal rumblings continued and the groves of rowans assumed the mantle of a conduit between the ageless oaks and wizened hazels. The rest of the forest leaned in closer trying to eavesdrop, impatient to understand what was unfolding.

The station inhaled air that was laden with the rich aroma of larch, lichen, and anticipation from the forest. Esther's time was coming.

6

THURSDAY

THAT NIGHT, WHEN the dream came, Esther was ready. Each night had brought changes with it, subtle at first, but now gathering a pace that was impossible to resist. She allowed herself to be swept up by it, all the while aware of the dichotomy between her two realities. By day, with Dan, she had resented the changes, fought against them. At night, in her dream world, she made peace with the earth, allowing its ancient magick to flow over her, through her. The more she submitted, the more she understood.

She started running, and as she sped over the frozen earth, the world fell silent save for her heartbeat. She found a place to sit and wait, gazing at the moon. The forest invaded her. Its smell clung to her hair, its sounds rang in her ears. The night breeze moved the freezing air around her and the trees sighed. Esther closed her eyes and listened.

She could hear gurgling as the water chased over the stony river bed, escaping from the mountains above. She changed course towards it, all the time listening out for the hunter behind her. The trees thinned and the shallow water beckoned. She hopped across from boulder to boulder, her gown trailing in the stream until it was no longer clear where the dress ended and the water began. Across the bank, the oak watched her pick her way through the water. She half-remembered being here before, but the last time she was fleeing from the hunter. She replayed the scene, the fear and panic she'd felt then just a distant memory. She was here on her own terms now, actively seeking the answers that evaded her waking hours.

Guided by instinct alone, she ran low to the ground, the owls screeching encouragement. Too late, she realised she was at the stream and about to fall down the bank again. The hunter would not get a chance this time. At the very last second, she jumped, aiming to clear as much of the burbling water as she could.

Esther climbed the bank, using the tree roots to pull herself up and smearing soil across her cheek as she pushed her hair away from her face. She spotted the door carved into the trunk of the ancient oak. It was closed. Where did it lead? Did she have the courage to find out?

She knelt and ran her hands over the edges of the door. It was about three feet tall, maybe a little taller. She pressed all around the sides, like a safe-cracker feeling for the right combination. Perhaps it was an elaborate joke. After all, if she did open it, it couldn't lead anywhere. She sat back on her heels, perplexed, and it was then that she noticed the small gap under the door; the kind of gap where shadows could slip inside and where secrets hid.

The sky above tinged with pink as the moon set. Soon it would be light. The forest had told her as much as she needed to know for now and she sat with her back against the carved door, watching the creeping dawn. Before long, she felt her thoughts drifting as her body relaxed.

The hunter settled into the bushes across the riverbank and watched as she slept.

❧

Dan was downstairs when she woke, clattering dishes in the kitchen as he put them into the cupboard. She hadn't been aware of him at all during the night, so deep was her sleep, but at least he'd come to bed, judging by the rumpled sheets. She lay back, cushioned by the downy pillows, trying to work out whether there was any lasting damage from her exertions yesterday. She tightened and flexed each muscle group, feeling the tension evaporate as she relaxed. Apart from the odd twinge, there didn't seem to be anything to be concerned about. She'd been lucky. Her stump was a different matter though. She swung herself out of bed and grabbed her backpack from where it was hanging on the back of the bedroom door. Even before she inspected her thigh with the hand-held mirror, the crawling, itching tightness of her skin – like fresh sunburn – told her what she'd find. *Stupid, stupid, stupid.* How could she have gone to sleep last night without checking her skin? Sure enough, her skin was irritated, raw where the suction liner had rubbed. She would need help to deal with this.

'Dan?' Are you there?'

There was no answer and the noise downstairs had stopped. She lay back on the pillows, listening for some sign of life below. He couldn't have gone far. Perhaps he'd gone to fetch more logs for the wood burner. She watched the slow crawl of the minute hand on her alarm clock. After ten minutes, there was still no sign of him.

'Dan!' She shouted as loud as she could. 'Dan!'

What if he'd gone out? Was she on her own? *Oh, God!* This was her worst fear. Being marooned here, in need of help and completely at the mercy of someone else. How had he ever talked her into it? She knew this would happen. Knew that coming here was a bad idea. She knew she'd never been very good at being independent, that she relied on Dan for more than she should, but it was easier somehow. Easier to let him look after her. Easier not to make a fuss about things, to do everything his way. Now she was helpless and alone – and in pain.

A new thought occurred to her. It wasn't just her that relied on him now. She had the baby to think of. All the worries she'd put behind her came flooding back. How could he think it was a good idea to move here now? Didn't he want his child to be safe? If she started to miscarry now, she didn't even know how far it was to the nearest hospital, or whether they could even get there. The bridge was out, the fog was treacherous, they had no way of calling for help, and the car was in a ditch somewhere. Her emotions spiralled, adrenalin heightening the anxiety she felt, until all her simmering frustrations spilled over.

She hurled the hand-mirror at the wall. It caught the edge of her jewellery box and knocked it off the dressing table, the contents spilling out over the floor. Immediately remorseful, she sat on the floor and inched her way over to the carnage, careful to avoid the splinters of glass from the mirror. Among the jumble lay the two pregnancy test wands and the amber brooch.

'Oh!' she cried out, picking up the ballerina. The leg she pirouetted on had almost snapped in two, connected to the foot by the merest sliver of plastic. Esther tugged on the ballerina, severing her from her pedestal. *Now we're both stuck here waiting to be rescued.* She immediately felt bad for breaking the figure. It wasn't often that her temper got the better of her. She'd ask Dan to fix it.

Now her anger had dissipated, she took stock of her situation. She was alone, in an unfamiliar place, unable to make sense of what was happening to her. Wasn't this scenario exactly what she faced each night in her dreamscape? And she'd survived, becoming stronger, adapting to the world around her, taking advantage of the secrets it revealed. It was just a dream, she knew that, but it was teaching her something, showing her that she had inner strength. She could deal with the pain in her leg. Nothing was going to happen to the baby, and if it did, she'd be prepared. When Dan got back, she'd make sure he had detailed plans in place in case of an emergency. Just a few more days without a phone. She'd get through this.

She heard the front door close, felt the change in the air temperature creep up the stairs.

'Dan? Is that you?'

'Yes, love. Everything alright?' He poked his head around the bedroom door and surveyed the scene in front of him. 'Hell! Es, are you okay?'

'I got myself into a bit of a pickle. I'm sorry,' she said.

'Stay there, don't move. I'll get something to clear up the glass, then we'll get you sorted.'

She heard him banging about downstairs and when he came back up he'd brought a dustpan and brush, and the cylinder vacuum cleaner. He put his arms under her shoulders and lifted her off the floor, setting her down onto the bed while he picked up the largest slivers of glass with his hands.

She watched him as he swept the remaining shards into the dustpan, plugging the vacuum cleaner in to pick up any loose fragments. When the slooshing-tinkling sound of glass against the metal tube, he stopped and pressed the off switch, taking the plug out of the wall. He retracted the cord and carried the machine out onto the landing.

'What happened?'

'Oh, Dan. I don't know. I did too much yesterday and my leg is on fire. So I tried to deal with it myself, but couldn't. Then you weren't here and I was on my own.' Aware how needy she sounded, she cast her eyes downward, shrinking back into herself, all her bravado gone.

'You silly girl, why on earth didn't you say anything last night?' He stroked her hair, his eyes full of concern.

'I know. I'm stupid and stubborn. But Dan, I was frightened when I called for you and there was no answer. What if I did need help? What if there was something wrong with the baby? We're so isolated.'

He nodded. 'I have it covered. Trust me, I know what's best. Once the phone line is fixed, you'll have more peace of mind. We both will.'

'I need you to check my leg. What do you think?'

He took her right thigh in his hands, watching her wince.

'It's certainly inflamed and you've broken the skin in a few places. I'll bandage you up and then I'm putting you on bed rest. No arguments.' He reached into her bag for the bandages and anti-septic cream. 'The minute – I'm serious, Esther – the minute the pain gets worse, tell me and I'll go up to Mike's and ring the doctor.'

'Okay,' she said, her voice small, her spirit defeated by her body.

'What would you do without me to look after you, eh?

She gave a small smile in return. Wasn't that the very thing she was most frightened of?

For most of the morning she slept soundly, the kind of deep sleep that comes only when the tiredness is bone-deep. She had no recollection of her dreams when she finally woke just before midday and she lay there for a few minutes, yawning and stretching. Her muscles had begun their protest at the exertions of the previous day, but her leg seemed to be no better, or worse.

While she'd been asleep, Dan had put a little hand bell on the bedside table, with a note saying 'Ring me.' She smiled, wondering if he'd consciously referenced Alice in Wonderland, then dismissed the idea. He was just being practical. She rang the bell.

'One sec,' he shouted up the stairs to her.

She could hear him pottering about in the kitchen below and after a couple of minutes he appeared with a tray.

'I thought you might be hungry, you missed out on dinner last night, and you have to keep your strength up.' He set the tray down beside her and sat on the edge of the bed.

'Thank you.' She smiled at his thoughtfulness, wishing at the same time that she didn't feel like such a burden to him. 'I'm sorry, Dan. I'm really sorry.'

'How are you feeling now?

'Better, rested. I slept well, but the painkillers are wearing off.'

Wordlessly, he reached into his pocket and pulled out two blister packs of tablets: paracetamol, and ibuprofen. He popped two tablets from each blister and handed them to her, with a glass of water from the tray.

'You had me really worried.'

To anyone else, it might have seemed like a reasonable statement for him to make, but she could hear the mild rebuke, the spike of disappointment in his tone where she should have heard concern. She knew she'd be saying sorry to him for a while yet.

'I won't do it again, Dan. I was going stir crazy being cooped up.'

He nodded, seeming to accept what she said, but she knew it wouldn't be that easy.

'You know, Es, your mood has been really up and down since we arrived here. It's kind of pissing me off, to be honest. I think we should get the doctor out to see you, after all.'

'What do you mean?'

'I'm worried about you.'

'But why? I feel okay. My leg will be alright in a day or two.'

He turned to face her, with no trace of the softness in his eyes that she'd been used to seeing.

'I'm not talking about your leg. I think the stress of the move on top of everything else has unsettled you and I'd prefer to get you checked over.'

'Unsettled me?' She held his gaze, not liking what was reflected back at her.

'I'm no expert, but you've been saying some very strange things recently – and Mike said you pretty much accused him of keeping something from you. I think you're becoming unhinged.'

She laughed, expecting him to join her, but when he didn't she stopped, abruptly.

'Oh, God! You're serious? You think I'm having a breakdown?' She could barely get the words out.

'I'm saying I don't know, but I think you need help.'

Major Tom nosed through the crack in the bedroom door and tried to jump on the bed. Dan swatted the cat away with his hand and it slunk off, tail twitching.

'I don't want that thing around until you are feeling better. Nasty, disease-ridden creature.' He squirted some hand gel onto the palm of his hand and started his cleansing ritual.

Esther took a small bite of the toast. It scratched her throat, like forcing down thistles. He wasn't going to make things easy at all.

'Es? There's a box here you might want to put somewhere safe.' Dan put the box down next to her side of the bed.

'What's in it?'

'Papers and funny things you've collected over the years.'

'Is my diary there? I can't remember where I left it.'

'No.' He smiled at her. 'Trust you to lose it. You are a scatterbrain sometimes. It'll turn up.' He ruffled her hair and went back downstairs, whistling.

She smoothed her hair down again. He was right. She needed to pay more attention to things. But that was the problem – she knew she'd been careful with her diary. The photos of her mum and dad were precious to her and she wouldn't risk losing them. Her stomach lurched. What if she hadn't put it in one of the boxes but instead left it in her handbag? She could have left it on the counter at a service station on the way up, or dropped it on her way back to the car. It could be anywhere.

She picked up the box and set it onto the bed. Her life in

a box. Nostalgia swept over her as she took the lid off and surveyed the contents. Her 25-metre swimming certificate. Two badges that were never sewn onto her Brownie uniform: Hostess; and Book Lover. She remembered looking down the list of badges and feeling overwhelmed. They all seemed so difficult or needed things she didn't have access to. In the end, she settled on the two that seemed the easiest to get. She'd loved books and reading from a young age, so that wouldn't be a hardship for her. The Hostess badge was trickier, but she'd be able to practise setting the tea tray at home. Anthea would help her with the kettle on the gas stove.

Going to Brownies hadn't lasted long. Her father had been keen for her to go, to make friends with other girls her age, but her mother was less enthusiastic. Why was that? Was it because Anthea wanted Esther at home with her, as a form of protection? It hadn't stopped the arguments; her parents fought whether she was there or not. She continued rummaging through the box. If only things weren't so complicated. Anthea was so reticent to talk about Patrick and Esther's memories of him were distilled into a dozen, maybe slightly fewer, anecdotes. She longed to be able to have conversations with Anthea that began, 'Mum, remember when we all . . .' but each time, Anthea would shut her down by changing the subject and so Esther learned to stop asking about her father at all.

She spotted a dog-eared and stained envelope addressed to Anthea. On the back was the start of a shopping list and a reminder to pick up a prescription. She opened it and in doing so, one of the sides came apart in her hands, and a handful of photographs spilled out onto the bed. Young faces beamed out at her full of hope, swagger, opportunity. In one, Patrick was sitting on a sofa, with a mini-skirted Anthea on his knee. Friends flanked them on either side and everyone in the photo was smoking or drinking, or both. In another, Anthea stood holding onto railings, looking out to sea. Her hair was blowing in her eyes and she was squinting into the sun. The mustard coat she wore was too big and she'd pulled the belt at the waist tight in an obvious effort to stop it flapping in the wind. The seafront looked like Blackpool, or Morecambe.

Esther scrutinised the photo; Anthea was wearing a wedding ring. Was this their honeymoon? Esther had seen the photos before, many years ago, but couldn't remember her mother giving them to her.

In another, both her parents were on the beach, him in trunks and her in a swimming costume. Anthea was holding out a towel to the side and Patrick was pretending to be a charging bull. Esther gave a short laugh at the sight of them, the fun evident on their faces, captured forever. She may not have found her diary, but these photos were better than the dog-eared one tucked inside it. She mouthed a silent prayer of thanks.

When did it stop being fun? When did he start drinking? She had so many questions. The prospect of being a mother brought it all into sharp relief for her. She wanted her baby to know where she'd come from, who her grandparents were, how she and Dan had been shaped and formed. She couldn't put it off any longer, she had to get Anthea to open up. Maybe the idea of being a grandmother would soften her, make her more interested in participating in their lives. Location needn't be an issue as the phone and internet would be installed next week. Esther resolved to try to make progress with her mother, little by little, both to improve communications between them and to help with her search for Patrick. That just left Dan to deal with.

'Do you want some company?' Dan appeared in the doorway, bearing a tray of soup, sandwiches and a pack of playing cards.

Esther smiled. The pain in her leg was easing and she felt fully rested. She moved the magazines and books she'd been leafing through in between dozing and made a space for him to come and sit down next to her. Her stomach rumbled, she was hungrier than she'd realised. She hoovered up the soup and demolished the sandwich, barely pausing to breathe as she ate.

He reached out and brushed a stray lock of hair away from her face. 'Fancy a game of rummy?'

'Why not?' she replied, arching an eyebrow in acceptance of his challenge. It was a shared joke between them that he always beat her at cards. One day, his luck would run out.

Dan dealt and Esther picked up her hand. A pair of kings and a pair of threes, straight from the deal. She tried to keep her face solemn.

'How are you feeling now?' He picked a card up and laid a four down.

'A lot better. Thanks for putting up with me.'

There was a flicker of a smile from Dan as she laid down an eight. He picked it up. 'That's my job.'

She'd have normally bridled at his response, taken it the wrong way, like he thought she was a burden to him. Looking at him now with his head bent in concentration, she understood he didn't mean it that way, that he thought his role as her husband was to look after her. There were so many ways they miscommunicated.

She picked up a card from the pile, shuffled it into her hand, then laid it back down, trying to put him off the scent.

His eyes gave nothing away as he also discarded a card he'd picked up from the pile. A king.

Instinctively, she snatched the card then cursed inwardly. She should have paused, lingered, pretended to consider. This was why he beat her at games: she was too open. Perhaps the only way to win was to turn to stone. She looked at the remaining cards in her hand and put down a six.

'Are you still hungry?'

She shook her head.

He placed a three down and her body tensed, ready to snatch the card off the pile, but then she relaxed, took her time, thought it over. She made as though she was going to lay one of her cards down, then at the last minute, changed her mind and picked up his three. Better. Now he wouldn't be so sure what her strategy was. She needed one more card, a king or a three, to win.

'Were your parents happy, Dan?'

'Yeah, I guess. What makes you ask?' He put his cards face down on the bed.

'I was going through that box earlier and I found some photos of Mum and Dad. They looked really happy and it just got me thinking about what could have gone so wrong between them.'

He looked like he was about to say something, then changed his mind. Instead, he half-shrugged. 'Who knows what goes on inside a marriage? People change, move apart. What does Anthea say about it?'

'You know she doesn't talk about it. Don't you think I've tried? Do you think the same will happen to us?'

His face clouded. 'Why would it?'

'I don't know, Dan. I just feel like we aren't on the same page at the moment.' She plucked at imaginary hairs on the duvet cover.

'I don't know why you'd say that. We're here, making a life together. What else do I need to do?' His tone was clipped, tense, ready to retaliate.

'I was so frightened this morning. I thought I was alone and it made me realise how much I depend on you.'

He scooted up the bed and lay beside her, his head on her chest. 'To have and to hold, in sickness and in health. That's what we said to each other and it's as true today as it was when we took those vows. More so now that this little fella is on the way.' He passed his hand over her swelling stomach.

She played with his hair. 'That's it, though. We're so far from everything here. I don't know where the nearest hospital is, or even how to contact a doctor. Dan, what if something goes wrong?'

'Don't be silly. Nothing's going to go wrong, you said so yourself. Besides, you've got me to look after you.'

'We're totally trapped here.' *I'm totally trapped here.*

He didn't answer and she realised from his steady, rhythmical breathing, that he'd fallen asleep. Without disturbing him, she eased out of the bed and started to gather the cards up. She turned over his hand and saw that he'd had one of the cards she needed to win. Some things never changed. The thought should have been comforting to her; she knew she was fighting against all the changes she was facing. But as she held onto the card, a lick of resentment flared inside her. Dan always had the upper hand.

❧

Outside, the earth wore the fog like widow's weeds. But below the surface, the transformation had begun. Flint chafed against amethyst. Lead rubbed against mica. The spaces between rocks, mulch, stones, expanded and contracted, expelling the seeping damp.

The mountains, ominous by day, sheltered the glen at night. Moonlight picked out paths through the trees, ready to lead her to the places in between, and the cathedral of trees rejoiced in the knowledge that soon she would claim her rightful place.

7

GOOD FRIDAY

THE FOREST WAS different tonight, more vivid. Like it accepted her – like she'd passed some kind of test. The sentinel oaks whispered their welcome, ushering her forward. She didn't need to look down to know that she was again evenly connected to the ground, she felt the balance from within.

An owl hooted in the distance, echoing through the pews of spruce, breaking the silence. A thin mist chased into the shadows, searching out the secrets that lurked there. Esther wanted to stay in this moment, wanted to savour the anticipation she felt. The oaks took up their hymn, reminding her that he was coming. Like she could forget. Like he'd let her forget. But for now, a curious peace settled over her, spiralling outwards from inside her as she walked through the grove.

For the first time, she noticed the changing colours of the bark, through the length of each trunk. She could see the difference between the dense blue-grey spruce and the Scots Pines. The spruce grew straight up from the ground, spear-carrying warriors, but the branches of the pines twisted and curled, like signposts offering different choices of route to take. Near each base, the gnarled covering was russet-coloured and the deeply-rutted surface formed a network of pathways and footholds for squirrels and insects to navigate. At eye level, sections of the bark had been stripped away and the exposed wood resembled the milky-almond hue of the lattes she used to buy on her way to work each morning. Bristol. So far away now. Daily, she felt its influence slipping from her and, for the first time, she didn't feel the customary sting of regret.

Towards the crown of the tree, the colour changed again; a subtle shift through amber to a deeper red, like the orange-pink light reflected from an open fire. How had she not noticed the range and depth of all the different colours before?

She brushed her hands over the trunk of the nearest tree, feeling the roughness of its skin against hers. The bark gave slightly, under the pressure of her fingers, rippling to close the gap between the outer and inner layers. The sensation was familiar to her and she smiled, wryly. In the past year, she'd developed her own bark and fitted it tightly around her. Time had moved things on, stretched her protective covering and she knew the day was coming where it would no longer hug her close.

The forest floor flexed beneath her feet as she walked. Crushed leaves, mosses, and fallen pine cones created a musky incense as she passed. The moon smiled down on her, its light dancing with the shadows created by the feathery canopy overhead. The resistance Esther felt to the world around her had almost disappeared. Before she knew it herself, the landscape had detected the change in her and welcomed it, marking time until she embraced the earth for what it was - solid, ancient, and nurturing.

She wouldn't wait for the hunter tonight. Instead she pressed on, deeper into the trees. He would find her in the end, but for now she was content to explore her surroundings and take in all the detail she'd previously ignored: rowan trees, warding the pines from evil spirits; the withered, white wood of the holly; bark nibbled by red deer and mountain hares.

She plucked a holly leaf from a nearby bush and studied it. She considered the contrast between the plumpness of the waxy leaf between her fingers and the sharpness of the spines, pushing the pad of her index-finger gently against the jagged edges. What did the forest want her to know? A twig snapped behind her and she took flight, instinct carrying her to the burn and closer towards the doorway in the tree.

As she leapt across the bank, she knew something had changed forever. The separation shuddered through her body, through her consciousness. Eyes, skin, hair, teeth, bones, muscle, sinew. In that instant, everything she knew splintered and fragmented. Her thoughts de-laminated, de-bonded.

Time sped up.

Stopped.

Sped up again.

Slowed.

It was the same feeling she'd had during the car accident, like she'd stepped outside of herself and was watching it happen. The trees grew giant around her, the bushes loomed. Used to the feeling of falling, this felt different. The movement was all wrong. She landed on the other side of the bank, close to the ground. Something was off balance; her perspective had shifted almost as though she'd taken a shrinking draught. Her peripheral vision was now in sharp relief as she realised she could see both in front of her and behind her at the same time. Her view of the world had changed. Frozen with fear, nothing felt right.

There was something else. She struggled to get a hold of the thought, feeling it slipping away. Even her ideas were different. She wasn't just thinking in words, but in shapes and colours and sounds. There was another dimension at work, as though she'd been able to step into the pages of a book and have the words of the story dance around her. Noise from all directions hammered into her brain. The sounds of the night came at her: bats pushing the air as they sped past; fireflies humming; the ripples on silky moth-wings. She could hear it all. The moon called her and she gazed up at the bright disc, as though seeing it for the very first time, the seeds of understanding planting and rooting inside her.

Pine needle fringes chimed in the breeze and she heard the sound they made, saw the tiny hairs on each needle, recognised their song as her sadness.

Details that would normally pass her by completely flooded her senses. Juniper, yew, alder – all layered their scents with delicate mushroom and sharp, vetiver mosses. The sounds and smells had intensified in the space of a few seconds, though she had no accurate way to measure time, which seemed to bend and curve around her.

As still as a rock, she tried to shut out the forest, tried to focus all her thoughts just on herself. She shivered and felt her heart rate increase, pulsing in her ears as if it was threatening to burst out of her chest. She tried to stand, raising herself off the riverbank, but her limbs wouldn't listen to her and she remained half-crouched, every nerve-end jangling. She tried again, stretching an arm out in front of her, shocked to see a covering of white fur where the sleeve of the gown had been.

Her ears tuned to the tinkling water, tumbling like liquid silver over the riverbed, and she loped carefully to the edge of the stream where the passing water was calmer. She peered into the water, but there were too many ripples to see her reflection properly. It didn't matter, she knew – in the same way she knew how to breathe – that she had been transformed, that ancient magick flowed through her blood. The water stilled, just enough for her to make sense of what she was seeing. As she looked at the reflection of the mountain hare staring back at her from the depths of the pool, Esther finally understood.

❧

Dan's side of the bed was cold, the sheets and pillows smooth. *Had he even come to bed?* Maybe he'd slept downstairs to give her room to move around without risking knocking into her leg. Esther wondered why his disappearances were bothering her so much. She didn't expect him to account for his every move, but his recent behaviour was so far from his normal routine. What was normal, though? They'd only been here a few days. Hardly time for anything to feel settled. If she closed her eyes and blocked out the possessions they'd brought from Bristol, she could easily make herself believe they were on holiday. Even so, as she tried to shrug it off, her instinct told her not to relax, not to stop watching for the small lies that hid the bigger ones. That was something she'd learned in the last year.

Dan seemed increasingly at ease when Mike was around. He laughed more than she'd ever known him to and she was convinced he'd received a text message the other day. The disquiet she'd felt when he'd lied to her about it pulled at her thoughts. She knew that type of smile.

He's with Mike.

She held her breath, waiting for anxiety to make her stomach drop like a lift car plummeting to the basement. Nothing happened. She considered the implications. A thousand questions came at her from all directions and her suspicions began to coalesce. She had to consider the possibility that there was more to her husband's relationship with Mike than she wanted to admit. The thought should have stirred up some emotion in her, but she was oddly calm. It would at least explain his strange behaviour, his deflection, his mood swings. If Dan and Mike were lovers, what did that mean for her?

Unable to think straight, she pulled herself up in the bed, testing out how much pressure she could put on her leg. Her hands pressed gently on the bandages, then firmer once the streak of pain she expected failed to materialise. Her leg was tender, but not painful. Dan might try to insist on another day of rest for her, but she didn't think she could face it. Ennui rendered all the books they'd brought disinteresting, and there was no aerial on the roof so he couldn't even rig the TV up for her. He'd tried to get it to work downstairs using a wire coat hanger, but was rewarded for his efforts by static snow. The surrounding mountains shielded Rosgill from all outside interference. Besides, the echoing thoughts in her head threatened to burst out of her skull. She had to find something to keep her occupied.

Her bandage would need changing soon. She rang the little bell to summon Dan, but there was no answer. The panic that she'd felt threatened to reappear, but she swallowed it back down. She'd overreacted yesterday and wasn't going to do the same again.

Leaving her prosthetic leaning against the wall, she chose the crutch. On other days, she wouldn't have given it much thought, often choosing the crutch over Peggy. But today, having to use it rankled, her freedom of choice restricted further. She swung her way to the top of the stairs, then sat down, finding it easier to shuffle down them on her bottom. It was an action she'd carried out thousands of times without thinking, but today it underlined her dependence and she felt a sharp sting of injustice. She needed to knock herself out of this mood; she knew it would lead to more bickering.

She opened the front door and looked along the length of the platform as best she could. The fog blanked everything out, creating a void around the halt, but she could see enough to tell that he wasn't out there either. Major Tom shot in past her, tail quivering. She stroked the cat's ears and was instantly rewarded with a deep, rich purring sound, matched by the rumblings of her stomach.

'Breakfast, that's what we need.'

The cat watched her move around the kitchen as though it agreed with her. She spotted a note propped against the kettle.

'Gone to see if I can fix the car. I might also try to find a church service, so don't worry if I'm gone for a while. D x PS Look in the fridge'

Good Friday. No wonder he'd want to look for a church. She felt stupid for doubting him, even more so when she opened the fridge to see he'd prepared her a breakfast of bananas and yoghurt. 'Yum,' she said, in the general direction of the cat.

After she finished eating, she was about to put the bowl

down for the cat to lick, and immediately stopped herself. Dan was right. Why take risks with her health? Still hungry, she cut two slices from the loaf Mike had baked and put them under the grill to toast. Out of habit, she picked up her phone. It felt solid in her hands, a link to her other life. Like the carving. She swiped the screen and the low battery icon flashed at her. Then she spotted the text message alert. She scrolled to the icon and opened the message.

From: Soph

I'm here. Shoes are clues.

Esther kept her finger on the screen, hardly believing what she was seeing. Someone was playing a cruel joke on her, there was no other explanation. Who would be so mean? Dan? What reason could he have? The screen darkened as the battery died. She looked round for the phone charger, trying to remember where she last saw it. It was on Dan's desk a couple of days ago. She got up and walked past the mirror, avoiding glancing at it, not wanting to see anything it had to tell her. Not wanting to consider that she might be losing her mind.

The charger was where she'd left it. Plugging in her phone, she had to wait a few minutes for sufficient power to reboot and she cried out with frustration when the screen booted up but the message had disappeared. She couldn't have imagined it. It had been there, right before her eyes. Frantic, she scrolled through every menu, checked every folder. Nothing.

Fat, salty tears coursed down her face. Whoever was doing this to her was cruel in the extreme and she didn't know how to react. Was someone watching her, waiting for her to break?

She was close to it, she knew that. Her stomach churned against a potent cocktail of grief, anxiety and fear. She had an overwhelming urge to vomit and just managed to reach for the waste-bin as her stomach did its best to expel her misery. Trails of saliva dangled from her mouth and she used the back of her hand to wipe them away. *Shoes are clues.* The pleasant bakery smell of the kitchen turned acrid and sour. Something was burning. The toast!

She turned off the flame and pulled the grill pan out. The two pieces of bread lay on the wire like little blackened tombstones. Her mouth tasted of metal and bile. Turning the cold tap on, she let the water run for a few seconds, then sluiced her mouth. The cold, clean water shocked its way down her gullet. She filled a glass and took it into the living room where she sat on the sofa, mulling things over. *Shoes are clues.*

The carving, still hidden under the seat cushion, pressed up against her leg as though she was the princess who couldn't rest because of the pea under her mattress. She fidgeted, then reached underneath the cushion and pulled out the carving, steeling herself against another vision. This time there was no fleeting glimpse of the forest, no vibrations, no message for her in a language she had never heard but knew intuitively. It was just a carving. She turned it over and over in her hands as she sat and thought, allowing her mind to navigate the possibilities she'd been resisting. If all the things that had been happening to her weren't just a mean trick, then what was the other explanation? Could Sophie be trying to tell her something? Was that possible? Were there forces at work which she couldn't explain? Threads of thoughts knotted and tangled as she tried to make sense of them.

The cat jumped onto the sofa next to her. Absent-mindedly,

she petted it, while holding onto the carving in her right hand, trying to place her thoughts into some recognisable form. The carving began to gently oscillate, like it was waking up from a deep slumber. Instead of being surprised or frightened, she smiled, understanding that it was a conduit carrying a message that was meant for her.

The blue shoe-box.

Whatever the secret was, the shoe box was the key. She had to find it; had to know what was inside. The carving stopped vibrating and she tucked it under the cushion again, scanning the room for the box. There was no sign of it. Looking at Dan's inventory wouldn't help as he hadn't listed it, but she knew it had to be close by; it was just a matter of putting herself into Dan's mind-set. He would approach the task logically, systematically.

The temptation to tear the unopened packing boxes apart was strong, but she resisted. Instead, she carefully opened each one, checking the reference number Dan had written on the side against the spreadsheet on his laptop. Kitchen equipment, books, board games; all matched the list.

Once she was satisfied that the shoe box hadn't been hidden among the cartons she'd searched, she turned her attention to the remaining boxes. More books, blankets, bedding, table lamps. It wasn't there.

Think. Think! Where else has he been? As she scanned the room once more, the mirror caught her eye. *The store room!*

Remembering to take the bunch of keys with her from the kitchen drawer, Esther made her way through the house. Major Tom trotted along beside her, but when she stopped at the store-room door, rummaging to find the right key, he suddenly shot off back in the direction they had come from and disappeared into the fog.

Opening the door, she fumbled for the light switch, but nothing happened when she flicked it on. It was hard to see in the gloom and the shelving racks obscured her view further. She walked past them, not sure what she was looking for and disappointed when it seemed there was nothing to find after all. Yet, instinctively, she knew she was right and this was the most logical place he'd have hidden it. The rabbit paw-prints Dan had called her to see led into the room, but not out. Were they also a sign to her, or had everything taken on such significance that she saw meaning where there was none?

She visualised the trail and, as her eyes became accustomed to the gloom, spotted another cupboard, set into the alcove next to the chimney breast and painted to match the rest of the walls. She looked through the bunch of keys, trying to find one that might fit. The fourth key she tried twisted in the lock and she pulled the door open, holding her breath as she did so. The cupboard was deeper than she expected and fitted with shelves on three sides, like the walk-in pantry at Eric's house. She scanned them: all empty. With a sigh, she was about to give up when she spotted something tucked behind the door frame on the bottom shelf. She reached inside and pulled out the blue shoe-box.

Esther's hands shook as she held the box up to the dim light from the doorway. A length of parcel tape around the box sealed the lid. She'd need scissors to open it, and once it was opened, it would be obvious that the box had been tampered with. What secrets lay inside? It was clear Dan didn't want her to find it, didn't expect her to find it. Or perhaps he'd set this up, hoping she'd stumble across it. Thoughts tumbled and whirled, their meaning always tantalisingly out of reach.

How long had he been gone? She wondered how much time she had as she closed the cupboard door and tucked the shoe box under her arm, locking the store-room door behind her. She needed to find a place where she could open the box without being interrupted, but she knew it wouldn't be that simple. He would find her wherever she went.

Dropping the keys into her coat pocket, she made her way up the stairs to the bathroom and ran the shower. If he did come back, he wouldn't think anything was amiss. She locked the bathroom door behind her and sat on the little stool she used to assist her in the shower, the box on her knees. She couldn't remember ever seeing it before, and knew she would have done as it was such a vibrant shade of blue, the colour of summer skies before storm clouds gathered. Time was running out, and yet . . . and yet, opening the box might change things forever. Her heart fluttered in her chest as it pumped adrenaline around her body.

She looked inside the medicine cabinet for something sharp to slit the parcel tape with. If she did it carefully enough, perhaps he wouldn't notice. She couldn't see any scissors, but spotted the metal nail clippers. It came with an integral nail file, the tip of which ended in a hook. It was perfect. The tape gave a satisfying 'pock' sound as she sliced through it. Then she lifted the lid and set it aside on the floor, next to her feet. Her hands shook. Whatever was in this box, whatever it was that Dan was trying to keep from her, there was no turning back now.

The letters stared up at her, like they'd been caught red-handed. There must have been a dozen, maybe more. She rifled through them, the sick feeling inside her growing as she read the front of each one. The letters were addressed to her. Some had HMP postmarks. Some had her father's prison ID number written across one corner. One of the letters had been sent to the apartment. *Oh, God!*

All the strength poured out of her and she bent double, hugging her knees, her mind in a tailspin. Esther now knew two things for certain: the letters were from her dad, and Dan had kept them from her. Her blood chilled and slowed even as her heartbeat hastened. Another betrayal. Maybe worse than before.

She didn't know how long she sat there, the water running in the shower, the box on her knee. Time had stopped inside the bathroom as her emotions created wormholes through everything she thought she knew. Perhaps he'd hidden the letters because her dad hadn't wanted to see her? *Stop making excuses for him. You always do that. When will you learn?*

The door handle to the bathroom rattled, bringing her back to the present.

'Es? Esther? You okay?' Dan shouted through the closed door to her.

'In the shower,' she called back, surprising herself at how normal her voice sounded. She was not ready to confront him, she needed to get things straight in her own mind first. He'd make her feel like she was being unreasonable, emotional, if she spoke to him about the letters now.

'Okay. You've locked the door. You know I don't like that. What if you fall over?'

She gritted her teeth, every muscle in her body resisting the enforced normality.

'I'm sorry. I won't do it again. I'll be right out.' She

struggled to keep her voice normal, neutral, and hoped that the sound of the shower had masked her discomfort.

Dan's footsteps receded. It sounded like he'd gone downstairs. She had to find a place to hide the shoe box so that she could go through the contents before he realised it was missing. Thinking quickly, she undressed and put the box at the bottom of the laundry bin, placing her nightclothes on top. Then she splashed her shoulders and face with water, as though she'd just stepped out from the shower, and wrapped a soft towel around her. Sliding the bolt back, she opened the bathroom door and jumped to see Dan standing there unsmiling, holding a mug towards her.

'Tea?'

Esther pulled out a red mohair jumper from the chest of drawers, and put it on, along with her brightest smile. Dan sat on the edge of the bed, watching her dress. The only thing she could think about was the shoe box. Could he tell? Could he sense her agitation? His face was expressionless, like he was waiting for her to make the first move, to break cover.

Unable to bear the silence any longer, she asked, 'Did you get it fixed?'

He was staring at a fixed point in the distance and didn't answer. She tried again.

'The car. Did you manage to fix the car?'

Her question seemed to snap him back into the room.

'No. I think I might have to get it towed. I'm worried I bent the axle when I ran off the road.' He ran a hand through his hair. 'Nothing seems to be going right since we got here. I'm sorry I brought you to this place.'

'You ran off the road? I thought it was just a puncture.' She wanted to sit beside him, to hold his hand and touch his cheek. He looked so worried. But he'd betrayed her again and until she had chance to read the letters, to know why, she couldn't risk letting him ensnare her.

'It was a blow-out. Unfamiliar road, poor visibility with the bloody fog. I was stupid to even try. It's no wonder I ended up in a ditch.'

He looked away and it hit her. He could have been killed. No wonder they'd rowed when he got back, he'd been in shock. Had it been preying on his mind since?

'Dan, I . . .'

He shook his head. 'No need, Esther. No need to say anything. I didn't tell you because I didn't want you to worry. And look at me, I'm fine.'

But he wasn't fine, the shadows under his eyes told their own story. She relented and sat next to him on the bed, putting her arms around him. Every cell in her body screamed out against her duplicity, but she had to pretend everything was normal; behave how he'd expect her to. Unconsciously, she grimaced and he caught her expression in the mirror.

'What's the matter?'

'Nothing. Why?'

'You pulled a face. What aren't you telling me?'

She drew away from him, covering her discomfort with a small laugh. 'Just aches and pains. I slept funny and my neck is a bit stiff.'

The ease with which she lied surprised her. Is this how it had started for him? With small lies?

'Ah, right. The heat from the shower didn't help, then?'

Puzzled, she opened her mouth to reply, then remembered she was supposed to have had a shower. Hastily, she changed her answer. 'Yeah, a bit. It's just a twinge every now and again.'

He knows I'm holding something back, I'm sure of it.

His eyes scanned her face. Esther, unused to such scrutiny, was almost ready to give in – to ask him about the letters – when the cat jumped onto the bed between them and started to wash his face with his paw.

'Did you manage to find a church?' She kept her voice as bright as her smile, showing just enough interest to throw him off the scent.

'No. It doesn't feel right not going to a service on Good Friday. It's not the start here that I had planned.'

'I've been thinking about that, Dan. Maybe I should come with you. Perhaps it's time I embraced your faith. What do you think?'

'You should do whatever your conscience tells you.'

Even though his response was without encouragement, he allowed himself a small smile in response and she knew she was winning him back round.

'What are your plans for the day?' She wanted to gauge his movements, assess what opportunities there were to read the letters.

'Mikey's coming over. We're going to knock down that lean-to over the other side.'

A curl of excitement unfurled in her stomach. Mike's presence would give her the perfect excuse to read the letters while they busied themselves with the renovations.

'No sign of the fog lifting?' Before she'd asked the question, she knew the answer.

He shook his head. 'Maybe the weather will break for the weekend.'

What had Mike said about glen fog? Did that mean that

it was clear higher up on the mountain? A thought began to coalesce in her mind.

'Yes,' she replied. 'Maybe.'

Esther busied herself with small tasks. They served two purposes: to take her mind off the shoe box, and to give her an excuse to follow Dan from room to room. He was unhappy that she wasn't resting, but she told him she felt much better and wanted to spend time being close to him. He'd smiled then and patted her hand. Finally, she heard the latch lift on the front door as Mike shouted through to them.

'In the sitting room,' Dan shouted back.

Mike stood in the doorway, and again Esther was reminded of someone else, but she couldn't place who or where.

'Hey! You're up and about.' He looked pleased to see her. 'I'm sorry I wore you out. Dan's chewed my ear off about it.'

'Well, I wish he hadn't. I'm perfectly fine, just needed to catch up on some sleep.' Esther glared at Dan, but he didn't seem to notice. Or maybe he had noticed and didn't care.

Mike half-shrugged. 'I still feel bad about it.'

'Take no notice, she's been cranky all day.'

Esther stared at Dan, surprised that he'd criticise her so openly. Mike shuffled from foot to foot in the doorway.

A plan began to form in her mind and she willed the two men to leave her alone so that she could put it into action.

Esther grabbed a role of parcel tape from Dan's desk, then went upstairs and retrieved the shoe box from the laundry bin, taking it into the bedroom. She pulled the box of memorabilia out from under the bed and selected a few items: certificates, school reports, a couple of cards she'd received on Valentine's

Day. Turning her attention to the shoe box, she lifted the lid and took out the contents, replacing them with some of the things she'd taken from the memory box. Finally, she carefully sealed the bright blue box with the parcel tape, taking care to match the original tape lines. It wouldn't hold up to scrutiny, but it wouldn't be immediately obvious that the shoe box had been tampered with either. She slid it under the bed; she'd have to find a way of putting it back in the store-room cupboard the next time Dan disappeared. If there was one thing she had observed over the last few days, it was that he would disappear again. The memory box was at her side, so if Dan suddenly came into the room, it would look like she was still sorting through it. She felt a stab of satisfaction at how resourceful she'd become.

Taking a deep breath, she picked up the letters. The ones with the prison postmarks were very old. Should she read those first? Or start with the newer one? She stared at them for a few moments, knowing that whichever order she chose, her life was about to change in some way. Not knowing how much time she had before she was disturbed, she summoned up the courage to open one.

She lifted the flap of the envelope carefully, like it was a plaster she was afraid of ripping off her skin. The letter was handwritten, on paper thin enough to see through; the type of paper Anthea used for sending airmail letters to her sister in America. The words swam into view, formed by solid strokes on the page, slanting to the left. Looking backwards. There was no date on the letter, so she checked the postmark again: 10th October 1991. He'd been in jail over a year by that point.

Four years he was sent to prison for. Custodial sentences for drink driving were only handed out when someone had died. She'd overheard snatches of conversation between her teachers who had unwittingly provided her with details her mother had tried to hide. She'd never forget the judgement, the pity, the embarrassed smiles. Memories bubbled to the surface now she'd removed the cap that had kept them sealed for so long.

"Terrible tragedy."

"Is it a tragedy, though? The man was drunk. It could have been prevented."

"A mother and baby – wiped out in the blink of an eye. What that other child must be going through doesn't bear thinking about."

"He'll have seen it all happen too. Poor lamb, no mother to look after him now. There's the tragedy."

"I heard the mother's sister was taking him in."

"And little Essie, a cripple. He should be locked up for life. Four years is nothing."

Anthea had hidden the newspapers from Esther, though she needn't have bothered. The children at school were all too happy to tell her what her father had done. A young mother, taking her children to the park. A baby in a buggy and an older child – a boy? She couldn't remember the details. The older child survived. The mother and baby had paid with their lives. Esther often thought about them, about what had happened. All those lives changed in an instant. She knew she was lucky to be alive, but in the months following her accident, through the pain of recovery, there were times she'd wished she had died too. Thinking of it all now gave her goose bumps. How terrible for a child to wish to die.

Steeling herself, she forced the words into some semblance of order on the page. Reading aloud made them stop dancing.

"Dear Essie, I wish you'd write. Your mum says you are back at school and that you are doing really well."

Wiping tears from her eyes, she put the letter down, the first stirrings of anger eddying inside her. She hadn't been doing well, she'd hated school after the accident. All her friends had drifted away now that she couldn't play the same games as them. She lost herself in books, spending break-time in the Reading Corner, with the companions that would never let her down: *What Katy Did*, *Heidi*, *The Secret Garden*. Her childhood heroes, Katy, Clara, Colin, had the same thing in common: they'd all had to learn to walk again. The realisation was brutal. She resumed reading.

"I don't really have any news to tell you. Every day is the same here. The cells are unlocked at about 7.30, but we eat breakfast there. It's usually cereal and juice which they give us the night before. Then we have some time to exercise, shower and clean our cells. It's not so bad, you get used to the routine. I don't think I'll ever get used to the smell of my cellmate's feet though."

Despite herself, Esther laughed. She pictured her father tilting his head towards her, his features sharp and angular, as though he was imparting an important confidence that may or may not have been rooted in truth.

"Afternoons are often spent working, or in the library. I work in the laundry and it's good to have something to do. It keeps me fit. Please come and visit me. All my love, Dad x"

She felt hollow, like someone had spooned out her insides. Whatever it was she expected from the letters, it wasn't that. Anthea had been right to keep them from her, to protect her, and now Dan was doing the same. Did she want to read on? Did she need to? It was so hard to process her feelings; they came at her from all directions. Sadness, anger, love, shame, guilt. There was a part of her that understood the loneliness and isolation he felt. After just a few days at Rosgill, with limited contact to the outside world, thoughts of escape occupied her. She wondered if it ever crossed Patrick's mind to escape, or whether he'd decided to knuckle down and accept his fate.

She picked up the next envelope and ripped it open. There was only one way to be sure, to rid him from her life forever, and that was to know everything he had to say. The envelope contained a birthday card with a big 10 on the front and a picture of a princess in a pink dress.

More letters followed the same form as the first, telling her about his time in prison, begging her to visit. None of the letters told her anything new. She sighed, a long and deep letting-go of her expectations. There were two letters left, both addressed to the Bristol apartment. How had he known where she lived? And why hadn't he come to see her? She couldn't figure out how Dan and Anthea had colluded to keep this from her. And Sophie, what was her part in all this? Esther was certain Sophie had guided her to the shoe box, and she'd read the text messages between Sophie and Dan. Sophie must have known, must have been urging Dan to tell her. The text messages between Dan and Sophie started to make sense.

The writing on the last two envelopes didn't match. One was from Patrick and the other was from Anthea. She opened Patrick's letter first.

"*Darling Essie,*

I know it's been a long time since you heard from me and that you've grown up now, with a life of your own. When I didn't hear from you, I stopped writing. Your mother tells me that she never passed my letters on, that she thought it best to cut all ties. I don't agree with her, but I had to respect her decision. So much time has passed and I wanted to have one last chance to set the record straight with you. I never apologised for my actions, but I want you to know that every single day, the thought that I hurt you has nearly killed me. I hurt you, Essie. Me. I should never have let you into the car that day. I should never even have been driving. When you've been drinking for as long as I had been, all reason goes out of the window.

Addicts are manipulative, weak, spineless. I am all those things and it's taken years of therapy to admit it. I haven't touched a drop of alcohol since the day of the accident. I've been tempted, sorely tempted, on many occasions. The night times are the worst, the loneliness, the enormity of what I've done hits home. I've altered your life forever. My own daughter. And I've killed a woman and her child. That weighs heavily on a man's mind.

I don't want you to forgive me, it's too much to ask of anyone. Your mother has been the one steady force in your life and that's why writing this is so hard. I must do it though, Essie. It's part of the programme, to accept what I've done, and why, and to try to make amends.

I drank to hide my shame. In those days, people didn't talk about domestic violence, not in the way they do today. The first time she hit me, I was mortified."

What? Esther re-read the line again. That couldn't be right. What did he mean? She continued reading, confused.

"We'd been arguing over something, then she lost her temper and pushed me against the wall."

A doubt crept in, sitting in the corner of her mind. Had she seen her father hit her mother? She thought back through all the worst memories. Her mouth dried. She couldn't remember one instance where she'd seen her father raise his hand to anyone, let alone her mother. But she'd heard them fighting and seen her mother crying.

"That was the start of it, but it progressed. Slaps across the face, blows to my chest and body. She'd throw plates at me, chairs, anything that came to hand. I was raised not to hit women, but I didn't know how to deal with it. It wasn't something I could talk about with my mates, they'd think I was a poof. Essie, I'm not telling you this to make you hate your mother. She's a good woman, we were just bad together. I'm telling you this because I want you to know why I started drinking. I had to find a way out of the misery. I should have just left, I know that now, but when you are in that situation, when everything is crumbling around you, you just don't see things the way you should."

Tears streamed down her face. She'd heard so many similar stories working at Helen House. It had never, ever occurred to her that her own circumstances were not what she believed. Yet, his words had a ring of truth. Anthea did have a temper on her. She thought about her jewellery box, the original one that had been smashed. It was Anthea who had smashed it, swiping it off the windowsill after Esther had refused to tidy her room.

Reality bit. All this time she hadn't been able to see what was now plain. What else had she got wrong? She almost didn't want to finish the letter, to face the truths coming at her from all sides.

"It was my fault, Essie. *My failing. I was too weak to leave her, and I was frightened for you. The day of the accident had been particularly bad. I'd started drinking in the mornings, to give me courage to face the day.* Now, *I know it just made*

things worse. She came at me with a knife and I knew I had to get out of there. Taking you with me was the stupidest thing I've ever done, but in my head, I was saving you from her. You know the rest.

So, there it is, my darling girl. All I ask is that you read what I've said and make your own mind up. If you never want to see me again, I understand. I've lost you already through my own stupidity. I won't contact you again, but my phone number is at the top of the page if you do decide you want to talk. No matter what you decide, I will always love you."

She read the letter over again. Her first instinct was to reach for her phone, to call the number. To tell him that she had read his letter and wanted to meet him. No bloody signal. She thought through her options; she had two choices: either to wait a couple of days until the landline was connected, or to ask Mike if she could use his phone. That would be trickier and she'd have to explain to Dan what was so important. As she lay there wondering what to do, she remembered the final envelope with her mother's handwriting on. Frowning, she turned it over and saw that it had been opened, and the point of the flap had been stuck down with Sellotape. She ripped the envelope open and pulled out a newspaper clipping:

> ROSE Patrick Anthony. Passed away after a short illness at Southmead Hospital on 18th August 2013, aged 61 years. Funeral service to be held at South Bristol Crematorium, 09:30 a.m. on Tuesday 1st September. No flowers please but anonymous donations to Helen House Women's Refuge welcome. For details contact . . .

The pain winded her. She folded into herself, numb with shock. Her father was dead. Patrick was dead. And Dan had known all along.

She didn't know how long she'd lain there for, curled up on the bed like a wounded animal, clutching the letters in her hand, but daylight was fading. All hope of a happy ending had been cruelly snatched away from her. She'd imagined a reunion, sunny days spent visiting him, birthdays and Christmases to catch up on. There was so much to take in. She had been ready to face the fact that he might not want her see her. She was strong enough to deal with the possibility of rejection, or that even if he did want contact, that it might fizzle into nothing. After all, they were very different people. She hadn't expected to find him, then to lose him again just as suddenly. It was such a waste.

Hearing Dan's footsteps on the stairs, she hastily hid the letters among the other items in the memory box and pretended to be asleep. She wasn't ready to face him yet. Not until she'd wrested her emotions into some kind of manageable shape.

"You awake, sweetheart?" His voice was soft, low, soothing, like he genuinely cared about her. Like he had her best interests at heart.

It took all her willpower to keep her breathing steady, rhythmical, but he finally turned away and closed the door softly behind him. She opened her eyes and stared at the wall, waiting for the huge, wracking sobs to come, heralding her loss. There was no good reason for Dan to keep Patrick's letters, or death, from her. And the same went for Anthea. How could she ever trust either of them again?

Did Dan think he was protecting her? Did he honestly think he was doing the right thing? She tried to see it from his point of view. Could she have kept a secret like this from him? She didn't think she could, but maybe he'd been waiting for the right time to tell her. The right time that never came because so many other things went wrong soon after. He'd shown no flicker of emotion when she'd talked about finding her father. In fact, he'd been supportive, suggesting they do it together, once the baby was born. The fact that he'd kept the letters must have meant he was going to tell her sometime. He could have disposed of them; she was sure Anthea wouldn't have objected.

She was doing it again. Making excuses for him. Trying to see him in a positive light, even in the face of such a stark betrayal. How was she going to face him, knowing there was such a big secret between them?

He'd tried to tell her.

The realisation landed with another thud in her gullet. He'd tried to tell her the other day, in the kitchen, when they'd reached an uneasy truce after their argument. He'd been talking about Anthea, about the accident. He'd been insistent that Anthea had lied. His words came back, ringing in her ears. *Sometimes we lie to protect the ones we love.*

That was the point their marriage had reached, the point where she couldn't, wouldn't, see what was going on around her. She'd thought he'd been referring to himself.

Outside, the fog shifted, drifted, finally dissipating so that the mountain air was clean and fresh. Far up above, where the inky sky met the heavy layer of clouds, Lepus disappeared over the horizon, with Orion in close pursuit.

Even as the fog evaporated overnight, the skies cleared and the stars shone with the luminosity of a bulb about to fizzle out. The velvet sky, blacker than pitch, wrapped around the earth, cleaning away the remnants of the smothering fog. Winter was not yet ready to go quietly and in one last showy display of power, breathed onto the earth below.

The station settled, the trees looked to the skies, and the first flakes of snow began to fall as the temperature dropped. Up above in the burn, the water slowed and crystals of ice began to form where the damp fog had clung to rock, to leaf, to branch.

The moon, full with promise, stood guard as inside the cottage Esther ran through a gauntlet of emotions. Her time was now.

8

EASTER SATURDAY

SNOW COVERED THE familiar path through the trees. It hardly mattered, for the course was so ingrained in her muscle memory now that she could run it blindfold. There was something in the air, other than snow. It tasted bright, sharp, like wine that had been open too long. Crystals of ice turned spider webs into doilies. Esther caught drifting snowflakes on her tongue, the transformed landscape adding a new sense of playfulness to her exploration. She was enchanted, spinning in circles and feeling a joy that had evaded her since childhood. Whatever was happening in her daytime reality seemed like it was another lifetime away. It was here, in her dreamscape, that she felt most alive, most connected to the world around her.

A pine marten stared at her from a nearby rock. Its piercing brown eyes ever watchful. She made no attempt to approach it, content to share the moment with her cat-like companion. The breeze picked up and the animal appeared to scent something more interesting, but before leaving her, tilted its head in her direction in deference.

She peered through the trees. How far could she get up

the mountain? She decided to try to see what was above the tree line and made her way up the slopes to where the trees started to thin. As the vista opened up she saw the expanse of forest for the first time, understanding how small Rosgill was in comparison. It was like looking at the stars; the reality of the earth's existence a simple co-incidence in a universe she could never hope to understand. The thought was sobering, and yet she firmly believed that there was an order, a plan, that life wasn't just a series of random events. This was her world and she realised she didn't need to try to make sense of it any more.

It was time to make her way back down the mountain. The hunter would already be waiting, stalking. He had the advantage now and she had a lot of ground to make up.

Ever watchful, Esther made her way to the stream, but as she reached the edge of the water, she heard a movement behind her. Instinct took over as she jumped the stream. As on the previous night, she felt the change fire through her body and, as she propelled herself forwards, the mitochondria in every cell ignited to generate the power she needed. By the time she landed the change was complete and once again she had become the Hare.

The doorway in the oak tree beckoned. She ran towards it, long strides covering the distance without effort. As she approached, she looked back over her shoulder, but saw no sign that the hunter was following her. She relaxed, sinking low into the undergrowth. A whistling sound high in the air – a sound she couldn't place – broke the silence. Then came the pain and her scream as the arrow pierced her flesh. She looked around to her right flank, at the source of the pain – red hot, pulsing out from the point of impact. The arrow shaft lay on the ground next to her, the tip tinged with her blood. It was a glancing wound, for which she was grateful. Gingerly, she tested the leg and found she could put some weight on it. Her eyes ached for the tears that would not form. Sensing he was nearby and watching her, she ran through the doorway.

Inside the tree, a white staircase spiralled into the earth below. She limped to the bottom, all the time on her guard. Far below the ground, the staircase opened up into a round chamber. Brocade cloth, the colour of the midnight sky, draped the walls. Silver threads in the cloth picked out the constellations and her eye was drawn to Orion, the hunter. A dais in the middle of the room supported a low, circular bed, richly dressed with purple silks and thick, inviting furs. A fire blazed in the hearth and the room seemed both familiar and foreign, like everything else that was happening to her. Was this his lair? She had to get out, quickly. He would know this place, know to follow her here. But tiredness overcame her. Limping to the bed, she sank into its softness, stretching out – once again taking her human shape – enjoying the sensation of the silk and furs caressing her body. *It would be so easy to lie here and sleep.*

Knowing that she couldn't afford to waste time, that the hunter would be following, she sat up and pulled up the hem of her gown to inspect her leg. The wound seemed to be superficial and had stopped bleeding. She didn't hear the footsteps on the stairs until he was almost at the bottom. Startled, she pulled the covers to her, knowing they offered only flimsy protection.

He stood at the entrance to the room, wordless, eyes glowing yellow behind his mask. He brought with him the smell of loam, of peat, of twig nests and mountain water. The reflection of the flickering flames danced off the edge of the curved blade that hung from his belt.

Esther swallowed hard. Her mouth was dry and her eyes darted around the room looking for an escape route. Her only chance would be to transform again, to trick him in the hopes that she could outrun his arrow.

The hunter took a step towards her and drew the knife from his belt.

Esther tensed her muscles, readying herself to spring from the bed, hoping that she had enough strength to complete the transformation again. Her eyes locked on his, unblinking.

In one fluid movement, the hunter put the blade on the floor between them, and remained on one knee before her, head bowed.

The move was so surprising that Esther let go of the covers, her eyes never leaving him. The hem of her dress was still pulled up, exposing the wound.

Your leg.

Yes, she replied. You shot me. You could have killed me and my child.

The man was silent and she realised he was crying; one of his tears splashed to the floor. As the stone flags absorbed the liquid, a tendril of green pushed its way up through the dense surface followed by another, and another as each tear struck. They twined around each other, the green shoots snaking their way towards her. At the same time, buds appeared, tiny at first but swelling and flourishing before bursting into colour, delicate pastel petals overlapping and forming a multi-coloured carpet of flowers until the floor of the chamber was covered. The scent rose up and filled the room,

Rest now. I will watch over you both.

Esther lay back on the bed, the hunter still kneeling by her side. Nothing more was said between them.

❧

Esther lay in bed, not wanting to open her eyes, not wanting to face the day or the secrets she'd uncovered. Multi-faceted grief tugged at her every thought. Her first baby, Sophie, her father, the extent of Dan's duplicity – and now his new secrets. Layer upon layer of sadness smothered her until she thought she might suffocate under the weight of her sorrow. She sat up, gasping for breath. Dan's sleeping form in their bed was an affront to her state of mind. Why couldn't she have woken up alone, like so many other mornings since they'd arrived? Why did he choose now to be the dutiful husband? His time had passed.

She sighed. In the last twenty-four hours, everything she thought she knew about her life had shifted, become distorted, like she was looking at it reflected in a fun-house mirror. Except nothing about what she'd learned brought her any happiness or peace.

Dan stirred. She looked at his face, the face she had trusted with her deepest secrets, and felt nothing. He'd beaten her. Worn her down. She had nothing left to give to him, to their marriage – and now she had to decide what to do next. Staying with him was not an option; their marriage had foundered, was unsalvageable. And yet, she was so dependent upon him. How would she cope on her own? How could she escape?

Dan reached out for her in his sleep, but she edged away, not wanting to feel his touch. He opened his eyes and smiled at her.

'Come here.'

'Sorry, no can do. Need the bathroom.' Surprised at how normal her voice sounded, she reached for her crutch and slid out of bed.

'Come back to bed then. It's lovely and warm.'

On any other morning, Esther wouldn't have been able to resist him, snatching the opportunity to share the same space. But now she couldn't bear to breathe the same air as him. The thought of his hands on her body made her want to scratch her skin until it bled.

'No. I'm too restless. I need to be up and about.' *I need to keep busy. I need to stop myself from screaming.*

'Spoilsport. Okay, then. I'll get up too – though I was looking forward to a lie-in with you.'

'Stay in bed then. There's no reason for us both to be up.'

'It's okay. I'll make breakfast.' Dan swung out of bed, pulling a t-shirt out of the top drawer.

Esther clenched her jaw and locked the bathroom door behind her.

She didn't recognise the reflection staring back at her from the bathroom mirror. Scrutinising her image, all the component parts were there. Dark eyes. High cheekbones. Nose just a little too large for her face. But her image had taken on a harder quality, like her expression had been laminated and all the softness had been lost. She tucked her hair behind her ears and splashed her face with cold water, enjoying the sensation of her skin tightening. Reaching into the medicine cabinet for the tube of moisturiser, she pushed Dan's shaving gear to one side, separating the items from her things. Was this how it began? With the division of possessions? He'd notice, she knew that, but he wouldn't appreciate the significance, would think that she'd simply tried harder to be neat and tidy. For five years he'd complained about her things getting mixed up with his. It wouldn't be a problem for much longer.

She sat on the edge of the bath, staring at the contents of the medicine cabinet. Would it be so easy to leave him? Staying with him was unthinkable – he'd pushed her love too far. No matter what his reason was for not telling her about her father's death, there was nothing he could say that would make her think any differently about his actions. Her marriage was over.

'Esther! Come and see!'

She closed her eyes tightly, trying to shut out Dan's voice. Just a few more days of pretending everything was okay. Once the telephone line was connected, she'd be better placed to escape. She had a few days to think about the practicalities, to plan.

'Es? You have to come and look at this.'

She sighed and went to the top of the stairs. He was waiting at the bottom, the door to the platform open. An icy blast from outside rushed up the stairs to greet her and she shivered.

'The fog's gone! Look, we've had snow!'

At any other time, she'd have been excited by his child-like enthusiasm. She assembled a smile. Snow was the worst weather for her to cope with and her body tensed instinctively as she surveyed the white world that lay beyond the threshold.

'How can something so beautiful be so treacherous?'

'I know it's not ideal, but at least the fog has lifted. I'll soon have a pathway cleared and we'll be able to get out and about.' He put his arm around her shoulders, seeming not to notice her flinch.

'We don't have the car, remember?'

He reddened. 'No, I know that. But the fog's gone, I'll be able to see the damage properly. Why do you always have to be so negative, Esther?' He pulled away.

She opened her mouth to reply, but thought better of it. What she had to say could wait.

'Come on, close the door, it's freezing. Let's have that breakfast you promised.'

Esther sat at the kitchen table, playing with her porridge while Dan wiped the kitchen counters down.

'What's up? Not hungry? You need to eat.'

Stop it. Stop it. Stop it. Don't pretend you care about me.

'Just don't fancy porridge. Sorry.'

'No matter. I'll make you something else. Boiled egg?'

Dan didn't wait for her to answer. He busied himself boiling the kettle and took two eggs from the box. She studied his every move. How was it that she knew so little about him? How could they live side by side but be so far apart? She'd never felt so alone.

He placed the eggs on the table in front of her. 'Eat up. Full of goodness. Got to keep that baby strong and healthy.'

The mention of their child stirred something inside her. She had to get as far away from him as possible. They had to disappear and the disappearance had to be total, final, leaving no clue behind. She watched all her dreams of a secure home with two loving parents for her baby turn to smoke. A plan began to form. Hard though it was, she had to keep her own counsel for as long as she could. How quickly love turned to hatred.

She ate the eggs – forcing each mouthful down, resisting the urge to gag. Long-suppressed memories of painting eggs for Easter surfaced; symbols of rebirth and new life. She felt like she was devouring her own child and pushed the plate away, unable to finish.

'Feeling queasy?'

She knew from the tone in his voice that his concern was genuine; that it came from a place where he believed they were both still a unit. The urge to ask him about her father was fierce, but she ignored it, letting it gnaw away inside her instead.

'Let me know if I can get you something else.'

She nodded and he removed the plate, scraping the contents into the bin, the noise of the knife across the ceramic surface setting her nerves jangling.

'What are we going to do, Dan?' She hadn't meant to voice her thought, but it cut across the kitchen.

He seemed to take her question at face value. 'Do? Well, there's still some sorting out to get on with. Or we can just relax if you want?

'Sure.'

He squatted beside her, taking her hands in his. 'I'm sorry. This week has been really difficult, particularly for you, stuck here. It's not how I expected our first few days to be. I wanted to show you how beautiful it is here, wanted to see you fall in love with it the way I have.'

'I know. It's just . . . '

'We'll get there, Es. It'll be okay.' He squeezed her hands.

She wondered how to steer the conversation round to the topic of her father. Then she remembered.

'I'm going to see if I can find my diary. It's got Mum and Dad's wedding photo inside it. It's pretty much all I have to remember him by and I'm terrified I've lost it.'

As she spoke, she watched his reaction carefully. His face could have been carved from stone; there was no flicker of emotion at the mention of her father. He was never going to tell her, unless she forced him to. A plan began to form in her mind.

'Okay,' he said, his voice bright. 'I'll crack on with clearing the snow outside. We don't want you slipping over now, do we?'

Esther set to work in the spare bedroom. She knew the diary wasn't in the kitchen or sitting room. *Unless he's hidden it, or moved it.* She shook the thought away. He wouldn't have hidden it. He understood her well enough to know she wouldn't forget it, that she wouldn't let it go until she found it again.

Even though they'd only lived at Rosgill for a week, the spare room was beginning to resemble a church-hall jumble sale as they'd dipped in and out of various boxes, looking for items of clothing. She started on the pile nearest to her and began to fold the clothes that lay rumpled in a heap. Memories came back to her as she handled the fabrics. A shirt of Dan's he'd worn to a gallery opening. A sparkly top she'd fallen in love with on the sale rail, but which still bore its tags like it was an item of lost property waiting to be reclaimed. Each fold felt like she was packing her life away, tucking it neatly into a box that she could tape shut.

She sank down onto a pile of towels and bedding in the corner of the room. Was she being unfair to Dan? Did she expect too much? *Don't go down that road again, Esther.* It was too easy, making excuses for him, shifting the blame onto herself. Although she'd never admitted it before, she was the same as the women she'd tried to help at Helen House. He may never have been physically violent to her, but he'd never been emotionally available either. She'd allowed it, excused it, enabled it. And it was clicking into place, the teeth aligned on the cog. She and Dan would never be quite right together. But Dan and Mike . . . well, that made more sense. And now it was time to put a stop to it, to grow a pair – as Sophie would have told her.

The future stretched out in front of her. Instead of fearing what it would be like to live without Dan, she felt a tentative fluttering of hope. Wherever they ended up, whatever she had to endure to make it happen, she'd create a world where her child was secure and loved. Just a few more days and the next stage of their journey could begin.

'It's you and me, Kiddo,' she said, her hand smoothing her top over her stomach, her wedding ring catching on the fabric. 'You. Me. Us.'

Mike's voice wound its way up the stairs. *Thank God.* There was only so much time Esther could spend folding clothes so that she didn't have to share the same space as Dan. Although she didn't want to spend any more time with Mike either, but at least he'd be a diversion. He'd probably take Dan off somewhere, leaving her to be alone with her thoughts. And she had so many things to think about.

When she reached the kitchen, the two men were sitting

at the table. Dan's hands were mottled and raw from the cold and he was blowing on them.

'Hey, Esther. How'ya?'

Mike half-stood as she entered the room and she almost giggled – his chivalry seemed out of keeping with his lusty approach and crude sensibility. And the fact that he was fucking her husband.

'Hey, Mike. Good to see you.' She surprised herself. Out of habit, her eyes flicked across to check Dan's expression, but he was still trying to warm his hands and didn't look up at her.

'I see you've had this fella hard at work already. He's done a grand job of clearing the snow off the platform.'

'Great – thanks.' It was hard to summon up any enthusiasm, but she knew that if she didn't respond, Dan's gimlet senses would needle away at her until he'd provoked her into speaking her mind.

'I brought some more bread. It's still warm.'

Again, she had the feeling he was somehow putting a on show, that the real man was partially obscured by the veneer he'd crafted.

'Thank you.' Her manners rose to the surface. 'You can't keep giving us treats though.'

A fleeting shadow passed over his face. 'It's no bother. And it's not like you've been able to get out much, is it? Just being friendly.'

I'll miss it here.

The thought was unwelcome and unsettling. She'd only been there a week, not enough time to form any type of bond with the place. Leaving Dan meant leaving Rosgill far behind. Dan was her connection, the tether that bound them. To her surprise, she could feel tears beginning to form and looked away in an attempt to regain her composure.

'Well, I'm happy to eat as much bread as you can make.'

Esther started. She'd almost forgotten Dan was in the room still.

Mike chuckled and Esther joined in, but to her own ears she sounded forced, strained. She hoped Dan wouldn't pick up on it.

If only things were different. From her initial misgivings about their move, she could now see that she might have been happy here. Dan's vision for their business and their life here was seductive. She couldn't allow herself to be derailed.

Mike broke the silence. 'D'you guys fancy going for a ride?'

Dan appeared startled and shot Mike a quizzical look.

'You know, in the Land Rover? With your car out of action and the fog, you've not been able to get around and explore. Just thought it might be nice to get out of here.'

The couple spoke at the same time.

Esther: 'Yes!'

'No, thanks.' Dan.

'Jeez. You two are in a weird mood today.' Mike shook his head. 'Dan, do you mind if I take your lovely wife out for a ride?' He raised his eyebrow suggestively.

Esther could tell Dan was scowling, even without looking at his face. His ears gave him away, just a fraction flatter against his skull, the tips white, as though they had been pinched, hard.

'Fine.' Mike stood and opened the door to the outside. 'See you tomorrow.'

'Yeah. See you.' Dan barely acknowledged the other man leave.

Even though she didn't want to engage Dan in conversation, Esther couldn't understand why he'd been so rude.

'What's wrong? What's with you and Mike? Lover's tiff?' She glared at Dan.

'What? Bloody hell. You've really lost it.'

'Maybe if you paid me the same interest as you give him, there wouldn't be a problem.'

When he didn't respond, she got up and went outside, slamming the door behind her. The force made the mirror rattle against the cottage wall. Mike and Dan were welcome to each other – and she intended to tell them.

❧

Outside, the calmness brought by the snow belied the turbulence within the cottage. Animals slumbered in dens, dreys, in the crooks of trees. But the trees knew that the end was approaching and their boughs sighed and creaked under the heavy burden.

Somewhere close by, an owl hooted, calling for the audience to once again take their places as the final act began.

9

EASTER SUNDAY

THE FOREST EMBRACED her as Esther danced across its expanse. This was where she wanted to be, where she belonged. She'd shrugged off the shackles of her daytime life and found the place where she felt happiest. Spirits called to her from the cracks between rock, between layers of bark. Fern fronds unfurled as she passed, stroking the air behind her. The rocks in the stream, vaguely square in shape, led her eye further up the hill to where the trees thinned to make way for the bracken, gorse, and heather that hugged the gentle curves of the glen floor. She picked her way through the boulders, lifting the hem of her dress out of the way as she clambered over the obstacles.

Deep inside her, she knew the hunter wouldn't come to her again and with that knowledge came freedom. She had made peace with him, shown him that strength takes many forms. The freedom to explore, to exist, to understand her place in the world, was all laid out in front of her. She reached the edge of the forest and studied the undulations of the glen ahead. Her breath misted about her face as the temperature plunged.

Overhead, stars glinted and glimmered; shards of ice

studded into the fabric of the sky. The moon, now at its fullest point, illuminated the glen, and Esther paused, savouring the view as the expanse of land opened up before her. She ran forward, as fast as she could, hair streaming out behind her. Before she'd even become aware of it, the change happened and her speed increased as she took on the now-familiar hare form. Energy coursed through her body, its animal shape seeming to skim the earth's curves as she sped across the fields. This was what living felt like; how freedom tasted. She'd heard friends talk about dreams of flying, but the image was meaningless to her. For her, freedom was the ability to run great distances with the speed of the wind, to zig-zag through long grass, and feel the impact on her muscles – in one heartbeat at full stretch, in the next tightly coiled, as she turned the world with her heels.

No longer afraid of her appearance, she revelled in the liberty she'd gained, leaping from rock to crag, pausing to sniff twig and leaf. It was as though she'd never seen the world before. Every time she turned her head, there was something new to behold. The earth was getting ready to greet Spring and she felt the welcome rising upwards through her feet into her body. The sound of water lapping against stones piqued her curiosity and soon she found herself staring into the pewter waters of the loch.

As she drank from the edge of the water, she remembered something Dan had said on their first evening. The loch was a man-made reservoir, made by flooding the original Rosgill village. Despite her warm pelt, she shivered. Deep below the surface lay the backbones of houses and shops that had witnessed so many lives passing through. If they could talk to her, what would they say? It didn't matter, she realised, they couldn't make her change her mind. She was just as much a part of this landscape as any other living thing. Without knowing how, she'd become embedded, entangled, her night-time reality at odds with the claustrophobia she felt during the day. Leaving here would take all her strength, but she knew that time was coming.

The chanting started as a low rumble in her chest, spreading outwards, carried by the haemoglobin in her blood. It was the same sound she'd heard when she found the wooden carving, only now it was more distinct and she could make out the words – even if she didn't understand their meaning.

O-*nam, gho rehsh nA'tham.* O-*nam, gho rehsh nA'tham.*

She stood with her eyes closed, reclaiming her human shape, reaching out to the moon as though to pluck it from the sky.

O-*nam, gho rehsh nA'tham.*

The words formed in her mouth easily and as she spoke them, she became aware of a new force flowing through her, quiet and determined – a force that brought with it truth and clarity, pushing away the last remaining doubts and insecurities that lingered from her waking moments.

The car. If Dan had nothing else to hide, the car would be abandoned at the side of the road like he said.

Esther opened her eyes, grimacing as she looked at the clock. Almost 7 a.m. and she was alone again. Dan was making it too easy for her. Now she was sure there was only one place he could be – Mike's croft. She felt her leg, getting ready to wince, but there was no arc of pain, no tell-tale heat indicating an infection. She reached out for Peggy and leaned her weight onto the supporting shaft. Her hands trembled as she made her way down the stairs, adrenalin replacing her blood. She was tempted to rush up to the croft, but held her instinct in check. She'd need to be prepared, to approach it logically, if she was to stand the best chance of finding out the truth. If she faltered, Dan would spot it and use it against her, confusing her, coaxing her into thinking that she had it all wrong.

Mike had said he lived to the north, about two and a half miles away. She was confident she could walk that distance if she was on the road, even in the snow. Walking the lane from the Halt to the road would be more difficult. She grabbed her stick from the coat rack and at the last moment, picked up the spare car keys, just in case the car was driveable. She caught sight of herself in the hated mirror. There was a wildness in her eyes, emphasised by the dark shadows beneath, her pale skin punctuated by high colour in her cheeks. She attempted to smooth her hair with the flat of her hand, but it had little impact.

'What are you doing, Esther? Do you really think the car will be there, just because you dreamed it?'

Her voice sounded out of place in the still air of the cottage. Her reflection stared back, unable to provide her with any answers. She pulled her woollen hat down firmly over her ears and brushed her fringe away from her eyes. She was ready to face the truth.

The world outside the front door was cosseted by a fresh layer of snow. She inhaled deeply, the clean mountain air chilling her lungs, enjoying the cleansing sensation after being cooped up in the cottage. The powdery coating crunched underfoot as she followed the indentations Dan had made earlier. She started off by overlaying his footprints with hers, but his stride was longer and they were soon out of sync. She pushed on, mouth set in determination.

The sun appeared over the tops of the trees, its watery rays glinting off the white ground, picking out the dimpled drifts. She felt the ground change beneath her, the start of the shallow incline to the road. She stopped to look back at the Halt, nestled into the mountainside. Mike had been right. It was enchanting, and for a moment she felt wistful that her time here was coming to an end.

As she reached the top of the incline, she let out a sigh of relief. Getting up the lane had been harder than she'd anticipated, but the snowplough had been through the glen, clearing the top road, pushing the snow into the ditches on either side. She decided to continue, at least as far as the place where Dan said he'd abandoned the car.

The sheen of the wet tarmac contrasted with the opaline earth. The snow was patchier up here, with most of it settling around the Halt and in the ditches. There was a new type of silence, not the dank, smothering silence of the fog, but a silence full of promise, as though the atmosphere had been purified. She continued, settling into a rhythm as she passed tree branches bent heavy under their icing-sugar burden.

Chandeliers of tiny icicles hung from fence rails and road signs. She'd been walking for about thirty minutes and guessed, at her pace, she was probably half-way to the croft. There was no sign of the car. The snow was piled high, taller than her in some places, but she was sure she'd have been able to spot the car if it had been where Dan said he'd left it.

So her fears were confirmed. She should be hurting, her heart should be pummelled into fragments. Yet she felt calm, serene, resolved. A quiet peace settled on her and she pulled its mantle tighter around her.

Esther eyed the ditches warily. If she heard Dan coming, would it be better to hide, or stay put? The decision was made for her; she couldn't risk falling into the ditch and harming the baby. She'd stand her ground, making an excuse for why she was out there alone. Even though the road had been cleared, it was still heavy going underfoot and she had to be careful not to slip in the treacherous conditions. Her whole body was tensed and she knew she'd pay heavily for her exertions, her muscles cramping with cold and her gait uneven.

By the time she found the sign for the reservoir she was panting heavily. Taking a moment to rest, she spotted the track that led to the left, to Mike's croft, just as he'd said. She took a deep breath. There was still no sign of the car and she didn't want to think about what that meant.

As soon as she left the road, snow covered the ground again, but she used the tyre tracks to guide her. They were fresh – or at least, they had been made sometime after the last of the heavier snow fall.

After a short distance, the trees along the lane thinned, opening out onto fields covered in downy white. A dark smudge on the landscape ahead gave away the position of the crofter's cottage, smoke rising from the chimney stack. As she approached, she noticed Mike's Land Rover was parked outside, along with the silver Toyota. Vindication rang hollow around her ribcage; she'd been right, there was nothing wrong with the car after all. He'd lied again. Had he ever been truthful with her? It should have hurt, she knew she should have felt her stomach lurch as the depth of his betrayal hit home, but the only thing she felt was a renewed determination to find out the truth, no matter what the consequences were.

She stalked around the outside of the croft, getting her bearings. The single-storey stone building rose out of the earth, the only man-made marker in the bleak landscape. At the east end of the cottage was a lean-to with a woodpile and workshop. At the other end, there was a squat chimney stack. Further away, there were two over-ground tanks; she assumed one was the oil storage tank and the other the septic tank. The quarter-light above a window with frosted glass – the bathroom she presumed – was open at the rear of the house, even though the temperature was icy. She could make out male voices inside, but not what they were saying. She moved closer, crouching under the window.

'She's been really weird the last few days. Do you think she knows?' Dan's voice.

Esther's breath caught in her throat.

'About her father? Yes. I told you she found the letters. There's no way she was just going to leave them be.' Mike answered.

Confused, she leaned against the croft. How could Mike know?

Dan said something she couldn't make out and Mike responded again, this time his voice sounded closer, like he'd moved nearer to the open window.

'She read those letters, I'm telling you.'

The only way Mike could have been so sure was if he had been there, but he was with Dan all day. It had only been her and Major Tom in the bedroom and the cat was hardly able to tell tales.

Her heart jumped against her breastbone. What if . . . what if— *No! Don't be ridiculous, Esther.* There had to be another explanation, an explanation that made sense. But the thought was insistent. She was beginning to accept that there were many things she'd never understand. Rosgill was a gateway between two worlds and, somehow, she'd found the key that allowed her to travel between them. Perhaps Mike had been having the same dreams.

'Is that all she knows?' Dan's question sliced across her thoughts.

'You mean, does she know about us? She's a cold fish that one, but I don't think she'd be able to hold something like that back. She'd be all too ready to tell us what she thought.'

She felt sick. What did they mean? The unfairness of Mike's assessment of her stung, but what was behind Dan's question? And what was Mike referring to?

Her spine turned to ice as Mike spoke again.

'Let's ask her. She's outside.'

She froze in place under the windowsill, her back pressed against the thick stone wall. The back door opened and the two men stepped out into the snow.

'What are you doing there, Esther?' The tone Mike so often used for teasing her, now took on a sinister note. 'Cowering like a frightened little rabbit.'

Using her palms for leverage, she pushed herself up the wall to her feet, not taking her eyes off either man, her spine crackling with dread. Whatever was about to happen, she wouldn't make it easy for them.

'What's going on?' She tilted her chin, hoping her eyes were flashing the defiance she felt.

Dan looked away, unable to meet her gaze.

Mike beckoned her inside. 'Come on in, we'll explain everything to you.' His tone was conciliatory, coaxing.

With her hands numb and blue-tinged with cold, and her breath misting in front of her, she couldn't see many other options. She followed Mike into the cottage, passing Dan as he held the door open for her. She searched his face, looking for clues, for reassurance, but found none.

The inside of the cottage was basic. Two leather armchairs in front of a wood burner, a small side table with a haphazard pile of newspapers, and a single bookshelf in the alcove. The room was open plan into a small kitchen and dining area. Underneath the kitchen counter there was a jumble of clothes, camping equipment, boots, and a washing machine. All the kitchen equipment was displayed on shelves, saucepans, dinner plates, bowls, glasses. Stone flags ran the length of cottage. She was left with the impression that his life could be packed up in minutes, that he could leave and never be traced.

Mike signalled to one of the armchairs and Esther, tired from the walk, sat, grateful to have the weight shifted off her leg. She looked from Mike to Dan, but both men were expressionless. Dan sat in the other armchair and Mike remained standing.

'So, Little Esther, how much did you hear?'

She opened her mouth to speak, but didn't know where to begin. This wasn't how she'd played the scene out in her mind.

'You'll have lots of questions, I expect?' Mike's eyes bored into her. 'No? What's the matter? Cat got your tongue?' Mike snickered and turned to Dan. 'Perhaps you should tell her?'

Dan put his head in his hands, but said nothing.

Esther found her voice. 'Tell me what?' When Dan didn't answer, she repeated, firmer this time, 'Tell me what?'

Her stomach lurched. Whatever he was going to say, she knew it was going to hurt.

'I'm sorry, Es. I really am. I never meant for you to be caught up in this.' Dan reached out for her hand, but she snatched it away. 'Mikey's right. It's time you knew the truth. I knew this day would come, but I didn't want you to find out like this.'

'Just tell me.'

'Yes, Dan. Just tell her. Get it all off your chest. Best to be out in the open.' Mike chuckled.

When Dan spoke again, there were tears in his eyes. 'I was planning to leave you. Rosgill was meant to be my new start, but then you told me you were pregnant and that changed everything.'

She waited for him to continue.

'You asked me if I knew Mikey before coming up here. I lied to you. I've lied to you about almost everything for too long. It's become that I don't know what's true any more.'

Esther eyed her husband warily; it was unlike him to be so candid. For a second, she wished she'd never followed him. She wanted to pull her marriage back from the precipice, but his betrayals had left raw welts on her spirit and she had to know the truth.

Dan looked defeated, but he continued, unable to look her in the eyes.

'I met him in Bristol, we caught the same train to work and over time got chatting. When I was made redundant I spent my days at his place, with him. I never meant for it to happen. I swear. I never meant to hurt you.'

Esther felt the blood drain from her face. Her tongue felt thick in her mouth, her thoughts congealed. With a flash of clarity, she pictured Dan washing his mouth out with the anti-bacterial gel and understood why. All this time he'd been seeing Mike. He didn't love her, didn't want her. Didn't want a life together. His protestations about homosexuality had been to cover his own conflicted feelings. She'd come here to confront them, to show them that she could accept their relationship, but the reality was too stark, too forceful.

'That's right, Esther. Me and your man here have become very close. Very close, if you get my drift.'

She wanted to smack the smug expression off Mike's face, but shock kept her arms rooted to her sides. She glared at him as Dan spoke again.

'I tried to leave. I did. But so many things happened. The miscarriage, Sophie. How could I leave you? You might not believe it, but I still have feelings for you and I'm not a cruel man.'

He was sobbing now, but Esther couldn't find it in herself to react.

'I was going to tell you—'

'You were with him when I miscarried.'

'Yes.'

The realisation came as a body blow and she barely registered his response. She laughed. A laugh that started small, but which grew in intensity until her body convulsed and she didn't know whether she was laughing or crying. Aware that both men were watching her, she regained control, harnessing her hurt into anger.

'All this time, I was trying to work out whether I wanted to be with you, to give you another chance, but you'd already made your mind up. For fuck's sake, Dan. You're such a fucking coward.'

Dan flinched as she spoke, but she wasn't finished. Twisting her wedding ring off, she read the inscription.

'You. Me. Us. Remember that? Remember our vows? That's how it was meant to be. All this time while I was torturing myself for not being able to forgive you, and you were hatching another plan. I was simply your Plan B.' She threw the ring at him.

Mike clapped. A slow clap that rang out like shots in the dense air.

Dan stood up and pushed Mike away. 'Stop it! Just stop.'

'Sit down, Danny-boy. You've done your bit, now it's my turn to tell some truths.' Mike stood with his back to the window, blocking out most of the weak light that was coming into the cottage. He half-rested on the windowsill, hands behind him.

A look of puzzlement crossed Dan's face and Esther took a deep breath, not sure what Mike was going to say.

'You see, that isn't all of the story. Not nearly all.' Mike picked up a pack of cigarettes from the windowsill and pulled one out of the packet, lit it and took a slow drag before he spoke again. 'I've been waiting a long time to tell my story and I want you to listen. To understand. I'm not Mike O'Rourke. I'm Michael Slattery.' He paused, waiting for the significance to sink in. 'The only surviving child of Maria Slattery, and brother to Sean Slattery, both of whom were killed by a drunk driver.'

The cottage was at sea. Esther cried out and put her hands on the arms of the chair to steady herself. This had to be a joke. How could he be so cruel? She looked at him, uncomprehending, squinting against the light of the window to try to make out his expression. His face was set like granite.

Dan was the first to speak. 'Did . . . did you know who I was? Did you plan this?'

'Yes. I knew who you were, Daniel. But this? No. This is better than I could have ever expected. I'd planned to get my revenge on that pathetic gobshite of a father of hers. But the bastard died.'

'But why go after her? She didn't hurt you. I don't understand.'

'What's to understand? Vengeance has no root in reason. My mother and brother died. I was robbed of a life with them and instead was packed off to Ireland to live with people I'd met a handful of times. I lost everything when that bastard chose to get behind the wheel. Everything. And I want her to know how that feels.' Mike paced up and down as he spoke. 'I was uprooted. Taken away from everything I'd ever known; everything that was familiar. I was a child for fuck's sake.'

'Don't you think she's been through enough? For God's sake, she didn't get out of that accident unscathed. And she lost her Daddy as a result. Not to mention everything we've done to her.'

Esther listened in silence, hardly able to comprehend what she was hearing.

'So yeah, once I knew he was dead, I looked her up. It's not that hard to find a cripple, even in a city the size of Bristol. And imagine my surprise to find she had everything she wanted. Everything I wanted.' He paused to relight his cigarette. 'You really are pathetic, Esther. All this time and you blindly followed where he led you. But she is right about one thing. You are a fucking coward, Dan. I was counting on that. A real man would have had the balls to tell her.'

Now it was Dan's turn to pale. Beads of sweat appeared on his upper lip and his complexion greyed. 'You said . . . you said you loved me.'

Mike shrugged. 'People will believe what they want to hear. I'll grant her this though, playing the baby card was a blinder. It forced me to rethink. Hacking into her phone took a bit of doing. Poor, screwy Esther, getting messages from beyond the grave. You have to admit, the result was pretty bloody inspired. In time, I could have probably convinced you that she was mad, leaving you no option but to apply for custody. Then she'd really have lost it all. Then we'd finally be quits.'

Esther flew at Mike, raining blows on his chest and arms. 'You evil bastard!'

She was no match for his size and strength and he shoved her roughly to the floor, kicking out at her in the process. A jolt of pain radiated out from her right hip, lightning striking every nerve. She whimpered with pain and scrambled across the floor trying to get away from him. As she did so, she saw the knife he'd been hiding behind his back on the windowsill, sunlight picking out the curved edge of the blade. She kicked out at him with her left foot, but she was kicking into air.

He snarled at her. 'Not so clever now eh, Esther? Not so brave.'

Mike lunged at her with the knife in his hand. Dan seized his chance, disabling Mike temporarily with a blow to his windpipe. Esther dragged herself to the cottage door. Using the door handle to pull herself upright, her eyes met Dan's and he signalled to her to run. She pulled the door open and staggered outside, gulping lungfuls of the biting air in her panic.

She felt in her pockets for the spare car keys, thanking fate that she'd had the foresight to bring them. Limping over to the Toyota, it was hard to keep her footing in the snow which was already showing signs of melting. She looked back at the cottage to see Mike and Dan as they tried to overpower each other, the window framing their struggle. She put the keys in the ignition, her hands and body trembling from a mixture of cold and adrenalin. She had to get away from here. Had to reach safety. She reached under the steering column to the pedals and flipped down the specially adapted accelerator. At the same moment, a single shot rang out and she froze.

Mike stood in the doorway of the cottage, the barrel of a rifle trained on her.

Where was Dan? Was he hurt? There was no time to go back for him, she knew she had to leave now or Mike would try to kill her. She had to protect her baby. Turning the key, she half-expected the ignition not to fire, but it exploded into life. She selected drive and pressed the accelerator to the floor, turning the wheel sharply to the left. Another shot rang out as she drove away and in the rear-view mirror she saw Dan pull Mike to the ground. She couldn't leave him. She reversed back towards the cottage.

'Leave, Esther! Just go! I'll take the Land Rover and meet you at Rosgill,' Dan shouted at her, waving her away.

She swung the car back up the lane, the front wheels labouring to gain traction in the icy conditions. The main road was quiet. It was like the struggle at the cottage was happening in a different world. All the time, she kept checking the rear-view mirror, expecting to see the Land Rover behind her, but there was no sign of it. Keeping watch for the turn-off to Rosgill, she slowed the vehicle as much as she dared. Dan couldn't be far behind her. She had to have a plan. Had to think about her next move. She was running out of options. Dan might be injured – or worse – but she couldn't think about that now, she had to protect herself and her baby. Getting away from the Halt and from Dan was her best option – she had to go back down the glen, to Invergill, for help.

Her mind raced. What a stupid fool she'd been. The knuckles of her hands shone white, so tight was her grasp on the steering wheel. She was vaguely aware that she'd clenched her jaw, shoulders rising as the cords in her neck tightened. She tried to relax, tried to force her shoulders back down, but her body refused to respond as the deep-seated anger she felt blazed through every cell in her body.

Dan had brought all of this on her. Dan with his secrets.

She should never have agreed to come here, to be uprooted. He didn't love her – not the way he should and she'd always known that, deep down. Tears threatened to appear, but she held them in check, too angry to submit to self-pity. Her desire for revenge burned deeply within. Leaving him wouldn't be enough. He'd follow her, apply to the courts for shared custody, maybe he'd even win. Thoughts tumbled across each other as she struggled to make sense of her emotions. She swung the nose of the car down the lane to the station. It looked just like it had a few hours earlier when she'd left, before she knew the extent of Dan's betrayal and the depth of Mike's hatred. Something in the air felt different; once again she had a feeling that someone or something was watching her. She'd been a fool to think she belonged here, and yet a small thought nudged at her subconscious. Perhaps this was exactly where she was meant to be. Perhaps it was Dan who was the intruder.

O-nam, gho rehsh nA'tham.

Saying the words aloud, she pushed all other thoughts away, trying to decipher the coded message. She hurried into the cottage and grabbed the carving from its hiding place in the sofa. It felt firm in her hands, unyielding. She traced the outline of the hares with her fingertips, feeling the notches where the whittling knife had scarred the surface. Closing her eyes, the sounds and smell of the forest invaded her senses. Cool spruce, scented ferns. Beetles chattered, mocking the posturing capercaillie.

O-nam, gho rehsh nA'tham.

Esther knew what she had to do.

Opening the kitchen drawer, she picked up a book of matches and put them in her pocket along with the carving. She opened the door to the outside. There was still no sign of Dan, but she knew she had to act quickly before he turned up and had chance to stop her. For a second, she thought about retrieving the photographs and letters from upstairs, but decided against it. They were part of her past now, just something else she had to let go of and time was running out. Ignoring the pain radiating from her leg, she limped down the length of the platform to the store room. The petrol cans were exactly where Dan had left them on that first evening. It seemed so long ago and yet it was only a week. So much had changed. She had changed. There'd be time enough later to process it all, but for now she had to focus on escaping and keeping her baby safe. The containers were heavier than she expected and she let out a grunt as she lifted them up.

She froze in place as she heard a vehicle pulling up outside. Blood pounded in her ears and she fought to control her breathing. She couldn't risk Dan seeing her, stopping her. She glanced around and spotted the interconnecting door to the ticket office. Pulling the keys from her pocket, she tried a few of the larger keys in the lock, her fumbling fingers working against her. If she could just make it through the inside of the building without going out onto the platform, she'd have a chance to stay one step ahead of him. She closed her eyes and focused, letting her subconscious take over. The keys in her hands began to vibrate so subtly that she wondered if she'd imagined it. She picked through each one, feeling for the key that would open the door, stopping only when the vibration dulled. Listening for Dan's footsteps outside the door, she turned the key in the lock as quietly as she could. It opened. She pushed her shoulder against the door, ready to stop if it protested, but it swung open soundlessly. She opened one of the containers and sloshed most of its contents around the store room and ticket office, making sure she coated petrol over as much of the wooden racking and flaking surfaces as possible.

'Esther!'

Her heart jumped into her mouth. *Mike!* Where was Dan? Were they together? Maybe they'd both come after her. She hurried across the ticket office to the internal door on the other side of the room. From there, she'd have to go outside to get to the cottage. She tried the lock with the same key, raising her eyes in silent prayer that it was a master key as she'd hoped. She emptied the rest of the petrol can onto the floor and walls, and threw a match into the store room behind her. Instantly, the vapour caught light and she half-closed the door, containing the fire long enough to give her time to escape. She scurried across the ticket office to the waiting room, this time closing the door behind her fully.

'Esther! Come out, come out, wherever you are!' Mike taunted.

The door handle rattled. It was locked. A dark shape loomed outside the window and instinctively she crouched down under it as Mike attempted to peer in through the acid-etched glass. Pain shot along her thigh and she had to put her hand over her mouth to stop herself from crying out. Tendrils of smoke snaked through gaps in the door frame. The paint on the inside of the door started to blister and the room started to fill with black smoke, acrid and choking. She had to make a run for it, before she was trapped. There was no sign of Mike. It was now or never. Grabbing the last full petrol can, she tried to open the lock from inside and dropped the keys in her haste. *Slow down, slow down.*

She picked them up, trying to steady her shaking hands, and inserted the master key in the lock. She pulled the door open carefully, ready to close it again if Mike lunged at her from the other side, but the platform was empty. The sound of a car door closing made her spin around to face the direction the noise had come from. It had to be Mike. What had he gone back for? Esther's t-shirt stuck to her skin under her hoodie. She tore off her padded waterproof and flung it into the waiting room. The trembling in her hands spread throughout her body and her teeth chattered with fear.

A single shot rang out, cleaving the air. He was going to kill her.

'Not if I get you first, you bastard.' She clenched her jaw.

Ignoring the pain and her body's protests, she heaved the petrol can into the cottage, splashing the volatile liquid liberally across anything that would burn. Mike wouldn't be foolish enough to follow her in to the burning cottage.

As she turned to leave, she jumped with fright. Mike was standing in the doorway, just like he had a week earlier, only this time he was pointing the barrel of a gun at her.

'Hello, little one.'

She stood, rooted to the spot. He could easily overpower her and she'd be left to burn to death.

He spoke as though he could read her thoughts. 'You've done my work for me. Inspired, Esther. I didn't know you had it in you.' He put the shotgun down onto the worktop.

'Where's Dan?'

'Dan? Even now, is he all you can think of?' Mike laughed, a hollow sound that echoed in her ears.

'You know, Mike, I can just about understand why you hate me. But he loved you.'

Admitting it should have felt like a defeat, the final betrayal, but she knew it was true, Dan loved Mike. Surely he felt something in return?

'He's at the croft. I'll deal with him later.'

So, he wasn't dead. Not yet, anyway. She took a deep breath.

'Let me go, Mike. I have nothing now. You've won.'

'Winning? Is that what you think this is about? You know, I almost feel sorry for you. Almost. But then I think of my mother and brother and all the things I've missed out on. How my life was shaped by something I had no control over. All the things they've missed out on. No, Esther. This isn't about winning. It's about getting even.'

There was a small movement to the left of Mike, Esther's eyes flicked across to it sub-consciously and Mike followed her gaze. He threw his arms up to protect his face as Major Tom lunged at him from the windowsill. Esther rushed forward, shoulder-barging Mike, who dropped the shotgun onto the floor. As he scrabbled to pick the gun up, Esther kicked out at him, sending him sprawling. He hit his head on the corner of the kitchen table and lay there, dazed for a few seconds.

Without thinking, Esther lit a match and threw it into the living room. She was rewarded by the sound of vapour igniting as she darted out of the cottage.

There was nowhere left for her to go. She'd never make it to the car before Mike caught up with her. She couldn't run any further, even if she hadn't been wounded. There was only one thing she could try, but it was a gamble. What if she was wrong?

Summoning her last shreds of courage, she put her hand on the waiting room door. It was cold to the touch. The fire hadn't taken hold inside the room yet. She hesitated, wanting to make sure Mike saw her go inside. Smoke blurred the air, darkening the atmosphere, making it difficult to breathe. She couldn't afford to wait any longer; she couldn't risk the fire taking hold. Pulling her hoodie up over her mouth and nose, she opened the door. Instinct took over. She had to be right. Not just for her sake, but for the life growing inside her. She crouched down and opened the cupboard door, squeezing herself in and pulling it shut behind her. Had he followed her in? She held her breath. Would he check the cupboard? The carving dug into her leg. She took it out of her pocket and put it down her top against her skin. It was time to find out if her instinct could be trusted.

There was a cold draught coming from the back of the cupboard, blowing onto her face. She twisted her body as best she could without kicking the door open and put her hands on the flimsy wooden panel behind her. It gave slightly. She pushed harder and the thin wood splintered around the edges. One final push and the panel fell away. Using her hands to guide her, she reached out into the void space, her body following where her hands led. She was in a tunnel of some kind;

it was hard to gauge the dimensions but she had just enough space to crawl forward, dragging her right leg. The blackness was overwhelming. She wanted to scream, to be pulled out wriggling and gasping into the clean, bright daylight, but she fought against her body's response and dragged herself further in. The air was much colder now and the draught was stronger. Her breathing came in short, rasping pants and she had to wipe her brow several times as beads of sweat bled down her face. With one final effort, her hands clawed into the floor of the tunnel, scraping away clods of what felt like mud and dirt. As she struck out again, she made contact with something solid. It was all that stood between her and escape. She pushed as hard as she could against the panel. It wouldn't budge.

'No, no, no. Not like this!' Esther felt the tears threaten to reappear. At the same moment, she felt something stirring inside her. It was a new sensation, like someone had run a finger across the inside of her belly. She waited for the wave of nausea to swallow her, but with a flash of euphoria, she realised it wasn't morning sickness at all, she was feeling her baby move for the first time.

With renewed purpose and strength, she shoved against the blockage. The panel fragmented and daylight poured in. Esther scrambled out of the tunnel, gasping into the fresh air. Her hands were covered with dirt and she wiped a cobweb away from her fringe. Still shaking from fright and exhaustion, she looked around her. She was at the rear of the station, the tunnel couldn't have been more than a few feet long, but crawling through the darkness had been the longest moments of her life.

Where was Mike? At any moment, he could come through the same passage. She knew she had to stop him, knew that she'd never feel safe again unless she knew he couldn't come for her. Every part of her ached. She had a deep scratch across the back of her right hand and blood mixed with the dirt like a distorted henna tattoo. Bending over to catch her breath, she summoned the last remaining remnants of energy and stalked around the outline of the station, clinging to the walls, ready to dart back under cover if she saw him. As she rounded the corner, he staggered out of the cottage, his jacket smouldering.

'Esther!' His roar was bestial. 'Esther! You'd better fucking come out now.'

She shrank back. He couldn't have seen her. The acrid air caught at the back of her throat and she had to stifle a coughing fit. She peeped around the corner again. He was coming down the platform towards her, but his shambling gait made him look drunk and unsteady. He stopped outside the waiting room.

'Playing hide and seek, are you? I have you now, little one.'

He opened the door and thick, dense smoke belched out from inside. He stood there, coughing, trying to wave the smoke away. It cleared just enough for Esther to see him go inside. This was her last chance. She made her way up the platform. Smoke billowed out of the broken window; he wouldn't be able to survive long inside. If he came out now it would be over. She had no strength left to fight him and nowhere to run to.

As she reached the door, she put her hand onto the handle to prevent him from turning it. She leaned back, shifting all her weight so she was a counterbalance, and with her free hand felt in her pocket for the bunch of keys. As her fingers closed round the familiar metal ring, he thudded against the glass in the door, his eyes wild and staring out at her through the filigree pattern in the door pane where the glass was unetched. She jumped backwards with shock, letting go of the handle, but grabbing it again before he could gain purchase. Sliding the key into the lock, she turned it, hearing the satisfying click as the latch slid into place.

'FUCK YOU!'

Her scream splintered the silence. The spell was broken.

'FUUUCK YOOOU!' This time, she drew the curse out, pouring every mote of hurt and anger into it, like it was the last time she'd ever speak.

It was done. Over. He was trapped. Cold logic flooded her brain. Kill or be killed. She felt no remorse as she studied the hillsides, looking for a place to seek shelter while she recovered. Without looking back at the Halt, she walked off the end of the platform, crossing over to the other side and began the steep climb up the mountainside.

❧

The spruce exhaled, their branches drooping under the weight of the unfolding drama below. The hare nestled into the mountainside, watching as a man fell out of the back of the blue metal beast. He stood, unsteady at first, then put his hand onto the metallic body to correct his balance. Even from this distance, she could tell he was wounded and she watched, unblinking, as he turned towards the station. He took five, maybe six, tentative steps, then fell to the ground as the station roared out its warning. Burning liquid, glass and metal shards, splinters of wood, all wheeled through the air and rained down onto the ground. The man covered his head with his hands.

Then came the noise. Birds scattered, tail feathers wagging with fright, the first to feel the disturbance as the air bent and rushed into the vacuum at the heart of the station. Later the trees would shrug off their shock, pretend they'd heard it all before, but the dropped needles littering the ground told their own tale.

'Esther!' The man on the ground laid bare his agony and the sound was so wretched, so primal, that even the granite responded, crying silica crystal tears into the burn.

'Esther! I'm sorry!'

The hare blinked, then she turned from the direction of the station and loped away, leaving the merest impression in the vegetation where she'd lain, and a strange wooden carving half-buried in the leaves.

THE END

ACKNOWLEDGEMENTS

I AM GRATEFUL to many people who have given words of encouragement or advice during (and post) the writing of *Liminal*. Firstly, thanks to Jen, Chris, and all of the team at Salt not just for having faith in this book, but also the vision to have built Salt into what it is today.

I must also thank Nick Royle, my tutor at Manchester Metropolitan, who continually pushed me and who always asked the difficult questions. His comma pedantry is legendary, whereas mine is a work in progress. Therefore apologies also, Nick, for the misplaced, misused, and wilfully abandoned commas I have subjected you to.

Livi Michael was also influential in the early stages of writing this book. The genesis can be traced right back to a writing prompt she issued while we were at Moniack Mhor together.

My fellow writers at Manchester Metropolitan have been nothing short of inspirational in terms of their encouragement and shrewd advice. Special mention goes to Helen Steadman, Zöe Feeney, Nicola Lennon, Dot Devey-Smith, Fin Gray, and Wyl Menmuir. I would also like to thank Sue Smith for her insight which led me to changing the title, and to Kerry Hadley-Pryce for her words of wisdom along the way.

Mike Irving also deserves my thanks for sharing his knowledge of the Scottish forests. I learnt a lot. I'd also like to thank Diane and Rob Hayes, who answered my questions about combustion, without panic or alarm - or accusing me of planning to carry out an arson attack.

But my biggest thanks are reserved for Diane Kingston (OBE) and her husband, Nigel, for answering my questions about amputation with good grace, patience, and humour. Without the insights I gained from my conversations with Diane and Nigel, I would never have been able to create Esther or an environment for her to interact with.

This book has been typeset by SALT PUBLISHING LIMITED using Neacademia, a font designed by Sergei Egorov for the Rosetta Type Foundry in the Czech Republic. It is manufactured using Creamy 70gsm, a Forest Stewardship Council™ certified paper from Stora Enso's Anjala Mill in Finland. It was printed and bound by Clays Limited in Bungay, Suffolk, Great Britain.

CROMER
GREAT BRITAIN
MMXVIII